GARDEN OF DESTINY

BY
MEARA PLATT

BOOKS FROM DRAGONBLADE PUBLISHING

Knights of Honor Series by Alexa Aston
Word of Honor
Marked By Honor
Code of Honor
Journey to Honor

Legends of Love Series by Avril Borthiry
The Wishing Well
Isolated Hearts
Sentinel

Heart of the Corsairs Series by Elizabeth Ellen Carter
Captive of the Corsairs

Also From Elizabeth Ellen Carter
Dark Heart

Knight Everlasting Series by Cassidy Cayman
Endearing

Second Chance Series by Jessica Jefferson
Second Chance Marquess

Imperial Season Series by Mary Lancaster
Vienna Waltz
Vienna Woods
Vienna Dawn

Blackhaven Brides Series by Mary Lancaster
The Wicked Baron

Queen of Thieves Series by Andy Peloquin
Child of the Night Guild
Thief of the Night Guild

Dark Gardens Series by Meara Platt
Garden of Shadows
Garden of Light
Garden of Dragons
Garden of Destiny

Rulers of the Sky Series by Paula Quinn
Scorched
Ember

Viking's Fury Series by Violetta Rand
Love's Fury
Desire's Fury
Passion's Fury

Also from Violetta Rand
Viking Hearts

Dry Bayou Brides Series by Lynn Winchester
The Shepherd's Daughter
The Seamstress
The Widow

TABLE OF CONTENTS

CHAPTER ONE

Two black dragons shall reign supreme.
Two black dragons shall unite the worlds of demon and man.

"LORD BLOODAXE, COME forward and rejoice with me," Brihann, High King of the Dragon Lords commanded the moment Bloodaxe stepped into the grand castle hall in response to the royal summons. Black and gold banners emblazoned with dragons covered the vast chamber and one enormous banner of the finest Italian velvet depicting a black dragon rampant upon a field of gold now draped majestically over the wall behind King Brihann's golden throne.

Bloodaxe made his way through the cheering crowd, his black cape swirling behind him as he strode forward on the long black carpet that was edged in gold. He tossed aside the demonic toadies who were waiting in line for an audience with the vengeful and wizened king and made his way toward the front of the room.

He hated these celebrations that could only mean the start of another war.

Brihann cast him a malevolent smile as he approached. Although Brihann had once been a prince in the realm of the Fae, hate had contorted his features over the past thousands of years so that he was now no more than a misshapen and unforgiving old man. "Ah, Lord Bloodaxe," he said with a wheeze, "we shall begin the festivities now that you've arrived. Do you have nothing to say? Did you not like my gift? She is yours to do with as you please."

"A gift?" Bloodaxe paused at the first of the three steps that led up to the throne which stood on a raised dais. He arched a dark eyebrow, understanding what Brihann meant for him to do with this benevolence he had supposedly received. "It must have arrived after I departed my fortress. But if this is yet another nymph you've sent to me, I have more than enough of them to service my needs."

"Ah, but this girl is like no other, for she is from the realm of mortals and her beauty is beyond compare. She's an innocent, untouched by any man. Enjoy her."

A mortal girl? A chill ran up Bloodaxe's spine. Had Brihann sent his demon spies to abduct this young woman? Fool, did he not realize the danger of bringing an innocent into their Underworld realm?

Brihann's smile turned venomous. "Will you not thank me for my generosity?"

"No." His insult resounded through the hall, immediately halting all cheers and chatter, and leaving only deathly silence in its wake. "You've just planted the seeds of our destruction. You would do this after the wounds you and Necros suffered at the hands of these mortals? Was losing an eye not enough for you? The merest gust of wind sends Necros into a tumble now that he's lost the tip of his dragon tail."

Brihann's wrinkled fingers moved to an even deeper wound, the one he'd suffered to his heart. That deep wound had been caused by a Fae dagger. His hand now rested above the spot that still festered and would never heal. It caused the prominent wheeze now plaguing him that left him straining for every breath. "Do you reject my gift?"

A murmur spread throughout the crowded hall as Bloodaxe remained defiantly silent, his gaze fixed on Brihann. Indeed, he dared not take his eyes off the old king. He did not need to look back to hear the scrape of talons against the marble floor. Those demons who'd packed the hall a moment ago were now running off in fear, for every demon knew of Brihann's explosive temper. None dared to linger and risk being scorched to ashes by his dragon fire.

Bloodaxe did not fear it, for he'd stopped caring about his own life long ago. Nothing could be worse than all he'd already been forced to endure since childhood. The boy that had once been Arik Blakefield, heir to the Duke of Draloch, no longer existed. All innocence had been tortured out of him years ago. He was Bloodaxe now, a feared and brutal Dragon Lord.

That indifference to his own wellbeing gave him power, allowing him to speak with reckless abandon. "I will take this mortal innocent back where she belongs. Send orders to your guards to allow me through the Razor Cliffs or I shall march my armies through their ranks and destroy every last one of them."

Brihann rose from his throne. "Be careful how you speak to me, Bloodaxe. We are the two black dragons and must stand together. You are my successor, but I am still High King and destined to reign in the Underworld for another thousand years."

"The Stone of Draloch is indeed powerful, but it does not rule our destinies. I will not believe it led you to deliver this dangerous girl to me. Speak the truth, Brihann. I must know why she is here. Did the Stone of Draloch command it? Or was this bad idea all yours?" He did not trust Brihann, for the old man was too lost in hateful schemes of lust and power to think clearly. Lies always spewed from his lips. Yet, to depose him was not possible. Brihann still held the loyalty of the other Dragon Lords.

He spared a glance around the almost empty hall. Where were Necros, Python, and Mordain? He should have easily spotted their robes of yellow, green, and red as he'd arrived and made his way toward the throne. These were their respective dragon colors and would have been worn for this royal gathering.

Brihann's fingers curled around his scepter, stroking it as he leaned forward. "Will you keep her if I say it is the Stone of Draloch who wills it?"

Bloodaxe saw through the deceptive workings of his evil mind. It still surprised him that others could not. But he had once been human and understood feelings that guided one's heart. The bad, such as greed and lust and envy, were pervasive in the Underworld. The good, such as honor and love, were no more than faded memories of an earlier life that was lost to him now. "I will keep her if you speak the truth."

Brihann released the rheumy breath he'd been holding and resumed his seat on the throne. "Be at ease then. The Stone of Draloch commands it and you have no choice but to obey. It is my will, as well. We must be friends and allies once more if we are to conquer other realms."

Bloodaxe nodded, deciding to relieve the palpable tension between them by bending on one knee and lowering his head in a subservient bow. "So be it." Although not in his nature to be humble, his fate and Brihann's were entwined. They were the two black dragons who reigned in the Underworld.

He was a mere pawn in the prophecy that was etched in the Stone of Draloch. It had predicted the defeat of the demons at the hands of the Fae. Was it now predicting a demon victory over the realm of man?

Two black dragons shall reign supreme.
Two black dragons shall unite the worlds of demon and man.

But there was a third black dragon, Bloodaxe's brother, Saron.

What ultimate fate awaited all of them, he did not know.

He chose to back down and rile Brihann no further. Whether or not he spoke the truth would not matter once their day of reckoning arrived. "I thank you for the gift, Your Majesty."

The demon minions who had fled Brihann's hall began to return. Bloodaxe heard the scratch of their hesitant steps as they approached behind him. He waited until Brihann was distracted and then left the hall to return to his fortress and the *gift* that awaited him.

Who was this innocent?

And how was his destiny bound to hers?

"WHERE AM I?" Lady Georgiana Wethersby asked, shaking her head in an attempt to clear the heavy fog from her brain as she awoke in unfamiliar surroundings. Her hair spilled over her shoulders in tumbling waves, but she quickly realized her messy tangle of hair was the least of her problems, for a handsome-as-sin stranger with hair as black as a raven's wing and exquisite ice-blue eyes was staring back at her.

He was not her betrothed.

Indeed, he was no one she had ever met before.

She shook her head again, confused by the lethargy in her limbs and the man's continued silence. The dank, oppressive heat of the elegant bedchamber felt amiss as well. It was Yuletide and there should have been a frosty chill to the air, but her body was warm and languid.

The only frost she felt was from the silver gleam in this stranger's cold eyes.

Mercy. Was she in his bed? She couldn't recall how she got herself into this compromising position, but gave silent thanks that he was seated on a stool and not stretched out beside her with her body wrapped in his massive arms. "Who are you, sir?"

She winced at the hoarseness of her voice, but her throat was parched and her lips, as she traced her tongue along them, felt cracked and dry. She took a deep breath to stem her rising panic as the dizzying scent of honey and tainted ash filled her nostrils, further muddling her senses. This was to be her wedding day, the day she and Oliver Cranfield, the Marquis of Linwood, were to exchange vows. Oliver was known for pulling pranks on his friends, but this was too cruel and went beyond any innocent jest that her betrothed might play.

Indeed, nothing about this dark and dreary morning felt innocent or right. Was it morning? Whatever potion had been used to knock her out was still working its way through her body. She did not know where she was and could not recall ever seeing this large, four-poster bed of polished ebony wood with dragon carvings on the footboard in her home. Nor did she remember donning her wedding gown or having her maid tie the intricate lacing along the back.

Thank goodness, I'm dressed.

Maintaining the appearance of calm, Georgiana sat up carefully for fear of damaging the pearl beads that had been sewn along the white satin hem in a patterned swirl that resembled ocean waves. "I must have wandered in here."

"You didn't wander in." The stranger raked a hand through the magnificent dark waves of his hair.

"I didn't?" Oh, everything felt so wrong about her situation. Especially this man clad in dark trousers and black leather boots who wore no shirt over his muscled torso and was still staring at her with eyes that reminded her of blue crystals trapped in ice.

They pierced her very soul.

"You're in my fortress. In my bed," he said as though she could possibly overlook the humiliation of it. His voice was deep and commanding, its angry timbre resonating through the richly appointed chamber. "Who are *you*?"

"Don't you know?"

"Answer my question." He spoke with regal authority and a marked impatience that caught her notice. Was it possible they'd both been victims of this unpleasant prank? No, he exuded power, strength, and danger. He was the sort of man who would unleash fire and brimstone upon anyone who ever crossed him.

Only a fool with a desire for an immediate and painful death would ever dare play such a jest on him.

Curiously, although she sensed this was a man to fear, she did not fear him. He stirred an inexplicable yearning deep within her. Did she know him? She felt the ache of a memory lost or an experience that had once connected them to each other.

What could she and this stranger ever have in common?

"There's been a terrible mistake. I want to go home." Pain shot to her temples when she attempted to scramble to her feet, all worry about protecting the delicate beading on her wedding gown now forgotten. She tried to stand, but for the first time noticed that her hands were loosely bound at the wrists. She studied the shimmering threads that appeared as delicate as a spider's web and then tugged on those silken bonds to break them apart. They held fast, tightening as she strained against them so that they now cut into her skin. "Untie me at once. Tell me why you've brought me here." Wherever *here* was.

Had he abducted her?

She couldn't recall anything after she'd gone to sleep last night at Wethersby Hall, the grandest house in the Lake District and home to the Duke of Penrith. Her father was the current duke and her wedding was to take place in their ancestral home this morning. Or had her wedding day already passed? "Answer me," she demanded, tipping her chin up and holding herself proudly. He wasn't the only one capable of exuding regal authority.

"Shouting will not get you what you seek." The man towered over her as he rose from the stool and took her hands in his so that she felt the roughness of his skin against hers. Surprisingly, his touch was gentle. Indeed, far gentler than she'd expected as he worked to further loosen her bonds. However, he did not untie her.

Had anyone missed her yet? Was anyone searching for her?

Did Oliver care that his bride was nowhere to be found?

She cleared her throat, deciding to take a softer approach. "I did not realize I was shouting at you. My apologies. I'm overset, obviously. I don't know how I got here or why you are holding me. Is it for ransom?"

She struggled to her feet, this time successfully, and realized she wore no shoes or stockings. However, the stone floor was warm despite it being winter and there being no fire blazing in the massive hearth which stood at the opposite end of the large chamber.

"I didn't abduct you. Nor am I holding you for ransom." Instead of releasing her, the man anchored her bonds to the bedpost so that it was impossible for her to leave his quarters. "Wait here."

Wait? While he went off and did what?

She tried to pull free again, but he stopped her by taking her hands into his once more. *Mercy.* He was quite tall and built like a warrior, his chest broad and arms seemingly sculpted out of stone. Despite his anger, there was something in his rough touch that felt protective and soothing. Why? Who was this man to her?

He scowled at her. "Stop struggling. Have you not learned your lesson? These ropes are thin and will cut through your skin like a razor."

"I've never seen such bonds before. They appear as fragile as silken threads, but they're impossible to break. Please untie me." She frowned back at him, still overset and confused, but determined not to show weakness. "I'd rather not bleed all over my expensive wedding gown."

Unimpressed, he turned and gave a sharp whistle. Two black dogs the size of horses trotted to his side. Georgiana stifled a gasp, for they'd been sitting so quietly in the shadows, she hadn't noticed them. "Your pets?"

He patted the slightly larger dog on the head, the casually affectionate gesture so at odds with the pervasive air of danger in the chamber. "This one is Charon." In response, the dog licked his hand. "And this one is Styx." If Styx had a tail, it would have been wagging. "They're friendly. But disobey me and they'll rip your slender throat to ribbons."

To prove his point, he snapped his fingers once and the dogs immediately tensed and began to growl at her, a soft and deadly growl emanating from deep within their chests. In this moment, they were nothing like pets and everything like predators about to trap and devour their defenseless prey. "All the more reason why you ought to release me. I can't possibly run away while they're guarding me."

He ignored her request and knelt to speak to his dogs in a language she did not recognize, perhaps an ancient pagan tongue. The words were enchanting as he spoke them, so she turned away to avoid accidentally being caught in his spell. There was something eternal and magical about this man, but not in a good or appealing way despite the masculine beauty of his form. "Please, don't leave me bound like this."

He continued to ignore her.

She released a shaky breath, her mind suddenly filling with thoughts of wild creatures, for he moved with the powerful grace of a beast from an ancient world, one that her heart recognized and wanted to protect. "My name is Georgiana Wethersby. Lady Georgiana, to be precise."

She'd given away nothing that he hadn't already known, for she didn't believe he was innocent in her abduction or ignorant of her identity. "Won't you please tell me your name?"

"You're Georgiana?" Despite the brutal coldness of his stare, she sensed a sudden surge of volcanic heat within him and feared he would unleash his molten fury upon her. "The daughter of Penrith?"

She shook her head. "If this is revenge for a business dispute, I can assure you–"

"I have no business dealings with your father." He moved close, and although he stood a full head taller than her average height, he seemed as big as a mythical leviathan looming over her. "I'm known as Dragon Lord Bloodaxe," he said in a husky rumble and then turned to show her his back and the black dragon emblazoned in ink along its broad and muscled expanse.

"I know this dragon," she said with a gasp. "It's the coat of arms of the dukes of Draloch." She reached out to touch it with her bound hands, spreading her fingers across his back so that her open palms pressed against his warm skin.

A flood of heat washed through her and seeped deep into her bones. Her heart began to pound with such force, she thought it might burst. "Dear heaven!" She struggled to hold back the tears suddenly threatening to spill onto her cheeks. Loss. Sadness. These were feelings that overwhelmed her. "Who are you to me?"

He shook his head as he turned to face her, his Draloch eyes the same compelling crystal blue as those of the black dragon etched on the muscled planes of his back. "I am Lord Bloodaxe," he repeated, but she knew he purposely avoided giving her the answer she sought. "I live and rule as a Dragon Lord in my realm."

She knew he was feeling the same powerful connection, he had to be. Her hands were still on him even though he'd turned to face her, now resting on his chest and splayed across his heart. She tried not to show her disappointment at its calm and steady beat. Hers was wild and pounding through her ears. She drew her tingling hands off his body. "What is a Dragon Lord?"

"A creature of the Underworld. One who reigns over the dead."

She shuddered, unwilling to believe the vibrant sensations he roused in her heart had anything to do with death. Was this a dream? Or had she somehow lost her sanity? Had he lost his? The man appeared fully in control of his senses, but spoke of a world outside of the quiet Lake District where she had been raised or the fashionable London society where she'd spent the past several seasons paraded on the Marriage Mart. "Is this a hoax? We must still be in England. You would not have had time to bring me somewhere else."

"I did not bring you here," he reminded her, unfastening the silvery bonds he'd wrapped around the bedpost moments earlier and taking her by the arm to lead her to the window. He opened it and allowed the hot wind to blow inside. The gentle gust unsettled her, for the winter air should have been biting and cold. "Look up there, Georgiana. Tell me what you see."

He stood close, his big body reassuring as she gazed at a red sky and the shadows of two moons. But she also saw a lake in the distance and several mountains that appeared much as one would expect an English lake or mountain to look. A bird flew by and landed on the ledge immediately below the window.

Georgiana peered out see what sort of bird it was, but it suddenly leaped up and tried to bite her. That fanged creature was certainly not a bird and would have embedded its sharp teeth into her skin if Lord Bloodaxe had not struck it with his fist and sent it tumbling back onto the ledge.

"Have a care." He slammed the window shut. "This isn't England."

"No, indeed it isn't." His world was the one warned of in biblical tales and church sermons. She hardly got her words out, for they stuck in her throat like lumps of coal. Her hands were still shaking from that frightening encounter and her legs were about to give way. "Am I dead? Is this why I'm here?"

"No, Georgiana." His voice was husky and soothing. In the next moment, he gave a slight wave of his hand and the last of her bonds magically disappeared. "You're very much alive and don't belong here."

Her eyes rounded in surprise. "Then you'll set me free?"

He traced a finger lightly along her cheek, as though he also needed assurance that she was safe and unharmed. But he was a sorcerer of some sort, wasn't he? Could he heal her if she were injured? "It isn't up to me," he said and drew his hand away.

"Who then?"

"I don't know yet." His crystal blue gaze stole the breath from her. "Maybe you."

"Me?" She wasn't certain what he meant by that. Was he suggesting that she pay for her freedom?

Mother in heaven!

What price?

CHAPTER TWO

"I F I DON'T belong here, will you take me back home?" Georgiana's eyes were soft and green as dew-soaked grass, big eyes that sparkled as she pleaded to be returned to the arms of her betrothed. Dark, velvet lashes enhanced their appeal. A riot of golden curls as vibrant as a summer sun tumbled over her slender shoulders. "Will you, Lord Bloodaxe?"

She tore at his soul, the very one he was certain had been lost for all eternity.

"I don't know. Stop asking me questions," he grumbled, uncertain whether his anger stemmed from finding her in his bed or from knowing that he somehow had to deliver her back to Wethersby Hall untouched. *Untouched.* She stirred the fires of his dragon lust and that was a dangerous thing.

Her green eyes widened and he noted a spark of fear in the emerald gaze she'd fixed on him. "Who should I ask if not you?"

"By the Stone of Draloch! Will you not give me a moment's peace?" The urge to stop her mouth with his was overwhelming. The urge to kiss her and take her into his arms, to feel her soft, sweet body pressed against his, had his own body shaking. He wanted to couple with her and feel the beat of her heart hammering against his chest, hear her breathy moans of ecstasy against his ear as he pleasured her.

She's an innocent.

Indeed, he had to deliver her back to her family soon. It was the only way to protect her, especially from him. He'd last seen Georgiana when he was a mere boy of ten and she was an infant, a baby girl too young to remember him. But he was a man now, and his body was responding as any man would to the beautiful woman who stood before him.

He turned away to finish dressing. She had regained consciousness shortly after his return from Brihann's royal hall, and he'd just gotten out of his bath. He always washed after an audience with the High King because he needed to scrub the pervasive stench of that foul demon off his skin.

Now that she was awake, he didn't know what to do with her. He'd been forbidden to return her to her own realm, yet he dared not leave her to roam free in the Underworld. He needed to come up with a plan to protect her. But who was the greater danger to her? Him or Brihann?

He made the mistake of glancing at her and saw her beautiful green eyes staring back at him. "My father is a man of means and I'm his only child. My betrothed is wealthy, too."

"Do not speak to me of your betrothed." Georgiana roused not only his dragon lust, but his possessive nature as well. A roaring heat now coursed through his veins and spread through his body like a wildfire out of control. It would take nothing for him to slip through a portal and turn her bridegroom to ashes with one blast of his dragon fire. *She's mine. No one else can have her.*

He turned away once more in a futile attempt to calm himself down.

But he heard her soft footsteps as she approached him. He ought to have kept her tethered so that she could not move around his chamber at will. "Am I forbidden to speak at all? You said not to ask you questions, so I didn't. I'm merely trying to make conversation."

The scent of wildflowers filled his nostrils. This was her fragrance, wild and delicate as the sweep of flowers across a summer meadow. She stood so close, he ached to touch her. He knew her skin would be soft as a rose petal. He yearned to kiss her as well, for she would taste as sweet as the wild strawberries that flourished in those summer meadows.

"Must we speak at all?" He pointed to his bureau. "I need a shirt to wear. May I dress in peace?" He arched a dark eyebrow. "Unless you prefer me as I am."

"As you are?" Her cheeks turned pink and she began to stammer, a sign that she indeed liked what she saw of his body. Dragons were not celibate creatures until they found their life mate. Till then, they indulged in carnal pleasures. He was well aware of the signs of desire in a woman, and Georgiana was exhibiting all of them. "Indeed, not! By all means, Lord Bloodaxe, cover yourself. I merely thought... I didn't..."

It pleased him that Georgiana desired him, no matter that she denied it.

She tipped her chin up in defiance when he grinned knowingly at her. "I forbid you to smirk at me."

"Forbid?" He slipped the shirt over his head. "This is my fortress. You are in my Underworld kingdom."

Now she was furiously nibbling her fleshy lower lip in dismay. "Yes, but you claim I'm not your captive."

"You're not." He slammed the bureau door shut, knowing the sound must have startled her. "Neither am I your servant. Do not ever issue orders to me."

"I'm sorry," she said in a contrite whisper, the gentleness of her voice like a punch to his heart. "If I appear flustered, it is merely because I'm scared. Please don't walk out and leave me behind."

He raked a hand through his still damp hair. "I have no intention of leaving you, Georgiana. You are under my protection now."

"Oh, I see." She rubbed her hands along the sides of her wedding gown. *Wedding. To another.* He had to get that odious garment off her before he did something foolish such as fly off and torch her betrothed. "Well, thank you for that. I... you must..." she said, continuing to stammer. Her eyes followed his every movement. "I'm sorry that I'm a nuisance to you. Are you in mourning?"

"No." He always dressed in black, for this was his dragon color. He took his time donning his battle leather, preferring the taut, tanned animal hides that clung lightly to his body and allowed him to easily wield his axe. The chain mail favored by many in the demon armies was too cumbersome.

He also found that he particularly enjoyed dressing in front of Georgiana. She could not hide her curiosity and blushed whenever he caught her gaping at him. *The innocent.* He was struggling mightily to keep her that way. "I'll have my servants bring clothes for you. Your wedding gown looks uncomfortable to wear."

"It is." She gasped. "I mean… the beading is very delicate… the laces are a little tight."

He'd noticed, for her bosom was pushed up so that the swells of her breasts were on tempting display. But her words signified more than a gown that was pulled too tight. He sensed that her wedding ceremony was an uncomfortable thing for her. No doubt she felt the same about the marriage itself. She did not love the man she was about to take as her husband. "I could loosen them for you."

She shook her head furiously. "No! It isn't necessary."

"You don't trust me yet." Or herself, he suspected, for the emerald glow in her eyes and the flush to her cheeks were unmistakable signs of passion. She was afraid of what might happen if he touched her.

So was he.

There was no telling what the demon part of him would do if he did not keep an iron control over himself. He was struggling already, his skin beginning to form dragon scales and his throat beginning to burn. She had ignited his dragon fire. "Remain in this chamber. Bolt the door behind me and allow no one in but me."

"You just said you wouldn't leave me." Her eyes grew wide with fright. "Where are you going?"

"To scout my borders." But that was not his only reason for escaping his chamber. He needed to shift into his dragon form and roar and spew flames until his dragon lust was spent. "I'll be back in a moment. Have you eaten? Are you hungry?"

"Very." She glanced at her stomach and nodded.

"I thought so. I'll bring us some food to share. I dare not take you into my dining hall just yet. We'll dine in my chamber this evening. You'll sleep here as well. It isn't safe for you to be anywhere else."

She grew deathly still at the mention of sleeping arrangements.

They'd discuss it when he returned.

He instructed his dogs to protect Georgiana while he attended to the true purpose for his departure, a purpose that had nothing to do with food, although he would remember to bring some back for them. The dragon fire now consumed his body. He had nymphs to take care of that need, but they no longer interested him.

He could have no other woman while Georgiana remained in his fortress. "By the Stone of Draloch, what's happening to me?" But he knew, for this was the curse of dragons. Georgiana was meant to be his mate. He'd known it even in childhood, felt that tug when he'd peered into her crib and first set eyes on her. She had been swaddled in blankets and had gurgled at him when he'd bent forward to kiss her on her drooling lips to seal their betrothal.

Their marriage had been arranged in that long-ago time when he was a boy in England and eldest son and heir to the Duke of Draloch.

None of it mattered any more.

Arik Blakefield no longer existed. He was Lord Bloodaxe now and his soul was beyond redemption. But he understood why Brihann had brought her to him. Brihann was the black dragon who ruled the Underworld, but as his power waned, so grew his fear. Especially fear of him, for he was Bloodaxe, the one who would take Brihann's place as High King. He was the next black dragon in the line of succession, the one who would eventually grow strong enough to depose the cruel and bitter king that was Brihann.

For some time now, Brihann had been plotting to weaken him. What better way to accomplish it than to deliver his dragon mate to him? "Georgiana," he whispered her name with an agonized groan. She was meant to be his. She was his weakness. Brihann would use her to destroy him.

Bloodaxe climbed to the parapets, shoving open the heavy door and allowing the tension to flow from his body as the hot wind blew on his neck. He removed his battle leather and clothing, the very garments he'd made a great show of donning in front of Georgiana because he'd enjoyed shocking her and thrilling her. Mostly, he enjoyed the feeling it brought to his heart, for that organ had lain dormant for so many years.

He felt his wings begin to form along his back. His body began to writhe and twist as he grew black scales and a black snout. His black tail was long and spiked and flicked through the air like the crack of a whip. He was no longer Bloodaxe or Arik, but an ancient terror who soared above his fortress and flew across the fertile lands and blue lakes that were within his realm.

His dragon eyes scanned along his borderlands searching for signs of Brihann's demon scouts. He peered over the mountain peaks, looking for signs of Brihann's armies on the march. All was quiet, but he knew it wouldn't be for long.

While Brihann meant him to be the next High King, he also feared his growing power and intended to keep him subdued until the very last.

But Bloodaxe felt his own power growing, and he was not one of Brihann's mindless toadies who would always bend to his will.

He raised his dragon neck and roared. He flapped his dragon wings and soared toward the clouds.

He blew fire across the water until his lungs ached.

Only when spent of his lust did he return to the parapet and quickly shift back into his human form. He picked up the clothes he'd neatly stacked upon the stones and put them back on. How long had he been gone? Perhaps half an hour at most.

He hurried downstairs to his vast kitchen. Cooks and scullery maids were bustling about to ensure food was always available to feed his own demon armies. He gathered bread, cheese, and a flask of wine. "I'll dine in my quarters this evening, Thomas. Bring me enough food for two."

"Aye, m'lord," his steward replied, casting him a knowing grin. "Only entertaining one nymph tonight?"

He winked back. "Bring up breakfast as well."

His demon minions were as trustworthy as any demon could be, which meant that most were not trustworthy at all. Thomas and a handful of others had his confidence, but within limits. The fewer who knew of Georgiana's existence, the better. He left the kitchen and took the stairs two at a time, eager to return to his chamber.

He hoped Georgiana had obeyed his instructions to keep the door bolted.

He trusted Charon and Styx to keep her close.

But as he approached his tower bedchamber, he saw the door flung wide open and heard his dogs barking fiercely.

Where was Georgiana?

Was that a pool of her blood on his stone floor?

GEORGIANA KNEW SHE'D made a terrible mistake the moment she opened the door, but the woman who'd spoken to her through it had said she'd brought food at Lord Bloodaxe's instruction. She'd sounded sincere, and the dogs hadn't barked a warning. Of course, that did not excuse her mistake in disobeying a simple command to keep the door bolted.

Three women pushed their way in the moment she'd thrown the bolt. "Witch!" the first one cried and spat in her face. Charon and Styx growled and immediately moved between Georgiana and these women.

"Good dogs," she muttered, taking advantage of the barrier they provided with their sheer size. She turned away and search for a weapon with which to defend herself. A candlestick or fire iron, anything to use in order to hold off her assailants, assuming any of them could get past the beasts who were determined to protect her.

But her assailants had come prepared. One of the women threw something into the eyes of Charon and Styx, a sparkling dust that suddenly blinded them. Instead of guarding her, they were suddenly howling and spinning in circles, useless to defend her from the attack these three had obviously planned.

Georgiana grabbed an ash shovel that hung from a hook beside the fireplace and used it as a makeshift sword. She began to swing it with all her might. "Who are you? Go away. You'll be punished if I'm harmed."

They shouted back at her, but their words were mostly unintelligible and they wailed whenever they glanced at Lord Bloodaxe's bed. Georgiana had never experienced a man's touch in *that* way, but she wasn't an ignorant dolt. These women considered her a rival for their lord's affection. *Mother in heaven.* If only she could make them understand. "You can have him. He isn't mine!"

Lord Bloodaxe would not care what happened to her, but he certainly would be unforgiving for the harm they did to his dogs. What had these women thrown in their faces? She needed to flush out their eyes as soon as possible. "Charon, Styx, are you all right?"

She couldn't tend to them while these three love-starved lunatics were lunging at her. Indeed, even while in a frenzied rage and maniacally distraught, they were the most beautiful women she'd ever seen. How could they be jealous of her? "Nymph," one said amid more shrieks and wails and lunges.

"You are his nymphs?" Georgiana had only read about these exquisite creatures in mythical tales, but these beauties standing before her also had bad tempers and were obviously prone to jealous rages. They wouldn't stop shrieking or clawing at her gown.

"Oh, dear heaven! You think I'm going to marry him?" Finding her in a wedding gown in their lord's chamber might have led them to that conclusion. "Lord Bloodaxe isn't my husband! You can have him. He doesn't belong to me. Can't any of you understand me?"

The nymphs were too busy tearing at her gown and attempting to gouge out her eyes to listen. Georgiana had no choice but to hold her own and continue to swing the ash shovel, cringing each time she struck one of them. But they wouldn't stop their onslaught and her life depended on holding strong until help arrived.

How long could she keep up her battle? She panicked as her arms began to ache and her breaths became labored. Her fingers were growing numb from the death grip she had on the shovel and every frantic swipe she took now caused shooting pains to run straight from her fingers to her shoulders and up into her throbbing temples.

Her strength was fading. She couldn't hold out much longer.

One of the nymphs caught her by the arm and sank her long nails into Georgiana's skin. She yelped in pain as those claw-like fingers broke through her flesh and drew blood. The shovel fell from her grasp and clattered to the floor.

"Die! Die!" the nymphs shrieked in victory.

Georgiana shrank back and covered her ears, for they now had her trapped against the wall and there was no escape.

She closed her eyes and waited for the killing blow.

Miraculously, it never came.

As though in answer to her prayers, Charon and Styx regained their sight and leaped between her and the nymphs. Their big jaws opened wide to expose the sharp teeth that would put fear into any being about to become their next meal. At the same time, Lord Bloodaxe stepped through the door and bellowed.

Georgiana cried out in relief and fell back, bloodied and exhausted. Her heart was pounding wildly and her entire body shivered so badly, she could no longer hold herself up. She sank to her knees in tears. His nymphs had done her some physical harm, but what were a few scratches on her arms and shoulders when her injuries could have been far worse?

"By the Stone of Draloch!" Lord Bloodaxe hurriedly set aside the food and wine he'd brought up and rushed to her side, sparing not a single glance at his nymphs. But they had to know that he was furious. What would he do to them? "Let me have a look at you, Georgiana. How badly are you injured?"

The nymphs ran off wailing and shrieking and leaving a trail of blood across the floor. She had done them little damage. Charon and Styx must have gotten their teeth into them and bitten down hard. Indeed, there was blood everywhere. Was some of it hers? "See to your dogs, I think they're hurt worse." She drew back when he reached out to gather her into his arms. "Don't touch me."

"Georgiana," he said gently, but she slapped his hand away.

She knew was on the verge of hysteria, but couldn't stop herself from tipping over the edge. Would he punish her for striking him? "What manner of world is this?" she cried between sobs and gasps and hiccups. "Your nymphs attacked me." *His bed mates.* "I tried to explain that I was nothing to you but they wouldn't believe me."

He frowned. "You opened the door. I warned you not to do it." But he sounded angrier with himself than he was with her. "The Underworld is a dangerous place. You won't survive an hour unless you do exactly as I say. Don't disobey me again."

He reached out once more to lift her into his arms and this time she did not resist. Charon and Styx came to his side as he carried her to his bed and eased her down so that she was now seated in the center of it. "Don't move." Although he was still frowning, his manner was surprisingly restrained. "Let me see what they've done to you."

She nodded, as yet unable to speak. Her heart was still madly beating a hole through her chest and she had several deep scratches along her forearms. Indeed, her arms had taken the worst of the damage. His nymphs had caught her by the arms and buried their sharp nails into her, but she'd also managed to break free and raise them in order to shield her face when they'd started to claw at her. "Let me go home. Please."

His dogs approached, whimpering. They began to lick her sore hands.

"Big babies," she muttered and patted them on the head.

Lord Bloodaxe arched a dark eyebrow in surprise. "They like you. I left them here to watch over you, but it seems you were the one who protected them."

She nodded. "Your nymphs threw something into their eyes. Thank goodness it was only meant to momentarily stun them. They seem recovered now. But I think we ought to flush their eyes with water, just to be sure."

"You care more for my hounds than you do for yourself." He

seemed surprised by her concern, but she had never been able to walk away from any injured creature. She watched as he took a moment to make certain they were well. "Go," he said in a whisper to each one and they immediately ran out of his bedchamber, their paws skittering on the stone steps as they tore downstairs.

He crossed the room to shut the door so that she was now left alone with him. "Where are they going?"

He returned to her side and stared down at her.

Although his eyes were the color of blue ice, there was nothing cool or detached in his gaze. The fire in his glance simply melted her bones.

She swallowed hard, for nothing stood between them but warm air and the remnants of her tattered gown. The beads that had been painstakingly sewn on by a team of seamstresses were strewn across the floor. "Um, why did you send your dogs out?"

"They'll be back soon." Which begged the question. Where had he sent them? Another shiver ran up her spine as she realized the order Bloodaxe must have silently issued to them. They were to find the nymphs. And do what to them?

Bloodaxe's gaze intensified as he probed her thoughts. "This isn't England. There is only my justice here, Georgiana."

She stifled a sob, uncertain why she should care about his nymphs when they had meant to kill her. This Underworld was a brutal place. She knew he wasn't going to be kind or forgiving. He confirmed it with his next words. "They knew the punishment they faced for breaking into my chamber and attacking you and my dogs. They'll die swiftly, that is the mercy I shall show them. But they must die."

"Is there no other way?" She couldn't remain silent and allow them to be put to death because of her.

"Imprisonment is an even crueler fate. It is a long, slow end to their miserable lives. Why do you care about them? They meant to kill you." He crossed to his table where an ewer filled with water and a basin stood. He poured water onto a cloth and lightly wrung out the excess moisture before returning to her side and settling on the bed beside her.

"Come here." He drew her onto his lap and began to carefully wipe the blood from her torn skin. "Let me know if I'm hurting you."

There was a darkly irresistible quality about him. He had a ruggedly handsome face and a magnificent warrior's body anchored to muscled arms as firm as granite that would make any woman sigh. His hard exterior was so at odds with the tender manner in which he treated her. "Why do you handle me with such care?"

He shrugged and paused a moment in his ministrations. "You were brought here for a purpose. I will protect you until I understand what that purpose is."

"And if I turn out to be useless to you, what then?" She dreaded the answer, but had to ask.

"I'll take you back to your home."

"England? Wethersby Hall?" But she dared not trust his response, for he might have said he would do so only to keep her calm. At the moment, she didn't care. She liked being in his arms and liked the touch of his rough, calloused hand on her waist as he held her close. She felt the warmth and strength of his body against hers and began to lean into him.

She quickly stopped herself.

He was a demon lord and not to be trusted… certainly not as completely as she wished to trust him. Although he'd denied it, he could have been the one to abduct her and bring her to his fortress. He could tell her anything and she'd have no way of proving it true or false.

"Yes, Wethersby Hall. I will return you to your father. Unharmed." He took her hands in his and carefully pressed the moist cloth against the scratches that ran along the length of each arm. He started with the one most badly injured, and after carefully clearing away the blood from that arm, he moved on to the other. "Your cuts are deep and must be properly cleansed. Whiskey ought to do the trick."

She shook her head, confused. "Am I to drink it?"

His lips turned upward in the hint of a smile. "If you wish, but it's better poured on the wounds. It will burn, but keep those cuts from getting infected."

He looked quite handsome when he smiled. She hadn't realized demons were capable of it. Nor had she realized demons could be so handsome. But he was proving her beliefs wrong. She returned his smile with a hesitant one of her own.

He lifted her off his lap and set her down in the center of his bed, the gesture so sudden, she almost lost her balance and fell flat against the mattress. She scooted closer to the footboard as he rose to his majestic height. His shoulders had felt big and solid when she was nestled against them, but appeared even bigger now.

"Um…" She tucked her feet under herself and began to nervously smooth her gown. "Oh, dear." She slid her hand along the fabric and felt nothing but rips everywhere. "It's ruined beyond repair."

He crossed to his table and returned with two goblets and the bottle of whiskey. The heady scent of spirits filled the air as he uncorked the bottle. "I'll help you take off the gown once I've finished cleansing your wounds. You can wear one of my shirts for now."

He stood looming over her once again as though waiting for her consent. He was a Dragon Lord, ruler of this nightmarish realm. Why would he show her any courtesy? "But you will find me suitable clothes to wear soon, won't you? I can't walk around in a shirt… your shirt. It will swallow me up and I'll look ridiculous in it." She cleared her throat. "I'll also need shoes and stockings. Do the women in your realm wear underclothing? Your nymphs didn't."

"Nymphs never do. They prefer to wear no clothes at all."

"Oh." Even while fighting for her life she'd noticed the delicately beautiful gowns they were wearing, the fabric ethereal and draping over their bodies in diaphanous waves. What a silly thing to notice. She hoped it didn't speak of her own shallowness in character to be thinking of clothes while struggling to save herself from death. "But surely you don't permit them to traipse around wearing nothing at all."

He eyed her speculatively. "Not outside of their private quarters. Or mine."

"Yours? Oh, I see." She cleared her throat again. "It's quite warm in here. Is it like this all year round? I enjoy wearing clothes. I wear them *all* the time. Lots of them. With thick stockings and heavy boots. It's winter at Penrith. I'd freeze if I were as scantily clad as your nymphs. You ought to purchase sturdier gowns for them. The slightest breeze will–"

"You may remain bound in your protective armor if you wish," he said, referring to her own gown. "But your lacings are obviously too tight and the fabric is tattered and bloodied." He handed her a silver goblet into which he'd poured a little of the whiskey. The goblet was finely crafted and there was a dragon etched into the cup. The design of the stem appeared to be a dragon's tail.

The amber liquid glowed within the goblet.

She took a sip.

Curiously, the dragon etched in silver seemed to come to life.

Of course, Lord Bloodaxe had marked all his possessions with the Draloch dragon crest. How was he connected to the family? And he'd muttered something about a stone of Draloch when he'd walked in on his nymphs attacking her. What did that signify?

The Draloch family owned properties not far from Wethersby Hall, but she knew little about the members of that family. Curiously, her father had never extended an invitation to the present duke even though they were neighbors and certainly traveled in the same *ton* circle.

Was there a feud between the Blakefields and the Wethersbys that she was unaware of?

Lord Bloodaxe poured a little of the whiskey into another goblet for himself and raised it in a mocking toast. "Drink up, Georgiana."

She toyed with the cup in her hands, twirling it lightly by the stem, but didn't put it to her lips again. "I thought this was to be used for medicinal purposes."

He gazed at her with an intensity that sent hot tingles shooting through her body. "Drink it. This is a medicinal use. You're talking too much and shivering. I think you're going into shock. This will warm you."

"And shut me up as well?" She grinned and took a second sip. "Oh, goodness. That's strong." She coughed and her eyes began to water. "I always talk too much when I'm overset. Can you blame me?" She took another sip. And another. The liquid felt like fire flowing through her body. "May I have some more?"

She held out the cup, surprised that she'd drained its contents so quickly and rather liking its mildly numbing effect.

He took it from her hand and set it aside. "In a moment." He drew her back onto his lap and began to run the cloth doused in whiskey on the hideous red welts and scratches running along the length of each of her arms.

She winced as ripples of pain surged through her. "It hurts." She tried to draw away, but he wouldn't allow it. Instead, he held her in a seemingly light embrace designed to keep her in place, but his arms were as hard and unyielding as the iron bars of a prison.

His words, however, were gentle. "Close your eyes and rest your head against my shoulder. It might help a little. I'm sorry, Georgiana, but I must do this or your pain will be a thousand times worse should infection set in."

"I thought demons liked to inflict pain. Why are you so considerate of me?" He'd said that he would protect her until he understood her purpose for being here, but his behavior toward her was far more than merely accommodating. One might think he cared for her. He certainly seemed to be indulging her.

"Perhaps tomorrow I'll show you a little of my lands. The Underworld realms are as different as the continents of your world." His voice was deep and soothing as he purposely ignored her question. She caught the light scent of whiskey on his breath. The scent was on her breath as well and soaking through her pores so that she now reeked of it. She wasn't used to drinking spirits of any sort and had imbibed too much all at once.

Her hiccups gave her away.

She alternated between sniffling, crying out "ouch" and hiccupping as he continued to treat her wounds. "I'm not being very brave, am I?"

"Your cuts are quite deep, Georgiana. You're holding up as well as any soldier would. Few men could endure this pain without flinching."

Her eyes rounded in surprise, for he appeared sincere and there was no hint of a sneer on his nicely formed lips. There was something in his gaze that tugged at her heart. He was one of those men who could endure incredible pain, and she knew by the darkness within the deep blue of his eyes that he had endured much. Yet, he was intent on shielding her from it. "Will you tell me more about your realm?"

It suddenly seemed important for her to learn as much about him as possible.

He gave a slight nod and resumed tending to her. "We have oceans and mountains and forests, such as you'll find in your world. But unlike yours, we have two moons that shine constantly in our sky. We live by moonlight. Our sun died out long ago. Indeed, so long ago that there are no ancients alive who remember it blazing in our red sky."

He continued talking to distract her from the burning pain that seared through her body whenever he applied the whiskey to her arms. She dared not get too comfortable beside him and was not about to rest her head upon his shoulder, no matter how appealing the prospect or how desperately she wanted to. He was a demon. A dangerous Dragon Lord. Why did she feel such a bond with him?

Although she remained on his lap, she insisted on sitting upright and did not close her eyes.

He arched an eyebrow, the slight gesture conveying he understood why she was sitting straight as a post. She tipped her chin up and glanced away, but felt the shrug of his broad shoulders against her skin. How could she not feel his every movement while splendidly trapped in his arms? "Please tell me more, my lord."

"Life here can be as peaceful or violent as in yours, Georgiana. But there are important differences."

She nodded. "The creatures here are quite different. Your justice is brutal and swift."

His expression hardened and his voice turned harsh, but she understood it was not aimed at her. "There is no system of justice in my world other than brute strength. If you anger someone, he will kill you. If you have allies, they will in turn kill your assailant. But tomorrow those same allies might decide you are now the enemy and turn on you." Now finished cleansing her cuts and gashes, he shifted her off his lap and sat her on the mattress. Grabbing his own cup, he refilled it and crossed to the window to stare out of it.

She watched him as he took a hearty gulp and then set down his goblet on the table beside him. Only then did he turn back to her, crossing his arms over his massive chest. "Power and retribution are the rules by which we survive. But that mostly applies to those who remain in the Underworld. Many are just passing through, not yet lost souls, but simply crossing through this realm on their journey to another destination."

Georgiana was enthralled. "To heaven?"

The mention of heaven must not have pleased him, for his expression once again turned quite forbidding. "Sometimes. Sometimes back to your world as a new soul."

Georgiana was eager to know more. She decided to press on until she sensed he'd been pushed too far. "And sometimes their souls are too dark to move on so they remain here?"

He glanced toward the window and his realm that lay beyond it. "Aye, trapped here for a myriad of reasons and doomed to remain for eternity."

"But they can die here as well. What happens to them then?"

He spoke without looking at her, his gaze still fixed on whatever lurked beyond these walls. "They no longer exist. They never return. They can never move on. They simply are no more."

She rose and walked to stand beside him, wanting to touch him, for this Dragon Lord could not hide the ache of his misery from her. The need to place her hand on him and comfort him was overwhelming, but he moved away before she succumbed to the foolish urge to put her arms around him.

He wasn't her friend.

He was merely her protector for the moment, and she wasn't yet certain he was that. At the same time, she knew that he was someone important to her. "Lord Bloodaxe, I won't deny that I'm desperate to return to my family. I'm terrified here and wish to go home." She paused a moment to nibble her lip in thought. "Yet, I'm not terrified of you. I know I ought to be, but there's something about you that is so familiar."

He would not look at her and his features remained expressionless, but she knew he was troubled by her words. She'd asked him before about their connection. They were more than strangers. Why wouldn't he tell her? She sensed something else was troubling him, was silently at war within him. "Lord Bloodaxe, are you afraid of me?"

He appeared startled for a moment, and then threw his head back and laughed heartily. "No, I'm not afraid of you. But an *innocent* does not belong in the Underworld. You were brought through a demon portal and should not have survived the journey, yet you are standing here beside me and very much alive. War will soon be upon us. Why are you here? Why were you given to me? What will happen to you if I take you back to your realm? I don't know if it is even possible to take you back."

"Why don't we try it and see?" She held her breath, knowing he wasn't likely to agree. But one could always hope. That was one of her strengths. She was always filled with hope. Indeed, she carried buckets full of it within her heart.

"Not tonight, Georgiana." His laughter faded as he studied her, his sensual gaze causing her blood to turn hot with a new sensation she knew had to be desire. She'd never felt this tingling need for any man before, not even Oliver. Is it possible she desired this stranger? For pity's sake, why? "But we will try soon."

Her eyes rounded in surprise. "We will?"

"Yes." He took a step toward her. "Dragon lords are as fickle as the dragons they shift into. There is no question that I must get you out of here, although I cannot tell you when that will be, only that it must be soon. I'm a dragon, Georgiana. Either I will take you as a bedmate, or... I will eat you for my supper."

CHAPTER THREE

THE HOUR GREW late and Bloodaxe was losing patience with Georgiana's reluctance to take off her gown. He had only himself to blame for scaring the wits out of her, but she needed to know what he was and the danger he represented to her. "I'm not going to eat you, Georgiana."

"So you say now. Is that supposed to calm me?" She was standing by the closed window, staring out at the two big moons that were floating like silver balls in the distant, dark red sky. Her long, golden hair spilled over her slight shoulders as she stood quite still, her injured arms wrapped around herself.

"You're too little and bony to make a decent meal." He sighed, realizing he was frightening her again. She looked so helpless and lost. How was he to keep her safe once war broke out? "I give you my oath. I'm not going to hurt you in any way."

She shivered in response.

"Here." He handed her one of his shirts, wishing he had the ability to heal her with a mere wave of his hand. But Underworld demons were not good healers, often causing more damage with their dark magic. Only the Fae had the ability to heal others and there were no Fae healers here. "You're cold and obviously tired. You didn't eat much tonight."

"I wasn't hungry. How could I be after what you said? Every bite I took only made me think of my body being chewed in your dragon teeth. Or are they fangs?" She tensed as he took her by the shoulders and turned her to face away from him.

"Snakes have fangs. Dragons have sharp teeth and spiked tails. And we don't slither on the ground. We have long wings that allow us to soar through the clouds and glide effortlessly on the wind over the lakes and forests we've marked as our territory."

She glanced over her shoulder at him. "How do you mark your territory?"

"Through conquest and bloodshed. We do not piss on the ground as beasts of your realm do to mark their corners."

"I didn't mean…"

"Yes, you did." But he wasn't angered by her impertinent question, for he was a beast. The primal instinct of survival was all that was left of him. "Hold still while I untie this tangle of strings that holds your gown together. How can you breathe in this contraption? It must be cutting into your ribs." He began to work the laces of her gown loose.

She tensed as his knuckles grazed her skin. "What are you doing?"

"I just told you. I'm taking it off you. Hold still." She had to know he wasn't going to allow her to sleep in this stained and ruined garment of hers. Indeed, she badly needed some rest. She'd been drugged and unconscious during her abduction. Those drugs and the strain of her journey into the Underworld must have taken a toll on her delicate body.

His nymphs had shown her no mercy and their attack had been vicious. Although Georgiana was not complaining, he knew those cuts were nasty and deep, too raw and exposed to overlook. Had his nymphs been true demons, the damage caused would have been far worse.

"Your gown needs to be burned." He ignored the softness of her shoulders and the sweet scent of her skin that stirred the dragon ache within his heart. "Take it off." He turned away and whistled for his dogs to settle on the floor at the foot of his bed while he kept his back turned and tried his best not to think of the sleek silk fabric sliding down her perfect body and falling in a gossamer pool of white at her feet. "Your undergarments as well."

"I can't."

"I'm not going to touch you," he said with a gentleness that surprised him even more than it surprised her. He'd lost such feelings long ago and never believed they were merely lying dormant for Georgiana to awaken.

His words seemed to calm her.

"Will you sleep in your bedclothes?" she asked as she removed the last of her garments and he heard the light *whoosh* as they fell to the floor.

"Of course. Wouldn't want to shock your delicate, English sensibilities." He usually wore nothing to bed, but Georgiana was already overset. Seeing *him* naked would likely send her into a fit of hysterics.

He didn't need a woman shrieking in his ear, not in that way. His usual evening entertainments involved bed games with two or three nymphs, and their shrieks were of the more sensual variety, of pleasure and desire fulfilled. But there would be no such sport with Georgiana this evening. Once she was settled in his bed, he'd grab a pillow and coverlet and stretch out on the floor beside the door. "Are you decent?"

He heard her small voice respond from across the room. "If you consider my wearing your shirt decent, then yes."

"Good." He turned to face her and instantly felt a slam to his heart. She was the most beautiful sight he'd ever beheld, even though she was almost lost within the folds of his shirt. She looked so soft and womanly. Her bare legs were nicely shaped. But her allure went far beyond mere physical beauty. Why did she mean so much more to him than that? "Get into bed. I won't touch you," he repeated, knowing she was not at all comfortable with their sleeping arrangements.

Perhaps he needed to caution himself as well.

He expected words of protest to spill from her lips and was surprised when she merely nodded and settled her body between the sheets.

Her unexpected compliance troubled him. Did she trust him?

She refused to look at him as she stretched out under the covers. Instead, she turned away so that her back was to him. He'd instructed her to take the far side of the bed, for he wanted to keep her away from any means of access. He and his dogs would put themselves between her and the door. His nymphs had already attacked her.

Who else would come after her in the dark of night?

He sat on the bed beside her, intending nothing more than to take off his boots. As he sat, the weight of his body put a dip in the mattress, causing Georgiana to slide closer to him. She quickly scrambled away. He sighed. "You needn't worry. I don't eat sleeping virgins either."

"Ah, thank you for those soothing words. I shall sleep ever so calmly now." Her voice was dripping with sarcasm, but she also sounded fatigued and could not hide it.

"I give you my oath, Georgiana. I will not harm you." He would repeat it as often as she needed to hear it. "I'm merely taking off my boots. I'll sleep on the floor tonight. Get a good night's rest. Tomorrow will be a busy day."

However, he knew his sleep would be as restless as hers was bound to be. *Georgiana.* She was his weakness. He longed to lie beside her and feel her body curled against his.

She would likely be the death of him. But what a sweet death it would be.

"What is to happen tomorrow?" she asked, her voice barely above a whisper as she struggled to hide her trepidation.

War. Danger. "I don't know."

"But you just said it would be busy. So why–"

"By the Stone of Draloch! Stop asking questions."

He groaned inwardly, knowing he'd probably frightened her again.

But she merely sighed with impatience. "You would be doing the same if our situations were reversed."

"Perhaps." But he knew it was not so. He wouldn't be bothering with questions. He'd be shifting into a dragon and setting his abductors and all they possessed ablaze. He'd be sweeping across their lands, a great dark shadow bellowing flames until all that lay in his path was scorched and burned to ashes. Indeed, he wouldn't bother with questions. Those foolish enough to attempt to take him had to know they would die.

She continued to study him, but her lids were heavy from fatigue and he noticed a yawn escape her generous lips. Those lips! They were perfectly shaped and would feel exquisite when they yielded to the pressure of his mouth. *When* they yielded? No, he wasn't going to kiss her. Not ever. He shook his head and studied her.

Her lips were adorably puckered and she was still frowning at him. "I don't think I can stop asking questions. I've been brought to a strange land against my will and attacked by strange creatures. I have a right to know what my purpose is here." Her breaths turned short and ragged. "Or if I am meant to survive."

"Damn it, Georgiana." He slammed his fist into the mattress, causing the entire bed to rattle. Blasted Stone of Draloch and the games it played with their fates! No doubt he'd frightened her again. "I've already told you that I don't know why you've been brought here. I have no answers for you."

She'd scrambled to the opposite edge of the bed again, but her gaze as she stared at him remained one of irritation and not terror. "My lord, is your disposition always so sour before bed?"

"Worse." He groaned and shook his head, finally giving in to the urge to laugh. She wasn't afraid of him which meant she trusted him not to hurt her. That pleased him more than he dared admit. "I'm usually much worse."

But her trust, coupled with the heat she ignited in him, dangerously stirred his dragon lust. He turned away from her. In any event, he needed to keep an eye on the door he'd made certain to securely bolt earlier. He'd also locked the windows to prevent unwanted creatures from flying in unannounced.

They were now sealed in his quarters and the air was so hot and stifling, the room felt more like a locked tomb.

But it couldn't be helped. Although he hadn't spotted them yet, he knew Brihann's demon spies were scouting outside his fortress. Brihann's armies would likely soon be poised on the border between their territories awaiting the order to attack his lands. That order would be issued the moment he attempted to return Georgiana to her home.

How was he to sneak her through a portal while the High King was watching?

He dared not risk it yet for several reasons, the most troubling one being that he was in no hurry to rid himself of Georgiana's company. He meant to take advantage of each precious moment spent with her, for war between the realms of man and demon was looming. He didn't know what the outcome would be or whether either of them would survive.

However, he was a warrior, a Dragon Lord, and expected to be in the vanguard of the great battles. He didn't care what fate awaited him. But what of Georgiana? Why had she been tossed in with him?

He needed to learn the answers from the Stone of Draloch. But the journey to the palace of the Fae king where that monolith stood would take too long, and after today's incident with his nymphs, he dared not leave Georgiana behind for any length of time.

Nor could he take her with him. Brihann was guarding the portals. In any event, travel between realms was too dangerous for a mortal. Especially when there were forces who did not wish her to leave. Brihann wasn't the only one to worry about. He doubted the Stone of Draloch would permit him to carry her off to safety when Georgiana had been brought into the Underworld for a purpose yet unknown.

If her presence was meant to shake him to the very depths of his demonic core, it had worked. There were only two beings across time and realms that he would sacrifice his life to protect.

Georgiana was one of them.

After an hour had passed, Bloodaxe quietly strode to the bed and knelt beside her small frame. Had she fallen asleep yet? Her eyes were closed and she was breathing calmly. He inhaled her scent and ran his fingers along her cheek that was warm and pink and tempting. "Georgiana—"

"If you're thinking of making untoward advances, don't. I took one of the dinner knives and hid it under my pillow."

He groaned lightly, amused by her attempt to protect herself. "A dinner knife? Why would you tell me that and lose the element of surprise?" He strode to the pallet he'd fashioned for himself by the door and picked up his battle axe. The weapon was almost as big as she was and probably weighed more than she did with boots on and sopping wet. He returned to her side and carefully propped it against the footboard.

"What are you doing?" she asked when he knelt beside her once more.

"Why do you think I'm known as Lord Bloodaxe? This is my preferred instrument of battle." He pointed to the blade that was within easy reach. "I always keep it finely honed and close at hand. Do you think your puny knife would ever save you from my axe?"

"No, but you vowed that you would never harm me."

He nodded. "I meant it."

She drew the covers up to her neck so that only her face was showing as she gazed at him. "Then why did you come to my side and whisper my name?" She sighed when he failed to respond. "Rest easy, my lord. I would never use my puny knife, or any weapon for that matter, against you. My heart simply won't allow it. I don't understand why I trust you so completely even when you've threatened me and purposely frightened me."

"Your heart knows I will not harm you."

"Then why are you still hovering over me?"

"I'm kneeling beside you. I merely wish to make certain you haven't developed a fever." He used the explanation as an excuse to run his knuckles across her cheek again. "How do you feel?"

She stifled a yawn. "Tired, but otherwise fine."

"Are you in pain?"

She nodded. "But only a little. My arms are throbbing. I'm afraid to sleep and yet my body is so weary, I yearn for it."

"Then close your eyes and stop fighting against your exhaustion." He settled his gaze on her, knowing he was making a mistake to remain so close, but he needed to breathe in her scent, that sweet, clean aroma of wildflowers and strawberries.

Stone of Draloch, I ache for this girl.

She was still huddled so close to the edge of his bed that the slightest movement would send her toppling to the floor. "This bed is all yours, Georgiana. Make yourself comfortable in it."

"How can I when it is your bed?"

"It isn't mine this evening." But he could not deny his torment. He wanted to wrap his arms around her and draw her up against his body. He wanted to claim her. Possess her. Spill his dragon seed into her. But that would be an incredibly dangerous mistake. She'd already smashed his iron control to bits.

He didn't dare couple with her.

She'd destroy him completely.

Her golden hair spilled across his pillow. Her womanly body was curled in a kittenish ball so that she looked small and lost amid the ocean of his satin sheets. Moonlight shone upon his bed, surrounding both of them in its gentle glow.

His blood was on fire.

He silently called out again to the Stone of Draloch. *Why have you brought Georgiana to me? She can only weaken me when I must be strong for battle.*

To his surprise, the Stone of Draloch responded. *Do not be foolish, son of Draloch. She is your greatest gift. Do not make her your greatest tragedy.*

Cursed stone! It spoke in riddles, never offering a clear path or a logical plan of action. What was he to do with Georgiana? Succumb to his dragon lust and claim her for his own? Ignore it and free her? He didn't know how best to keep her safe. "Georgie," he said in an anguished whisper, calling her by the name he'd used upon sealing their betrothal when she was but a babe in swaddling clothes.

Had anyone else ever called her that?

Perhaps her betrothed had done so, using it as his pet name for her.

His dragon rage ignited once more and he could not tamp down the urge to torch the blackguard with his dragon fire. *Mine. She's mine.*

Behave, son of Draloch! The Stone of Draloch was still in his head and reading his thoughts. But never offering help.

Why should I behave? What will you do to me? What can possibly be worse than what you've already forced me to endure?

The stone turned ominously silent.

"Georgie," he whispered again, reaching out to make certain she was still there and not swept out of his life as suddenly she had been brought into it.

She said nothing.

Exhaustion had finally conquered her. She had fallen asleep, the peaceful sleep of the innocent.

In the next moment, he heard her soft snores.

Stay. Stay with me, Georgiana. He thanked the Fates that she was still beside him.

How long before he lost her again?

"I'M SO SORRY," Georgiana said with a gasp, quickly shaking off the remnants of her morning haziness. She rolled to her knees and stared down in horror at Lord Bloodaxe's big, muscled body. His hugely muscled and shirtless body.

Did the man have no proper bed clothes?

"Oh, my goodness. I don't remember climbing out of bed." Had she spent the night on the floor beside him? Worse, had she slept all night with her body scandalously curled around his? "I… I must have grown cold."

It was an utterly ridiculous lie and he knew it.

He smirked and did nothing to hide his amusement. "In this stifling room?" He rolled to his feet, seemingly unaffected by her nearness or touch. Her heart was wildly leaping in her chest so that she could hardly catch her breath. Still smirking, he casually crossed to the large windows to open them and allow in a breeze.

He remained standing by one of the windows, his assessing dragon gaze fixed on the mist rising over the distant forest and thankfully not on her.

She had yet to recover from her embarrassment. Her voice was tight as she asked, "What are you looking at?"

He continued to scan the landscape. "I'm searching for signs of Brihann's demons. They must have been camped on the borderlands last night, but I still don't see them."

"How can you find them through that layer of gray clouds? Perhaps they withdrew, assuming they were ever there."

"They were and still are." He inhaled deeply.

"What are you doing now?" She marveled at how finely sculpted his warrior body truly was. There was nothing soft about him other than the occasional softening in his glance toward her when he thought she wasn't looking.

He remained by the window, standing as tall and proud as a monument. Indeed, he appeared to be shaped of granite and covered in taut, rippling skin.

Nicely bronzed skin.

Nothing pale or delicate about him, and yet there was no denying his regal elegance.

He inhaled again. "If they are out there, then their foul scent will give them away. Demon stench lingers in the air."

She quietly approached him, feeling quite small now standing by his side although she was of average height by London Society standards. "I don't smell anything. Do you?"

"Aye, I do." He glanced down at her and grinned. "It's your scent that fills my nostrils."

She gasped. "Mine?"

He caught her by the waist when she tried to draw away.

She squirmed in his arms. "Let go of me, my lord."

Instead, he laughed and drew her shamefully close.

She tried to push off him, but realized her mistake at once. His skin was warm and inviting. His muscles were… *Mother in heaven.* "I haven't bathed yet. Don't you dare breathe me in."

"You mistake my meaning, Georgiana. Your scent is that of wild-flowers and strawberries. Do you think any demon ever smelled so sweet?"

She stopped struggling but eyed him warily. "Then you weren't referring to my foul stench?"

"No." His regard almost appeared tender. "You are a rare nectar meant to be savored."

She knew he had to be teasing her once more, for only her parents had ever considered her rare or special. She was desirable to others because she was the daughter of a wealthy duke and considered pretty. She was not a perfect beauty like the young women considered Incomparables.

But Lord Bloodaxe sometimes looked at her as though she was. A rare nectar? The idea was laughable. "Do not compare me to drink or food," she teased, her humor returning as the shock of her scandalous thoughts began to diminish. "I am not a drink to quench your dragon thirst or food to satisfy your dragon hunger."

"*Georgiana.*" He spoke her name with an aching growl. "One taste of you would never be enough to satisfy me."

His voice resonated through her like a caress. No! Was she mad to have such feelings for a demon lord? "Why? Because I'm too little and bony."

"Aye, that." He lightly tugged on the sleeve of the shirt he'd loaned her. "Your strawberry scent clings to my shirt. It is all I will have to remember you by once I return you to your family."

She gaped at him.

A flame of hope kindled in her heart. "Then you truly meant what you said? You will take me home?"

"I gave you my oath. How many times must you hear it before you will believe me?" He appeared sincere, but could she ever trust the word of a demon? Yet, there was something about Lord Bloodaxe that inspired confidence. "You were a gift to me and mine to do with as I please. It pleases me to deliver you back into the arms of your family."

"Thank you." Relief washed over her. She hadn't believed him yesterday, not completely. She hadn't believed him until this very moment.

But having survived the night alone with him and knowing he'd behaved honorably even when she hadn't, somehow made his words ring true when they hadn't before. She rubbed her eyes as tears suddenly welled in them and began to spill onto her cheeks. "I thought I was trapped here forever."

Perhaps it wasn't the wisest thing to say to him.

He'd been nothing but protective and respectful of her. He'd treated her wounds with gentle care. "Not that you make me feel trapped. You don't at all… not very much. That is, I understand why you've confined me here. For my own protection. It isn't your fault that I can't leave your bedchamber. Or that you've ordered your dogs to stop me if I try." She was blathering, somehow demeaning his generosity because her gratitude sounded like an insult. Perhaps this is why she'd remained a spinster until Oliver had come along.

She sighed. "You have a way of overwhelming me. I suppose you do that to everyone. I'm terrified of remaining here. I'm terrified that you will change your mind. I'm terrified that—"

"Enough, Georgiana. You won't be here much longer. I'll get you out." His blue eyes grew dark and angry. "It is not me who traps you here. Do you think I enjoy playing nursemaid to you? You're a distraction and a nuisance. I wish to be rid of you as soon as possible."

There was a look of impatience in his eyes.

She held her breath.

No, it was darker than that. Perhaps anger or frustration.

He looked angry enough to eat her.

After a moment, she released the breath she'd been holding. "I'm so sorry that I'm a nuisance to you. It's my fault, I know. I'll do my best not to get in your way. Oliver didn't have much use for me either."

"Oliver? Your betrothed."

She nodded. "An arranged marriage. After five seasons, my family despaired of my ever making a match. You see, I'd held out for love." Heat rose in her cheeks. "A silly, hopeful dream. But I never felt anything for any of the gentlemen who courted me, so I finally gave up and settled for the amiable companionship Oliver offered."

She frowned and pursed her lips in thought. "You may think me foolish for what I am about to say. I've never experienced love, but I know in my heart how it should feel. At least, I think I do. Sometimes I feel as though I have experienced it, but I don't know where or when." She had been staring at her toes as she spoke, but now looked up at him.

She couldn't make out his expression, only that he no longer appeared angry. The frightening darkness had faded from his eyes. "Lord Bloodaxe... I..."

She turned away and gazed at her toes once more. How could she tell him the rest of it? He'd laugh at her and call her a fool.

How could she tell him what she did not believe possible herself? But there was no overlooking their connection. She dared not call it attraction.

He was a demon.

And yet, he was something more.

Someone important to her.

How was he important to her?

CHAPTER FOUR

I N THIS MOMENT, Bloodaxe wanted to tell Georgiana the truth. In this moment, he wanted her to know that he was once Arik Blakefield, the one meant to be Duke of Draloch and her betrothed. He glanced out the window at the two moons that always shone in the red sky. Bright by day and dim by night, but always there.

Always a reminder of the life he'd given up when following his little brother into the Underworld to rescue him. *Saron.*

He had succeeded in saving his brother, but had paid an enormous price for it. By rescuing Saron, he'd condemned himself to this brutal and soulless Underworld existence.

Even so, he would do it all over again without a moment's hesitation. It mattered not that Saron hated him and had sworn to kill him on sight. That hatred sprang from Brihann's evil doing, a monstrous act purposely designed to keep the Draloch brothers from ever uniting.

Two black dragons shall reign supreme.
Two black dragons shall unite the worlds of demon and man.

But which two?

He, Saron, and Brihann were the only black dragons. Three dragons. The words of the prophecy mentioned only two. *Which two?* He and Brihann who could unite both worlds by demonic conquest? Or was it possible that he and Saron would reconcile and unite both worlds by truce?

The Stone of Draloch could be interpreted in many ways.

What was Georgiana's part in his destiny?

He fixed his gaze on the moons that sat well above the horizon and towered over the thin tendrils of mist still clinging to the forest treetops. The mist was heavier than usual this morning. There was a dampness to the air which meant rain was in the offing.

The heat was already oppressive and stuck to his skin.

He glanced at Georgiana who was staring at him with her innocent green eyes and stirring his dragon lust.

There was no time to dwell on thoughts of her exquisite body, for a hot breeze now carried the scent of demon toward him. Brihann's demons were finally making their presence known.

There was no chance of taking her to the Razor Cliffs and freedom now. But he had a week before he was due to return to Brihann's palace for a war council with the other Dragon Lords. Seven days to form a plan to help Georgiana escape the Underworld.

However, this was not his only concern.

A great war was about to break out between the realms of man and demon, if Brihann had his way. How was he to keep Georgiana safe once she was out of his realm?

"My lord, is something wrong?" Georgiana was studying his scowling face and must have noticed his subtle tension in his stance. "What do you see out there?"

"There isn't much to see yet. But the day is young and the thick clouds will disappear once the storm passes. Ours is the same as your English rain. Just water and nothing for you to fear." However, he'd just caught Brihann's particularly foul scent and he was a creature to fear.

Why was Brihann out there?

It was one thing for the High King to send his demon scouts to spy on him, or to send his demon armies to block his path to the Razor Cliffs, for that was the access to the demon portal opening onto Friar's Crag. Georgiana's home was not far from that ominous red mountain no mortal man ever dared go near.

But it was quite another thing for Brihann to actually lead his demon armies. There was only one reason for it.

Georgiana.

He swore silently.

She had to escape the Underworld this very day.

Can I not have even one more day with her?

He knew the answer, and the Stone of Draloch's silence confirmed it.

Georgiana was not meant to remain with him.

She had spoken of love and betrothal. Perhaps she would not know love with the one she called Oliver, but it was best for her to go through with the wedding. Brihann would lose interest in her once she was wed to another.

There was no question that Oliver would marry her. As the wealthy daughter of Penrith, she would still be desirable to her betrothed. The blackguard would overlook all scandal to have her dowry.

He fought back the urge to kill Oliver.

The man would soon have Georgiana.

He sorely wanted to kill Oliver.

"You're angry again." Georgiana placed her small hand on his arm.

"Not at you." Keeping to his purpose and helping Georgiana escape was no easy matter now that Georgiana had lain beside him. She'd sought him out in her sleep last night, coming to his side in tears and pain.

"My arms hurt," she'd said.

He'd wrapped her in his embrace so that she might be soothed by the heat of his body, by the dragon fire she aroused in him.

Could he ever give her up now? The insistent urge to possess her, the unrelenting need to claim her for his own, grew stronger with each passing hour.

All the more reason to give her up now.

Another day. Another hour. And he wouldn't have the strength to let her go. He'd felt the soft perfection of her body against his and knew she was meant to be his dragon mate.

Brihann knew it as well and now meant to take her from him to use as a weapon against him. This must have been Brihann's purpose all along, to give him the hope of love and then snatch it from him.

Keep Georgiana safe.

She was his weakness.

She drove him mad with wanting.

Madness surely had taken hold of her as well last night. Had she been awake, she would never have walked over to his pallet and stretched out beside him. By the Stone of Draloch! She'd settled atop him so that her breasts were pressed against his chest and her slender legs entwined around his thighs.

She'd burrowed against him, clutched his shoulders, and held on as though she never wanted to let him go.

He did not think she could have acted so foolishly on her own.

Was the Stone of Draloch responsible for this mischief?

Or had Georgiana's heart led her to his side?

Dragon Lords were demons of the highest order, creatures of an ancient heritage who conquered and plundered. It would have taken nothing for him to roll her onto her back and bury himself deep inside her body.

Perhaps the same madness that lured her into his arms also prevented him from taking advantage and claiming her for his own.

There was no other explanation for his decision to rein in the violent urge to mate with her. "Are you hungry, Georgiana? Cook will have left a tray for us by the door." He needed time to think.

He needed time to teach her to defend herself.

She nodded. "Famished."

He crossed the room in three strides and paused at the heavy wood door. "I want you to eat quickly and get dressed."

"Very well, but I have no clothes. What am I expected to wear? Do you have something more colorful than your black shirts?" She grinned at him, but it quickly faded when she noticed he wasn't in good humor. "We're in danger again, aren't we?"

He decided to tell her the truth. *"You're* in danger. You must be ready to leave here at a moment's notice." He whistled sharply, summoning Charon and Styx who had been standing guard beside his bed to protect Georgiana.

They had quietly followed her to his pallet last night, but he'd ordered them to stay back. He hadn't wanted their big bodies snorting and drooling atop him.

No, he'd only wanted the pleasure of her soft body against his own. He'd been lulled into a peaceful sleep by her light, breathy snores against his ear.

When had he ever slept so contentedly, even if it was only for an hour or two?

His dogs now took up positions in front of Georgiana so that they stood between her and the door.

She continued to gaze at him in confusion. "Leave? But you just said you didn't know–"

"I still don't know why you are here or how to get you safely out, but there's far more danger in your staying. Brihann is approaching and he's coming for you. He can't be more than an hour or two away."

"Didn't he give me to you as a gift?"

"And now he's realized his mistake and means to take you back. Perhaps it wasn't a mistake at all, that he knew… never mind. The point is, he's dangerous to you." He picked up his axe and opened the door to peer down the hall.

Empty.

Only Thomas, his steward, was ever permitted to come up to his tower quarters without being summoned.

He glanced down and saw the breakfast tray. Thomas must have brought it up from the kitchen a few moments ago. Steam still rose from under the silver salvers that held eggs, kippers, and freshly baked buns. He'd purposely asked for foods that were familiar to Georgiana.

His dragon scent would detect anything amiss with this meal.

He inhaled lightly. No one had tampered with it.

He picked up the tray and set it on the table, then strode back to fetch the other packages that had been left beside his door.

Georgiana's new clothes and slippers.

Her wedding gown had been ruined, but he couldn't return Georgiana to her family wearing only his shirt. By the Stone of Draloch! She looked so beautiful in it, so naturally alluring with her tousled blonde locks spilling over her shoulders.

And her big, green eyes so trusting as she continued to regard him with confusion.

He knelt and held out the packages for Charon and Styx to smell. They would growl if these garments had ever been worn before. But his dogs didn't make a sound, merely continued to sniff the packages out of curiosity.

Georgiana shook her head. "What are they doing?"

Bloodaxe rose and placed the packages on the bed. "These are your new clothes. Slippers, too. My dogs are making certain no demon taint is on them."

She gasped softly. "I've just realized something. Oh, how stupid of me! You're a demon and yet you carry no such taint on you. Why is that?"

The comment surprised him even though he ought to have realized the special connection between them would affect her senses. "You're wrong. I do carry the foul stench of darkness. Perhaps it is not quite as foul as the High King's, but it is there."

"It isn't." She shook her head vehemently. "Your scent is that of honey. Mostly that, but there's also a masculine mix of pine forest and rugged mountains."

He crossed his arms over his chest. "I don't believe mountains give off a scent."

"They do. Cool air and rich earth."

"You're wrong, Georgiana. Dragons smell like slimy toads." Sighing, he motioned for her to sit at the table. "Let me look at your arms first. Your eyes look…" *Beautiful.* "Slightly glazed. You may be running a fever."

She obeyed his command and sat, but frowned at him. "I'm not running a fever."

He drew his seat close to better inspect her wounds. But as he took her hands in his and leaned in to roll up her sleeves, she surprised him by putting her nose to his neck and inhaling deeply. He drew back. "What are you doing?"

"Proving you a liar. I knew it. Your scent is that of honey." Her soft lips grazed his throat. "If I'm never to see you again, I want to remember all that I can of you."

Remember him? No, he would fix that by casting a spell of forgetfulness over her once she was safely back home. He didn't want her to recall their time spent together, for she needed to move on and put him out of her mind. Unfortunately, he could not do the same for himself.

He would never forget her.

But he could indulge himself in these last moments.

It would take nothing for him to turn his head ever so slightly and lower his mouth to hers. *One kiss.*

She would be gone from his life forever within a matter of hours.

Did he dare?

"Eat quickly and get dressed." He abruptly rolled down the sleeves of her shirt... his shirt... and strode to his night table where the ewer of water stood. He hastily washed and dressed and then told her to do the same. He opened the last of the packages that contained her new clothes. Would they fit her?

They'd been prepared in haste and without benefit of her exact measurements, only what he could estimate. He was familiar with a woman's body, but he was no seamstress and could only describe what he'd observed of her shapely body.

Her breasts were ample enough to fill the cups of his palms, but not so large as to be overflowing.

Her waist was small enough that his hands could span it.

Her hips were not much larger than her waist. She would have trouble delivering a child, certainly any offspring of his seed.

He dismissed the thought.

There would be no coupling with Georgiana. "Are you done eating?"

She nodded.

He handed her the new garments. "Wash and dress as fast as you can. Bolt the door behind me. Keep away from the windows. I'll ride out with my forces to see if I can distract him from his purpose. If I fail, be ready to leave here. We'll have to move fast."

He had dressed in his usual black. He wore the leather hauberk he always donned before a battle and secured his axe in its sheath at his hip.

He spared her a glance, finding it hard to part from her even though she'd been in his life no more than a day. She was holding up the gold kirtle and green overtunic he'd ordered sewn for her and inspecting them. The green was the deep, rich tone of new spring grass. The gold was the bright gold of sunlight, the one thing all demons feared.

She clutched the clothes to her chest as he approached. "I thought you were leaving."

"I am." He eased the garments out of her hands.

"Mother in heaven," she whispered as he caught her up in his arms.

And then he kissed her.

MOTHER IN HEAVEN.

Georgiana's heart soared the moment he touched her. She ought to have been terrified and fighting him off. Instead, she stood on her toes and circled her arms around his neck, eager to lean into his warrior's body and give herself over to the wondrous sensation of his kiss.

She knew his touch.

She knew his lips.

How did she know this man? She struggled to think, but his lips were on hers, probing and possessive, and she couldn't hold a single thought other than she wanted to belong to him. *Oh, his kiss.* So filled with longing and desperation. His mouth pressed down on hers, urgent and demanding, and at the same time it seemed as if he were reining in his passion, as though he feared to hurt her with the power of his need.

He wrapped his arms around her waist and lifted her against his muscled body so that she could feel the taut planes of his broad chest. Keeping one arm around her, he put his other hand to the back of her head, his fingers winding in her wild curls to hold her steady. Did he think she would pull away?

How could she ever want to draw away from him when the power of his desire filled her? His strength flowed through her like a molten pool of lava filling every lonely crevice of her heart.

The turbulent feelings he evoked in her were at the same time frightening and thrilling.

"I know you, my lord. Sweet mercy, how is it possible? Why is your kiss so familiar?"

"It can't be." His mouth closed over hers once more, the touch of his lips on hers sparking a fire within her that would not be quelled. But how? What was this heat surging through her body? She pressed her lips against his, and did not resist when he slid his tongue between them to tease them apart.

She breathed him in.

She tasted him on her lips.

She felt the iron strength of his arms that held her close to his body. Curiously, they were not confining. Quite the opposite, his touch seemed to set her yearning free. She ran her hands along his bulging muscles and down his broad back. She wanted to run her fingers along his hot, smooth skin, but he was dressed for battle and she could not dig through the layers that covered his body.

She clutched his shoulders, but only managed to clasp the worn leather of his hauberk and the soft linen of his shirt in her fists.

He thrust again to tease her lips apart. She opened her mouth to allow his tongue to slide in, for he was deepening the kiss and stirring her passion. She was a virgin, but understood the act of mating. How soon before he probed lower and entered her *there*.

And was she mad to desire it?

"By the Stone of Draloch," he said in whisper, easing his lips off hers and setting her down gently before moving away. "Why did you not stop me?"

Her heart was pounding like a war drum in her chest. "Could I have?"

He nodded. "Aye, a word from you is all it would have taken."

She doubted it, and yet he did not appear to be in jest. "I didn't want to," she admitted, although it was folly to do so. She didn't wish to encourage him, but neither was she sorry for this kiss that both of them appeared to need with an inexplicable desperation. "I've never kissed any man like this before. Not even Oli–"

"Do not mention his name." A darkness swirled amid the blue of his eyes. She'd seen it before. But it flickered out quickly. "I do not wish to hear about this man who intends to claim you as his wife."

"Assuming I make it out of here alive."

He appeared offended. "Do you doubt I will protect you?"

"No, I don't doubt you." She shook her head. "But you're worried that you might not succeed. This realm is a cruel place, or so you've told me. And I've experienced it." She held up her arms that were covered by the long sleeves of his shirt that she was still wearing.

He frowned, but gave her cheek a light caress. "I had better see what Brihann wants. Get dressed, Georgie. Be ready for my return. And if I tell you to run, then do it. Don't look back. Just keep the two moons to your right and that will keep you heading west. You'll come to a range of tall mountains. That's your passageway out of here. The mountain rock is sharp and will likely cut your hands, but ignore the pain. Keep climbing and don't stop for anything."

"Won't there be demons to stop me?"

"Lots. I'll take care of them. All you need to do is climb."

She glanced at the battle axe he carried so casually at his side. "Will you give me a weapon? Something more effective than the eating knife I took last night?"

"No. Your wits are your best defense." He studied her a moment longer. "Besides, you were brought here for a purpose that is beyond my comprehension. Whatever force placed you here is not about to let you die."

"Unless it is my time," she said quietly.

He placed his hands on her shoulders and drew her to him. "By the Stone of Draloch, it is not your time. I think I would feel it in my very bones. I would feel it in the last vestiges of the soul I thought I had lost years ago. You aren't meant to die."

Why would he feel it in his bones? Or to the very depths of his soul?

He couldn't unless they were connected somehow. They were. They had to be. He'd poured his heart into their kiss. Even though demons weren't supposed to have hearts or noble thoughts or feelings. But his every thought and act had been to protect her.

She gasped. "Do you believe you're the one who's meant to die?"

The possibility left her bereft.

He arched an eyebrow. "I am not afraid of death."

"No, I didn't think you would be. I also think there are times you long for it." She surprised him by rising on tiptoes to give him a soft kiss on his tense jaw. "If this is to be our last meeting... I want you to know that I shall keep you in my heart always."

He looked at her as though she'd stuck a knife between his ribs. "Don't you dare."

He strode out, leaving her behind with Charon and Styx.

CHAPTER FIVE

LORD BLOODAXE'S HOUNDS sank down on their hind legs and stood so still on either side of Georgiana that they reminded her of a pair of matched fire irons. "You are permitted to move about the room," she said, expecting they wouldn't understand a word of what she was saying. "But you'll have to turn around while I undress. After all, I'm a well-bred young lady and require some privacy."

She blushed when they nodded. But they remained as still as statues and continued to stare at her. "What are you trying to tell me? Very well, you're right. I didn't behave like a lady last night. But I couldn't help myself. Your master is…"

She picked up her new clothes and moved to stand behind the bed while continuing to chatter at her two intrepid companions. "I don't quite know what he is, in truth. But he must be someone special to me. Don't you think?"

Charon and Styx nodded again.

She eyed her two companions warily. "Is it truly possible you understand me?"

They gave another nod.

Was it just a trick or did they know what she was saying? She tipped her chin up in the air. "Then turn around while I slip off your master's shirt and don this gown. I won't have the two of you gawking at me."

Charon turned to face the door while Styx faced the windows.

"Sweet merciful heaven, you do understand." The realization rattled her, but also comforted her. She hastily washed and then put on her new garments. Her slippers turned out to be soft leather ankle-length boots that laced up the front. She nodded her approval. She'd be able to run in them if she had to. Her gown was a little too long and not practical for running, but she could gather up the skirts without much difficulty. "You may turn around now, gentlemen."

Charon and Styx immediately obeyed.

She laughed and shook her head. "What do you think of my outfit? The kirtle and tunic are a few hundred years out of fashion. But I'm not going to tea with the Prince Regent, am I? The linen is quite soft and the colors are very pretty, don't you think?"

They barked their obvious approval.

She sighed. "Who were you in an earlier life? Knights of King Arthur's round table?"

They didn't respond.

"I suppose not. Perhaps Knights Templar? Did you hide your treasure on the Isle of Malta?" She caught not even a blink from them. "Will you give me a hint?"

She sat at the table and nibbled on the last of her eggs and kippers. She'd already had her breakfast, but took a few more bites anyway to fill her belly and maintain her strength. But she knew better than to overdo it. If she had to suddenly run, she couldn't afford a stitch in her side to slow her down.

Yet, if she were on the run, she might have trouble finding food. She fashioned a pouch out of the kerchief that came with her gown and tucked some bread and an apple in it.

She turned to Lord Bloodaxe's hounds that were following her every move. "Am I permitted to feed you table scraps?" Charon's ears perked when she lifted a kipper onto her fork. She grinned at him. "Aha! You like fish, so you must have been a fisherman."

He cast her an exasperated look, as though she were so far off the mark as to be pathetic. "But I saw your ears perk. You–"

Both dogs suddenly turned to the window and started growling, all playfulness gone as they bared their sharp teeth and settled their bodies low on their haunches, preparing to leap at whatever threat was out there. In the next moment, an enormous, yellow-scaled creature made its presence known by smashing the windows with its spiked tail.

Georgiana fell back with a soft cry as the massive beast suddenly stuck its long yellow head through the gaping hole and tried to grab her in its snapping jaws. *Dragon.*

She meant to scream, but her terror caused her throat to constrict so that she felt strangled by her own fear. No! She had to keep her wits about her.

She rolled out of reach and scrambled to her feet to frantically search for a weapon while the growling dogs held the beast off. Charon lunged at its snout and Styx went for its throat. The beast momentarily withdrew, but Georgiana knew there would be no more than a few moments of respite before it demolished this stone tower and caught her in its bone-crushing grip.

How does one defend against a dragon?

This one looked similar to the one imprinted on Lord Bloodaxe's back, but it was an opalescent, yellowish amber and not nearly as majestic. Perhaps it was the lack of expression in its ebony-black eyes that diminished the nobility of the creature.

Lord Bloodaxe had taken his battle axe along with several daggers that he'd kept in a chest along the back wall. She raced to the chest, her heart once more thumping madly as she opened it to uncover a treasure trove of weapons, none of which she knew how to use.

The crossbow looked the most promising, but it was too heavy to hold in her hands and aim. She'd have to prop it up on something. The bed's footboard would do nicely. It would also provide a protective screen that she could hide behind.

But the footboard was merely carved wood that would split in half if the dragon whipped its tail and gave it a good *thwack.*

Mere seconds had passed but it felt like an eternity.

She glanced around, looking for something sturdier to shield her. Of course! Lord Bloodaxe's shield was hanging on the wall beside the chest. She used her shoulder to push it upward and off its hook and then winced as it noisily clattered to the ground. "Please don't be dented."

She wouldn't blame Lord Bloodaxe if he throttled her for damaging his precious armaments. But she'd worry about that later. She hoisted the shield onto the bed and propped it up between the footboard and the mattress.

Breathing heavily and grunting from the exertion, she then dragged the crossbow to the bed and propped it up against the footboard as well. She hastily dug through the chest and grabbed all the arrows she could find, loading one onto the crossbow.

"Blast, how does this thing work?" It was no easy feat to draw the bowstring taut and properly set it on the delicately poised spring. She finally managed it, but knew she would have only one chance for a good shot because reloading it would take more time than she had to spare under a steady assault.

"Charon and Styx, stay back," she warned. "I don't want to accidentally hit you while you're leaping in midair." Besides, there was shattered glass all around the front wall that might cut their paws.

Where was that yellow dragon?

She'd barely gotten the thought out before it reappeared, smashing the stones around the damaged windows with its whip-like tail. Her finger twitched as crumbling stones pelted the footboard causing her to accidentally shoot her arrow. It sailed off wide of its mark and disappeared into the dank air.

"Blast and bother." With shaking hands, she attempted to load another arrow onto the crossbow, but a deep and ominous roar filled the air and sent piercing waves of pain through her eardrums. The arrow fell as she dropped it to cover her ears. She'd never heard the full-throated, angry roar of a dragon before and never expected the resonant call to be so powerful as to affect all of her senses.

Unable to load the next arrow, she curled behind the propped-up shield as though it could hide her from this ancient monster. In the next moment, she felt a burst of heat and the bed quickly became engulfed in fire, all but the little square upon which she was curled. Incredibly, the flames whipped around the shield and struck everywhere on the bed but where she hid.

Thank goodness.

She dared not inhale, for the heat would certainly singe her lungs. She held her breath as long as possible, determined to hold it until she passed out, if necessary. But her head quickly began to spin and she heard another ear-splitting roar. Another dragon? The call sounded different from the first. Suddenly, the shadow of the yellow dragon that had cast a pall over this ruined tower chamber was no longer there.

The bed was still in flames so she quickly rolled off it and patted herself down to inspect her gown and hair. She gave silent thanks that there were no embers caught in them. But the beautiful dragon bed had been reduced to firewood and would soon be nothing but ashes.

The crossbow was already a pile of ashes.

She darted around the dying-out flames to Lord Bloodaxe's chest and withdrew a simple bow and a quiver full of arrows. She hoisted the quiver over her shoulder. The yew bow was not as effective as the deadly crossbow, but it was a weapon she could hold in her grasp and easily raise to take careful aim.

Young ladies were trained in the sport of archery.

She was an expert marksman.

But where could she strike a dragon with her arrow to cause the most damage? Unlike the crossbow arrows, these did not have the ability to penetrate a dragon's protective scales. The slender shaft would simply bounce off the dragon's thick body.

More earsplitting roars filled the air.

Mother in heaven.

How many dragons were coming after her?

She covered her ears yet again, her mind racing all the while. She needed to stuff them with something to mute the sounds. She dumped the bread and apple out of the kerchief, shook out the crumbs, and stuck one end of the kerchief into each ear.

No doubt she looked ridiculous, but this was necessary for her survival. She grabbed the bow and placed an arrow on it. *Aim for the dragon's eye.*

Yes, that was her best chance.

But when she dared to peek out of what remained of the window, she saw three dragons flying overhead. "Merciful heaven."

She couldn't fight them all.

No, she didn't have to fight them at all, she quickly realized. The black dragon with the blue underbelly had to be Lord Bloodaxe. She recognized the yellow dragon that had attacked her and quietly cheered as Lord Bloodaxe grabbed its flailing tail in his dragon teeth and flung its big yellow body with enough force to toss the beast into the distant lake.

The third dragon was an enormous, all black dragon with fiery red eyes and a mean disposition. The two black dragons now turned to face each other, their wings magnificently outstretched in an aggressive display as they prepared to fly toward each other in the first engagement of what had to be a deadly battle.

The yellow dragon was forgotten as each turned its feral fury on the other.

She was forgotten as well, for they probably believed her to be dead.

Charon and Styx drew close to her, their gazes also fixed on the black dragons soaring overhead.

Georgiana stared in fascination as they began to circle each other, the nostrils on their long snouts flared and the spikes that ran along their spines taut as sword points. To her confusion, the dragons exchanged no more than a few roars before the enormous black dragon suddenly flew off with a flap of its massive wings. The smaller black dragon made a graceful turn and was about to chase after his larger challenger when it suddenly stopped and turned back to circle the bedchamber tower that was now mostly in ruins.

Turbulent blue eyes met the worried green of Georgiana's gaze. She knew this black dragon was Lord Bloodaxe and quickly removed the kerchief stuffed in her ears so that he did not think her addled. She lowered her bow and stood in front of the broken window so that she was now fully exposed to his view. The dragon roared softly and she noticed a surge of relief in his eyes. "I'm safe," she mouthed, doubting he could see the movement of her lips.

With a powerful thrust of his long, black wings, he flew upward into the clouds.

She peered out of the empty space that had once been a window, careful to avoid the shards of glass that stuck to the sill and frame. More glass was scattered across the floor. The scent of smoke permeated the air. Had the windows not been broken, she would have suffocated from the smoke. But the opening served as a chimney flue to draw the worst of the smoke out of the chamber.

She tried to find him among the swirling gray clouds. "Where are you, Lord Bloodaxe?" she muttered, but there was no sign of a black dragon stealthily threading its way in and out of the clouds. Her gaze was still fixed on the thunderous sky when Charon and Styx suddenly left her side and raced to the door.

They weren't growling, but panting excitedly.

She was about to throw the bolt and fling the door open when she remembered her lesson with the nymphs. The dogs hadn't growled when they'd come to the door either. In the next moment, a mighty fist pounded against the thick wood. "Georgiana," was all Lord Bloodaxe needed to shout.

She cried in relief and opened the door.

He stood there looking magnificent, no matter that he was battle-worn and bloodied. "You're alive," he said, the deep rumble of his voice ragged and raw. He stood on the threshold and studied her. His gaze was intense, blazing a trail up and down her body. "By the Stone of Draloch, how is it possible? I saw Necros shoot his dragon fire straight at you."

"Is that what you call the hideous yellow beast?"

"Aye. He's a Dragon Lord, but was once a goblin. He's a brainless toady. I will kill him. There is nowhere in the Underworld he can hide from me." He swept her into his arms and kissed her with a depth of feeling that stole her breath away. He kissed her long and hard, and she returned his kiss with equal ardor. He chased the cold from her bones. He touched her heart as no other man ever could. "How did you survive, Georgie? What miracle occurred to spare you from his flames?"

She didn't know. "It wasn't so much a miracle as good fortune. I went to your chest and gathered some of your weapons," she said in a rush, now beginning to feel quite proud of her actions and pleased that he regarded her with obvious admiration. "I noticed your shield on the wall and decided to wedge it between the bed's footboard and the mattress. It looked sturdy enough to protect me from falling stones or from a dragon's tail smashing against the bed. But your crossbow is destroyed. I'm so sorry."

"Do you think I care? It is easily replaced. You're not." He lowered his mouth to hers once again and claimed her lips with a possessive hunger.

She trembled against his hard body, not from fear but from the passion he evoked in her. Her heart was racing and her senses were atilt. His tower chamber was in shambles. Smoke from the yellow dragon's flames still lingered in the air as did the odor of that foul beast. Ugh! What an unholy stench!

To counter it, she breathed in Lord Bloodaxe's honey scent as she eyed him with worry. "How soon before more dragons attack?"

"They won't." His smile made her heart flutter. "You've scared them off."

She shook her head and laughed softly. "I doubt it is me that has put them on the run."

"Indeed, it is." He brushed aside a few stray curls and kissed her on the forehead. "I warned them about you, but they wouldn't listen."

"Oh, am I that fearsome a warrior?" Her lips tilted upward in a grin, for she was feeling proud of herself again.

He lifted her into his arms and kissed her soundly again. "You even have me quaking, and I'm a bloody Dragon Lord."

She laughed heartily, for his teasing manner calmed her. Nothing mattered now that she was in his arms. All she'd thought about while the dragons had hovered overhead was of his safe return. Now that she knew he was unharmed, she wanted nothing more than to hold onto him with all her might. "Your dragon shield protected me. Necros' fire swirled all around me, but couldn't penetrate the shield."

She ran her hands up and down his arms and gasped when she felt a sticky warmth on his sleeve. "You're bleeding."

He shook his head. "No, just a scratch."

"Let me see." Her arms still pained her from the cuts and scratches she'd received when attacked by his nymphs. He'd taken on dragons and demon armies. "Scratches don't bleed this profusely."

"'Tis naught, merely a small spot on my sleeve and already caking dry. Hardly worth the mention." He ignored her concern and stepped into the center of his bedchamber to inspect the damage. "By the Stone of Draloch." He groaned in frustration. "Necros was angry."

She followed his gaze and grimaced. "I tried to get off a shot with your crossbow, but he startled me and the shot went wide. I did a miserable job of defense."

"My quarters will be repaired quickly. But we'll have to leave the fortress while my workers are rebuilding this tower. In truth, it may be for the best. Brihann brought you here and would know where to find you if we stayed." He stepped over the rubble to stand beside what had once been a beautifully framed window but was now a gaping hole. "There are many places to hide you within my realm. It is best you retreat to one of those. You'll have to slip out quietly. His spies are everywhere around my fortress, watching your every movement. Your escape will have to be well planned."

Her eyes widened in surprise. "Am I to be left on my own? Or will you be with me?"

He returned to her side, closing the small distance between them. "What do you think?"

She sighed. "I no longer know what to think."

"Yes, you do." The air felt charged between them, and his touch, when he gently cupped her cheek, felt like the strike of a lightning bolt.

Her heartbeats felt like hammer strikes against her chest. "I shouldn't trust you, but I do. I shouldn't like you, but…"

He did not smile as he spoke her thoughts. "But you do, even though I am a demon. You don't know if your ordeal has confused your mind, for how can you possibly have any affection for a shape-shifting monster?"

She wanted to tell him that he was no monster, but it wasn't so. He was a dangerous Dragon Lord and ruled over a demonic realm. She merely nodded in agreement.

"I can't explain it either. But it doesn't matter right now. You've survived Necros' attack and word of it will quickly spread throughout the Underworld."

"How is it significant?"

"You're a mortal girl who survived dragon fire. The only other young woman who managed that is the Fae queen, Melody. She was a simple vicar's daughter who fulfilled the ancient prophecy etched into the Stone of Draloch and gave the Fae their great victory over the demons of the Underworld."

Georgiana tipped her head in confusion. "How did she manage it?"

"It's a long story and one I shall tell you once I have you safely hidden away. Georgiana, ever since the demons' loss, Brihann has been ranting and raging about conquering the realm of mortals. The Fae and demons battled for thousands of years and all attention was given to the words of the Fae prophecy, but there was more written on the stone concerning the fate of mankind." He tipped her chin up to meet his gaze as he began to recite the two sentences from memory.

Two black dragons shall reign supreme.
Two black dragons shall unite the worlds of demon and man.

"You and your High King Brihann?" She pursed her lips. "Or are there more black dragons that exist?"

He turned away and rubbed a hand across the back of his neck. "There is another."

She waited for him to continue, but he said nothing more. "Must I ask you questions about this third dragon? I know how intensely you dislike questions."

He chuckled softly and returned his gaze to meet hers. "I will tell you about him another time. My concern right now is to keep you out of Brihann's grasp. There is no doubt that he purposely engaged me and my men in a skirmish to keep us occupied while Necros came after you. I don't know that he gave Necros the order to kill you. You're more useful to Brihann alive, but who knows what runs through his deranged mind? He may want you dead."

"If that is so, then why did Brihann not do it when he first abducted me?"

Lord Bloodaxe ran a hand once more through his dark hair. "I think he gave you to me believing I'd take you as one of my concubines. You were meant to be a gift to me to repair hostilities that have existed between us for quite some time now. He meant it as a gesture to unite the two black dragons in preparation for war against our mortal foe."

His mouth pursed in a thin, tense line as he gave the matter more thought. "It wasn't until he gave serious consideration to the words of the prophecy that he understood you could be the means to his undoing. He's just realized his mistake in bringing you to me. That's why he must now hunt you down and make certain you are destroyed before you can destroy him."

She shook her head, straining to understand the politics within this realm, but found it even more indecipherable than those of England. "But he flew off when you confronted him. If he's so desperate, why didn't he stay and fight you?"

"Because he and I may be the two dragons referred to in the prophecy. He isn't certain yet and for that reason, he won't risk killing me."

"That may explain why he spared you. I still don't understand what makes me so important to him."

He took a long moment to respond, frowning as though the reason was not to his liking. "Because you are important to me," he said finally and with such reluctance, it seemed as though each word had to be dragged forcibly from his lips.

"How can I be? You hardly know me." Even as she spoke in protest, she knew that she was wrong. They did know each other and it mattered not that she had no knowledge of where or how or when. He knew.

Why wouldn't he tell her?

A commotion at the door ended all chance for further conversation. "Lord Bloodaxe," said one of the demons who'd come running up the stairs with broadswords in their hands, "what has happened here?"

Surprisingly, these demons resembled men and all wore hauberks similar to that of Lord Bloodaxe, except for the man who spoke. His garments were finer, and by the set of keys dangling from his belt, she assumed he served as steward of this fortress.

Charon and Styx began to bark at the men who stood behind the steward with their weapons still drawn.

Lord Bloodaxe raised his hand and uttered a single word. "Quiet."

His dogs immediately obeyed.

He turned to the men who had yet to cross his threshold and would not do so unless permitted, and waved them in. "You may as well meet the cause of the havoc. This is Lady Georgiana Wethersby, daughter of the Duke of Penrith."

"The Duke of Penrith," his steward repeated in a murmur of surprise. He appeared to be a man of middle age with thin, gray hair, and resembled a clerk or professor, for he was not very tall, not at all muscled, and wore spectacles. The other men looked more like fighters and carried themselves as such, although none were as tall or broad in the shoulders as Lord Bloodaxe. "His estate, Wethersby Hall, is in the Lake District, is it not?"

Lord Bloodaxe nodded. "It is. Quite astute of you, Thomas. She is an *innocent* brought against her will into our lands. So now you understand why she is important to us all."

As one, the men fell on one knee and bowed before her. "We shall protect her at all costs," they pledged, their heads lowered in reverential respect.

To Georgiana's consternation, they remained kneeling and with their heads bowed as though awaiting a magical word or two from her. She gazed at Lord Bloodaxe in confusion.

"Do you not understand yet? It seems you are the one chosen by the Stone of Draloch to be our guiding light. You hold our destiny in your hands."

She refused to believe it. "Rise, gentlemen. I am no deity and do not presume to have any control over your lives." *Whatever the life of a demon might be.*

Lord Bloodaxe regarded her with a wickedly appealing arch of his eyebrow. "Even I misjudged your purpose in being brought here. Your powers may prove stronger even than Queen Melody's."

What nonsense is this? He'd compared her to the Fae queen, the mortal female that all demons feared. She studied his face for the hint of a twitch in his lips or a glint of amusement in his dragon eyes, but he did not appear to be jesting.

"Lady Georgiana, allow me to introduce you to the captains in command of my armies. Sir Artemis," Lord Bloodaxe said, nodding toward the burliest of the three demons who also appeared to be the oldest, for his hair was thick and bristly and almost completely gray. But she couldn't be sure of his age, for these captains had the look of men and yet they could be any form of creature. No man she had ever met had eyes as black as theirs.

Obsidian black and fathomless.

Lord Bloodaxe quickly introduced her to the other two who appeared to be fairly young demons. One had dark hair that was almost longer than her own locks, and the other had blond, wavy hair that fell just below his shoulders. He introduced the dark haired one as Andronicus and the light haired one as Dalgwynn. "All of them were once men. As was I."

Was that a hint of wistfulness she'd detected in his voice?

"Captain Artemis was a knight in service to the Duke of Poitiers.

Captain Andronicus commanded a Roman legion in Jerusalem. Captain Dalgwynn led several successful Welsh uprisings against the Marcher Lords who protected the English borderlands. The Welsh revolt failed once he was killed. In losing him, they lost their best military tactician."

Georgiana pursed her lips in thought. "I know it is rude of me to ask, but how do men such as you come to be here? How is service to your liege lord not honorable?"

Lord Bloodaxe placed a hand lightly on her arm. "Not all who pass through the Underworld are dark souls. This is a conversation for another time." He turned away from her and began to give orders to his captains and his steward about the repairs to be done to his bedchamber tower. "Thomas, prepare the south chamber. Lady Georgiana and I shall sleep there until the repairs are completed."

Heat flooded her cheeks. She wanted to protest, but thought better of it. Instead, she purposely kept her mouth shut. Expressing displeasure would only call more attention to their situation which was scandalous at best. She was an unmarried woman sharing quarters with a man... demon... Dragon Lord.

Mother in heaven.

Would anyone believe her tale, assuming she ever made it home to tell it?

Although these beings now thought of her as their possible savior, Lord Bloodaxe still meant to treat her as his captive. He might consider his nightly presence in her bedchamber as necessary for her protection, but the fact remained that she was subject to his will, and he was not letting her out of his sight.

She considered ordering Thomas to arrange separate beds for them, but chose to remain silent about that as well. She had already spent a night alone with their liege lord. Whatever damage to her reputation had been done. Far more important was the fact that she had not been *damaged* in any physical way. Lord Bloodaxe had fashioned a pallet for himself by the door and given up his bed to her last night. She had been the one to leave that bed and huddle beside him on the floor to seek the warmth of his body and security of his arms.

Her stomach began to twist in knots.

Would she do the same tonight?

If anything, the yearning to lie in his embrace intensified with each passing moment in his presence. Even now, the urge to melt into his arms overwhelmed her. But she was not so foolish as to do anything about it.

No, indeed!

She clasped her hands together to keep herself from reaching out to him, and then stood quietly beside Charon and Styx while Lord Bloodaxe reviewed the destruction with his captains. He assigned a task to each of them. Captain Artemis and his men were to clear out the rubble, and with the help of stone masons, rebuild the tower. Captain Andronicus was to secure the fortress and hunt down as many of Brihann's spies as could be found within its walls.

She couldn't hear what he commanded of Captain Dalgwynn, but saw the captain nod solemnly and stride out in a hurry. "Come, little savior. Take a walk with me in the garden."

Perhaps he meant only an affectionate jest in calling her that, but it distressed her all the same. "I'm no one's savior. I can't even save myself. I couldn't lift any of your weapons and almost put out my back lugging the few I could manage into position."

She noted the glint of amusement in his eyes, but in the next moment his expression turned contemplative. "The Stone of Draloch did not bring you here because of your physical prowess." But his gaze was approving as he slowly and discreetly raked it over her body.

She sensed the heat in his gaze signified more than mere admiration.

She tingled every time he looked upon her.

Mother in heaven.

Her own betrothed had never once made her feel this way. Oliver. What was she to do about him, assuming she ever escaped the Underworld? She suddenly gasped. "Has this changed matters? Will you still help return me to my home?"

Instead of responding, he led her down the tower steps and through the main hall. His dogs followed, taking positions on either side of her, but one walked slightly behind her while the other walked slightly ahead.

Lord Bloodaxe paused a moment to address the servants and his other subjects who had gathered in the vast hall to seek refuge from the dragons that had soared overhead a short while ago. "All is safe now. You may go about your duties. But before you do, I would like you all to meet Lady Georgiana. The rumor swirling about her is true. She is the young mortal who just bested Necros and survived his dragon fire."

Some of his subjects fell to their knees while others attempted to rush toward her to touch her, but his dogs growled at any being who dared come near. "She is beautiful, my lord," several murmured as they bowed to him and then to her.

Others wept. "She will save us."

Lord Bloodaxe surprised her by his kindness to his subjects, much as a king might walk among his subjects and inspire them with his mere touch. Nor did the regal aura of the hall escape her notice either. To her surprise, the stonework, elegant columns, and stained-glass windows reminded her of a charming, old English castle or a magnificent abbey.

"They think I'm special. You should not have introduced me as you did." She frowned at him when he did not respond. When that failed, she tipped her chin up in indignation. "You must tell them the truth, correct their wrong impression. I'm merely an Englishwoman."

"They won't believe me. They know you are more important than any of my nymphs."

Ah, his concubines. Even as they made their way through the swelling crowd, some of the demons were eyeing her with an avidity that made her skin crawl.

Lord Bloodaxe would have to be as dense as a post not to realize her displeasure. Was he purposely ignoring the leers she was receiving?

"They are looking upon you in adoration. Most are, anyway. Stop pouting and follow me." He held out his arm to her in an unexpectedly courtly manner so that those watching would understand she was a lady and he meant to treat her as such even though he had yet to formally acknowledge her as anything more than a guest. They must all believe he had already bedded her.

But he didn't slow his steps, and she had to scurry to keep up with him. She had no time to view the rooms they strode past. Some had rich carpets covering the floors. All was a blur, but she could not overlook their surprising opulence as glitters of gold and silver and crystal flashed before her eyes. "Your fortress is as elegant as any of my father's homes. Perhaps more so. I did not realize Dragon Lords lived as finely as dukes, even princes for that matter."

He arched an eyebrow. "Even beasts enjoy the finer things. Although, in truth, these trappings of wealth are more for show rather than for my own satisfaction."

She nodded. "I understand. It is meant to convey power and the depth of your resources should anyone attempt to attack you."

"It discourages the lesser demons, but is meaningless against Brihann." He led her through a room that could have passed for an elegant London townhouse sitting room and crossed to the tall, glass doors that opened onto a terrace. Beyond the terrace was a garden as lovely as any she'd seen in England. "Surprised?"

She nodded.

They descended a row of stone steps to the garden, the dogs now bounding ahead with a playful eagerness that belied their ferocity. While his beasts ran back and forth along the grass, chasing each other and then pausing to sniff along the sculpted bushes, Lord Bloodaxe slowed his pace to a leisurely one so that they now strolled along the flower paths instead of racing through them.

Perhaps he'd purposely brought her into the garden to soothe her frayed senses, for her heart was still tight and racing after her encounter with the yellow dragon. "You survived, Georgiana," he said quietly, placing his hand lightly at the small of her back in a gesture of assurance.

She nodded and returned her attention to the garden. The flowers were beautiful, but there were strange plants she did not recognize along with the many that she did. She noted the blood-red roses, pink lilies, silver foxglove, and pale purple periwinkles that seemed to thrive despite the lack of sunshine.

How odd that they should bloom so robustly under a red sky and the light of the two moons?

But there were oddly shaped flowers of russet and blue and deepest black with eyes in their petals and leaves that reached out to touch the hem of her gown as she passed. They seemed to be alive, small creatures rooted to the ground. A few even seemed to have teeth, and she was careful to step well away from them.

Lord Bloodaxe's lips were pursed as he resumed his earlier thought. "One would think Brihann had learned his lesson after the Fae victory, but it merely drove him further into darkness. His madness now has him in an unbreakable grip."

Georgiana was pleased that he was talking to her about the frightening incident and wished to encourage him to tell her more about this strange world. "How did the Fae defeat Brihann?"

"The Stone of Draloch, as ever, guided them. Lord Mordain and I were there to witness his defeat, our presence having been commanded by Brihann himself. He thought he'd lured the Fae king, Cadeyrn, into a trap and meant to use his victory to coerce us into joining him in war. Mordain and I had yet to be convinced that his endeavor was other than an old man's folly."

"What happened?"

"Brihann killed his own dragon mate, Ygraine, with his dragon fire." He paused a moment as though expecting her to understand the significance of that act, but continued when she obviously did not. "In doing so, he unwittingly fulfilled the ancient prophecy and handed the Fae their victory. His demon forces watched the moment unfolding and began to retreat in panic. All knew of the words written on the

Stone of Draloch."

She listened intently as he continued, eager to absorb all she could of their lore and the Stone of Draloch. "The ground quaked and I thought the Underworld would break apart in a great cataclysmic roar. No dragon has ever murdered his dragon mate. To this day, he has shown no remorse for this act against Ygraine. Nor does he understand that he alone led to the Fae victory and our near destruction."

Georgiana's hand trembled as it rested on his forearm. "Is a dragon mate similar to a wife?"

His gaze upon her remained thoughtful as he nodded. "Yes, but she is much more. The union of a dragon to his mate is no mere marriage of convenience or business arrangement designed to unite families and secure land holdings. When a dragon takes a wife, it is for eternity. For this reason, his selection must be based on love. He must know to the depths of his being that she is the one for him. From the moment he takes his marriage vows, there will be no other woman for him and can never be again."

"Is it the same for his mate?" She tried to keep the surprise out of her voice, but likely failed. Women were taught to keep themselves chaste, but no one ever frowned upon a man who spread his seed wide. At worst, he might be considered a rake. Even married men took on mistresses to tend to their carnal pleasures, and it was accepted among those in elegant society.

"I do not know." He considered her words a moment longer and nodded. "But I think it must be."

She could not quite bring herself to believe that Lord Bloodaxe would forsake his nightly trysts with the beautiful nymphs at his beck and call for the love of one woman. But he appeared to be sincere as he continued to explain. "Once they couple, their union is unbreakable. A dragon may have a heart that beats within his chest, but the dragon's true heart is now his mate. When she dies, his grief is unbearable."

Her eyes grew wide and she gaped at him. "I don't understand. Why would you then pledge your heart to a woman? Why would you agree to a few years of happiness knowing it can only lead to an eternity of sadness?"

Even as she spoke those words, she realized it would be no difficult choice for her to make if she were ever faced with it. She'd held out for love, hadn't she? Rejecting suitors because she wanted a marriage bound by more than columns of ciphers and land holdings.

Sadly, she'd betrayed her feelings by giving up on her convictions and accepting to marry Oliver. *Mother in heaven.* She couldn't bear to have him touch her now. She wanted... no, it was not a thought worth completing.

Or rather, the thought was too dangerous to complete.

"Why would I sacrifice my happiness?" There was a husky sensuality to his voice as he broke through her thoughts to reply to her question. Its deep rumble flowed through her body, stirring her as though his lips were on her skin and pleasuring her with fiery abandon. His gaze fixed on her, the turbulent swirls of his blue eyes seeming to reach out to drag her into their depths. "Because her love is worth it."

Oh, mercy. She was going to fall in love with this man if he didn't stop talking soon. Had any knight in shining armor ever sounded so chivalrous? The pulse at the base of her throat began to beat furiously. She swallowed hard and a sigh or two might have escaped her lips.

Lord Bloodaxe's gaze was smoldering. "You asked me earlier if I was still going to help you escape."

She bobbed her head up and down, for words failed her at the moment. She doubted her ability to string together a coherent sentence.

"I will help you." He placed his hands lightly on her shoulders. "It was my intent from the moment I set eyes upon you. My instinct, which rarely fails me, is still telling me that I must continue in this task. You do not belong in this wretched world of demons."

"I don't?" She slipped out of his grasp and turned away to hurry down the gently curved garden path toward... she didn't know where, only that she had to get away from him before he noticed her own broken heart. Which was a ridiculous way for her to feel about Lord Bloodaxe. She didn't want him. She was glad he meant to help her escape and even gladder that he had dismissed her as his possible dragon mate.

So why was her body crying out in sorrow?

"Georgiana, stop." He grabbed her hand and wouldn't let go, forcing her to come to a halt. "Did you misunderstand me? I said I would help you escape."

"I heard you." She tried to squirm away before he noticed the tears glistening in her eyes. She wasn't going to cry, of course. The notion that she would was absurd.

"Why are you overset?" He appeared genuinely confused.

In truth, so was she.

"I'm not," she insisted, concentrating on her toes. She was fighting the ridiculous impulse to behave foolishly and knew she'd make an utter goose of herself if she dared to look him squarely in the eyes. How could a demon make her feel this way? She wanted to throw her arms around him and beg to be allowed to stay. This desire to remain with him made no sense at all. No doubt, he'd be appalled if she ever made her feelings known.

Indeed, she was appalled by her wayward thoughts. His world frightened her, but she felt as though she could endure anything while he was by her side.

"Georgiana?"

Oh, my. The husky rumble in his voice was once again soothing and devastatingly alluring. "Perhaps I am a little overset," she admitted. "The way you spoke about your dragon mate just now… it's what I've always wanted. But I betrayed my principals and was ready to settle for someone I didn't love. I'm ashamed of myself. More so because I thought of you as a soulless creature, but I, not you, am that very thing."

He ran the pad of his thumb gently across her cheek. "Do not judge yourself too harshly. You're not wrong. All demons are creatures with damaged souls. Many have already lost their soul and will never reclaim it."

"But you still have yours." She finally mustered the courage to meet his gaze. If one looked beyond the layer of ice, one would find the heart of a gallant warrior.

He frowned. "Don't mistake my ability to reason for anything more than it is. I am a demon. I kill if I'm challenged and feel no remorse for my acts."

"Then why are you so gentle with me? Is not such tenderness reserved only for your dragon mate?"

He drew his hand away. "Let's walk. I need to consider how to slip you out of here unnoticed." He continued to glance at her from time to time as they made their way deeper into his garden. His dogs had stopped running about and were now stretched out and panting beneath a nearby shade tree. Lord Bloodaxe spared them a passing glance, but his attention was mostly on her. "Seems your gown is too long. I've noticed that you keep tripping over the hem as you walk."

She nodded. "It is nothing. I can fix it later."

"You?"

"Yes, me." Once again, she tipped her chin up in indignation. There was a dismissive quality in his tone that rankled her. "All I need is a needle and thread to… Why are you smirking?"

One of his dark eyebrows arched up. "Am I? I hadn't realized I was."

But she was determined to disabuse him of the notion that she was helpless in all things. "Do you believe I am useless because I'm a duke's daughter?" She placed her hands on her hips and frowned at him. "I'll have you know that my parents did not pamper me. I learned to sew and knit and embroider. I also learned to cook and bake." She paused, realizing that she may have taken offense when none was meant, and cast him an impish smirk. "Although I would not wish my biscuits on anyone. Cook broke a tooth when she tested one of them."

She simply melted when he graced her with a wickedly delicious smile in response to her admission.

"That bad?" The seductive smolder in his gaze sent her heart into palpitations.

She cleared her throat. "I was also taught how to manage an estate and keep accurate ledgers. They trained me to be a capable consort to... Why are you smirking at me again?"

"I'm not, Georgiana. I'm admiring you. There is a difference." He took a step back and gave a quick wave of his hand.

She felt a soft, tingling sensation rush through her body. "What did you just do to me?"

"Not to you, but to your hem. I fixed it." She barely had a moment to glance down and inspect his handiwork before he took her by the elbow and moved them along the garden pathway. "See, you're not tripping over it any longer."

She shook her head and laughed. "How are you with baking biscuits?" She was not surprised by his abilities whether in battle or in the domestic realm, for everything about this demon lord felt magical.

"Never tried conjuring them." His humor suddenly faded. "But I might have to resort to it once we're in hiding. I'll give you a pouch of supplies to take with you on your climb up the Razor Cliffs. You may need to hide out for several days afterward and will require food and drink to sustain you."

Georgiana felt her eyes well with tears once more, but managed to maintain control. She refused to turn into a watering pot at the thought of parting from him. He was a stranger to her and a dangerous one at that. She knelt, pretending to study a bed of red roses, for she did not want him to notice that she could not shake off her sorrow. "Will I see you again, assuming I ever make it out of here?"

"Hopefully not."

She shot back to her feet and turned to face him, all thought of hiding her feelings forgotten. "Why not? Why can't we?"

"By the Stone of Draloch," he muttered with a shake of his head, "you ought to be pleased that your nightmare will soon come to an end. Why would you ever wish to see me again? I can only bring death and destruction to your door."

"No, you would protect me." She was about to place a hand on his arm, then realized it was his wounded arm, so she set her hand over his heart instead. "Can you conjure a basin of water and a cloth? Is your wound deep enough to require stitches? If so, I'll also need a needle and thread to–"

"Georgiana, I will take care of it later. I do not need you to fuss over me." He drew back as though her hand was a flame and her touch had burned him.

"Forgive me." She had intended no insult, but he seemed to have taken it that way. "I did not mean to suggest you cannot manage for yourself. I only sought to be useful."

He sighed and raked a hand through his hair. "I know. But you cannot help me. No, let me correct that. You can only help me by getting out of here and then staying as far away from me as possible. You and I must never see each other again."

"Never?"

He spelled it out for her. "N-e-v-e-r. How much plainer must I say it?"

CHAPTER SIX

B LOODAXE STARED AT GEORGIANA, more confused than ever by the despair he saw in her eyes. Did she wish to stay with him?

Sweet madness! The fiery urge to mate with Georgiana already consumed him with a hunger that ate him raw. He needed no encouragement from her. Indeed, he wanted this innocent in his life for all eternity. He wanted her to stand by his side as she was now. He wanted to talk with her and look upon her beautiful face.

He simply wanted to be with her, that desire so desperately painful, it tore at his already aching heart.

But what he spoke and what he felt were different matters. He'd told her that he would help her escape and he meant it. The Stone of Draloch might prevent her leaving, but he didn't care. It was important that he follow his instincts to whatever fate was intended for them.

However, he would not allow any harm to befall Georgiana.

Not ever.

Necros did not know it yet, but he was a dead man… a dead goblin, for he had tried to harm Georgiana, and in that moment, had sealed his doom. Revenge would be exacted. But he would not go after Necros until this beautiful innocent was safely back in her realm. He did not want Georgiana to see him for the cold-hearted, blood-thirsty beast he truly was. He growled softly. "Don't look at me that way."

Her moss-green eyes widened. "How am I looking at you?"

"In a soft, adoring way." They were still standing in his garden, green grass all around them and green leaves above them from the overhanging tree branches, yet all he noticed was the green of her eyes. Her hair was a wild, tumbling gold that fell down her back and over her shoulders, a reminder of the sunlight he'd forsaken decades ago.

"Then how am I to look at you? By your own words, you've told me not to pout and now you don't want me to smile. I can't be angry with you and I refuse to cry. I've run out of suitable expressions." She frowned lightly and began to nibble her fleshy lower lip, the casual gesture sending flames of desire shooting through his body. "I'll do my best to look indifferent."

She trailed her fingers along the broad length of his chest. He almost leaped out of his skin. "What are you doing?"

"You didn't say not to touch you." She cast him an impatient look. "If you must know, I'm still concerned about the wound to your arm. The dried blood is sticking to your shirt and will start to bleed again when you take it off." She carefully began to poke around it. "It ought to be cleansed before infection sets in. Is that not what you said about my injuries?"

He glanced around and saw that they were alone for the moment. "Very well, let's sit over there." He pointed to a wooden bench under a willow tree and motioned for her to sit. He sank down at the other end and carefully removed his shirt. The blood had indeed caked and the fabric was now stuck to his flesh. The wound began to bleed the moment he threw off his shirt.

Sweet mercy. He felt the heat of Georgiana's gaze on him. She was dangerously arousing the dragon within him. Were he not bleeding, he'd be drawing her onto his lap right now and kissing her with dragon greed.

He'd be doing a lot more than merely kissing her. The overhanging branches of the willow would afford them privacy even if others came in search of him.

He wanted her.

His body cried out for her.

She was meant to be his dragon mate.

The urge to couple with Georgiana gnawed at his insides, but he was determined to resist temptation. He gave his back to her and spoke sternly. "I'll treat my wound now, but you're not to touch me or sit close to me. There are soul trappers in every demon's blood. They're harmless to us, but might leech onto you and bury themselves deep under your skin. They're deadly to you. Few mortals who are infected ever survive."

He heard her slide back to the very edge of the bench, her gasp betraying her alarm as he spoke his warning. "What can I do if one gets inside of me? Is there a cure?"

He nodded and turned to face her. "Aye, there is for you. But you will not like it."

"How bad is it? Very painful?" She shook her head as though dismissing the concern. "Worse than death itself?"

Not to him, for he could think of nothing better than to complete their joining. "Perhaps, if you're unwilling."

He glanced back at her and saw that she was shaking her head vehemently. "Why would I be unwilling? Am I to simply allow myself to die? I don't think so. What is the cure?"

"For you, the cure would be to mate with me." His loins responded at the mere thought of Georgiana pink and naked beneath him.

She shook her head once more in dismissal. "No, really. What is the cure?"

"No jest." His skin began to turn to scales, but he fought to regain control of his own traitorous body. "You and I would have to mate. I would have to spill my seed inside you in order to save you. It would not be gentle. Once aroused, I might become frenzied and unwittingly hurt you."

"Mating?" She regarded him as though he were mad. "So, if I were infected by a soul trapper, I would need to... um, do *that* with you, and I would be saved?"

He nodded.

"And you're not jesting?" Her voice was laced with doubt, not that he blamed her wariness. Not even he had believed such a cure possible, but it was the wise faerie, Ygraine, who had gone out of her way to tell him of this method of healing shortly before her death at the hands of Brihann.

Ygraine had powers beyond anyone's comprehension. Bloodaxe knew this healing wisdom had to be true. Even the Fae king had saved his queen in this way. Cadeyrn's love for Melody was boundless, as foretold in the prophecy etched in the Stone of Draloch.

Bloodaxe didn't know whether his heart was too damaged to save Georgiana, but whatever was left of that beating organ drew him to her with an overwhelming force. Was he capable of love, much less a boundless love? He had yet to join with Georgiana, but already his need for the girl was embedded within every beat of his heart and his every breath. "No. Unfortunately, there is no other way. As I said, I would try my best not to hurt you."

"Must it hurt? Is it different from the way people in my mortal realm mate?"

"No, it is the same."

"Then why do you think I would find it painful or objectionable?" She opened her mouth to say more, then changed her mind and snapped it shut. After a moment, she nodded and proceeded. "What if I were to become frenzied, too? Is this possible? Would I hurt you if I did?"

"By the Stone of Draloch," he said, laughing and groaning all at once. "Yes, it's possible you would feel this same frenzy. Sweet mercy, it's possible. And no, you would not hurt me."

He was still laughing and groaning as he quickly worked his magical incantation to stop the bleeding and heal his wound. The girl had never experienced the sexual ardor of which they spoke.

He wanted to be the one to show her.

He wanted to be the only one ever to touch her in that way.

Her betrothed, be damned.

But to claim her and bind her to him in this way was impossible. Were she anyone else, he wouldn't care, for the act would be a physical release and nothing more. The meaningless act was one he'd performed often enough with his nymphs.

But this was Georgiana.

If they mated, he could never let her go. It would be the same as taking a knife to his own heart and ripping it from his chest.

If they mated, they would be bound to each other for eternity.

If she did leave, the sorrow would kill him.

GEORGIANA HELD HER BREATH and gaped as Lord Bloodaxe twisted his lean torso this way and that, flexing his broad, muscled back and shoulders while he quietly worked on his wound until it had completely healed. She shook her head in wonder. "How did you accomplish this?"

"Dragon Lords have magical powers, as do the Fae. It is something all higher demons have acquired. But there are limits even to these powers. I can heal my own small injuries. Had the damage been greater, I would have needed a Fae healer to attend to me. I have no healing power over others. That is why I could not repair your injuries, much as I wanted to."

"Please tell me more." She was still seated at the far end of the bench watching him as he muttered a quick incantation to repair his shirt before he donned it. His body was now properly covered. She considered that a terrible shame. Such a body was a treat for the eyes. "Can someone like me acquire such powers?"

He shrugged his massive shoulders. "If the Stone of Draloch wishes it. Many believe that the Fae queen, Melody, is more powerful than all of us. Yet, she knew nothing of her powers before meeting King Cadeyrn. Even Anabelle–"

"Who is Anabelle?"

He refused to answer, now frowning as though irritated by the question. More likely, he was irritated with himself for allowing the woman's name to slip from his lips. "Is Anabelle the one you wish to claim as your dragon mate?"

Georgiana swallowed hard, determined to suppress the ache now gripping her like an iron clamp.

Did he love this woman? No doubt, she was beautiful and noble.

He regarded her with some surprise. "Anabelle?" He laughed and shook his head. "No, Georgiana. You have no competition for my affections."

She blushed.

He tipped a finger under her chin and forced her to meet his gaze. "But once you've escaped this Underworld, if you ever find yourself in trouble, seek out Anabelle."

"Who is she?"

"At the moment, the only person in your mortal realm who trusts me." His dogs suddenly scrambled upright and began to bark at the sky. Lord Bloodaxe glanced up and muttered an oath. "Brihann is circling overhead. He thinks I can't see him."

She followed his gaze. "Where? I don't see anything."

"You wouldn't. It takes the sharp eyes of a dragon to know he is soaring high above the clouds and plotting his next attack." He took her hands in his and nudged her to her feet. "Time to get you safely back inside."

She didn't resist, but one dragon had already destroyed his tower chamber. The mighty Brihann might bring the entire fortress down upon them. "Isn't there a safer place to go? He'll turn your home to rubble and who knows how many of your subjects will be killed in the attack?"

"I'm not staying, merely delivering you to safety." He turned to his dogs. "Charon. Styx. Protect Georgiana."

"Then where will you go? What are you going to do?"

"Kill him before he kills you," he said with a cold determination that chilled her bones.

His steward happened to be in the great hall when they hurried inside. "Thomas, is the south chamber in readiness?"

Thomas nodded. "It is, my lord. I was just about to go in search of you to report the news."

"Good. Take Lady Georgiana and my dogs there." He turned to

Georgiana and took her hands in his. He frowned. "Your hands are cold."

She nodded. "I'm not all powerful. Your world frightens me. In truth, you frightened me just now." She'd seen the demon in him for a moment. It was foolish of her to be surprised, for that's what he was. He'd warned her repeatedly, but she hadn't seen the evil in him until he'd spoken of killing Brihann.

This new knowledge only filled her mind with more questions. Why hadn't she seen this dark part of him before? Why was she seeing it now? These demons spoke of the Stone of Draloch as though it were a divine, spiritual force. Was it manipulating her? If so, she had to find out the reason. "Be careful, my lord."

He nodded. "I always am, Georgiana."

She was not quite certain about that. Although he was obviously intelligent and a brave fighter, there was an element of recklessness in him that worried her. Perhaps this recklessness went hand-in-hand with bravery, for it took a certain fortitude to plunge into battle knowing the odds were against you.

If this is what it took to hold his own against Lord Brihann, she was not about to undermine his confidence or distract him.

"This way, my lady," Thomas said, escorting her and the dogs up the stone steps to the south chamber. Although not as high up as Lord Bloodaxe's tower bedchamber, it was an elegantly appointed room with a very good view. "I hope you will find these quarters to your liking. I'll have supper brought up when his lordship returns. You needn't worry that harm will befall him. He will return to you, my lady."

"Thank you, Thomas." In truth, that his steward had faith in his abilities lightened her spirit. He'd also spoken kindly to her, with a gentle concern not expected in a demon. This world had many layers to it and she hoped to learn more before she made her escape. It felt important to do so, but she didn't know why.

He gave a quick bow. "You have only to tug on the bell pull if you wish to summon me. Please stay away from the windows, my lady.

We all know it is you Lord Brihann wants. It is you he fears."

Once alone, Georgiana began to pace across the beautifully patterned Persian carpet that covered much of the stone floor. The dogs quietly paced behind her. "Are you worried about him, too?"

Styx nodded.

Charon barked and then nodded.

"I wish there was something we could do," she muttered. "I don't like feeling helpless. My father often took me out with him to inspect his fields and visit the local tenant farmers. If the weather was decent, we'd ride into Penrith together and attend to business with the local merchants. I am an only child, you see. My father never had a son, so I think he resigned himself to teaching me whatever he would have taught his son."

The dogs listened attentively.

She wondered if they truly had the ability to understand her. She hoped so, but it didn't really matter. She needed to confide in a willing listener. Charon and Styx were more than suitable confidants. "I enjoyed being kept busy. I learned the proper duties of a lady, too. My mother insisted upon it." She grinned. "And then there was the training I endured, as all debutantes must, in order to make a proper entrance into Society."

She rolled her eyes, recalling those dull lessons.

Charon and Styx rolled their eyes as well.

She burst out laughing. "Yes, they were deadly dull." She stopped pacing and was about to kneel to pet her companions who stopped following her and were seated like bookends in the center of the room. As she was about to bend on one knee, each grabbed a sleeve and tugged hard so that she lost her balance and fell atop them. "What did you do that for?"

She'd hardly gotten the words out before one of the windows shattered and an arrow flew across the room directly over her head. It lodged with a *thwack* upon the mahogany headboard of the enormous bed. "Mother in heaven," she whispered breathlessly. Had she not been forced down at just that moment the arrow would have struck her between the eyes.

Charon and Styx, having released her, were now barking furiously. In the blink of an eye, they'd transformed from companionable dogs to growling, salivating beasts. They bared their sharp teeth and sprang through the window, shattering the remaining shards of glass jutting from the panes. "No! Stop!"

But her shouts were to no avail. Had they just jumped to their deaths? This chamber was on the uppermost floor of the fortress, only Bloodaxe's ruined tower and the parapets above this south chamber were higher.

She knew it was foolish to peer through the window, but she had to know his dogs were safe. The breath rushed out of her in a sigh of relief as she saw them tearing through the courtyard toward the main gate. The men-at-arms hurried to raise the gate, allowing Charon and Styx to cross the drawbridge and run toward the distant woods. In the next moment, an unearthly shriek filled the air.

Georgiana fell to her knees, trembling.

The dogs had found the assassin.

But she had no time to feel relief before the red sky suddenly turned dark and a great roar split the air. She covered her ears and peeked out the window in time to see two black dragons charge at each other. She knew Lord Bloodaxe was the smaller dragon, yet what he lacked in size was more than made up for by his speed and agility.

To Georgiana, they both appeared enormous and fierce.

Angry roars filled the air, and when they snapped their tails, she felt the cracks as sharp as bolts of lightning shoot through her own body.

Lord Bloodaxe suddenly soared high above Brihann, then turned and dove straight for him. Brihann avoided him and turned his body to do the same. Each spread his enormous black wings and soared effortlessly in and out of the clouds, but Bloodaxe was more adept and relentless in pushing Brihann away from his fortress and back toward their shared borderlands.

In truth, Bloodaxe almost seemed to be toying with Brihann. He was flying circles around him, bumping him off balance, and not a moment later, swooping across the border onto Brihann's land and emitting bursts of fire aimed at Brihann's minions.

He was skilled at that tactic, the bump and swoop accomplished with a balletic grace. However, she knew better than to impute nobility in his actions, for just like Brihann he was a hunter, a skilled predator and killer.

She covered her ears once more as Bloodaxe turned to face Brihann and roared to proclaim his dominance. Brihann roared back, and then both snapped their spiked tails. They reminded her of two knights preparing to joust, their tails serving as lances and their dragon scales used as protective armor.

They hovered motionless in the air for a long moment, then with a great roar and a quick flap of their wings, the two dragons flew toward each other. The ground beneath Georgiana's feet shook as each dragon landed a solid blow.

This jousting battle waged for a few minutes, although it felt like an eternity to Georgiana. Violent tremors rocked the solid fortress each time their bodies collided. Suddenly, Bloodaxe got the angle he desired and was about to sink his teeth into Brihann's thick neck, when the yellow and green dragons appeared. Their roars sounded more like shrieks of alarm than cries of war. But they managed to slam their dragon bodies into Bloodaxe and kept doing so in a frenzied onslaught until Brihann escaped.

Once their High King was safely away, they fled as well.

It suddenly turned quiet.

Only the smaller black dragon remained, his wings outstretched in a challenge no other dared take. "Bloodaxe," Georgiana whispered with relief, knowing it must have taken much out of him to battle three dragons. If they hurt him, he'd never show it. He was too proud to show his pain.

He'd fought for her.

He'd risked his life to save her.

Perhaps he'd been commanded by the Stone of Draloch to do this, but she indulged in the notion that he'd done it because she meant something to him.

After taking a majestic turn across the red sky, he flew toward the fortress, his sleek body gliding low. He landed silently on the parapet immediately above her chamber. Georgiana knew he would come to her as soon as he'd shifted back into his human form.

She hurried to the door, about to lift the latch to allow him in when it suddenly lifted by itself. "Lord Bloodaxe?" Was he using his magic to raise the latch with the simple wave of his hand?

She stood back, expecting him to storm in, cursing and in a temper. He did exactly that, striding in with ten of his soldiers beside him. To Georgiana's surprise, they were disciplined men and did not so much as blink an eyelash upon seeing her standing in the center of the room.

Bloodaxe paid her no notice as well as he began to command his soldiers, giving them more orders. Some were to secure his fortress and realm, while others were to push Brihann's forces back. "You have my authority to cross into his realm. March deep into his territory, as far back as his castle. But do not attempt to breach it. Lay siege to it. Keep him occupied, defending himself."

"Aye, my lord," several of his men said at once.

"Go now." He looked to his steward. "Give them all the supplies they'll need. Do not disturb me unless we are once again under attack."

He kicked the door shut in frustration once Thomas and his men had disappeared downstairs. "Bloody demented faerie!" He winced as he landed the kick and clutched his side.

Were his ribs broken?

Georgiana hurried forward. "Let me see." But she knew better than to touch him without his permission. Not that she was being obedient. She merely needed assurance that he hadn't been cut by Brihann's dragon tail. She had no desire to be infected by his soul trappers. "May I?" she prodded when he failed to immediately reply.

"Hell, no. I'm fine."

She rolled her eyes. "I can see that you are in the pink."

He growled to mark his annoyance, but took only a moment to calm. He managed a wincing smile in response to her dripping sarcasm. "Perhaps I'm not at my best just now."

She nodded. "Are you bleeding?"

"No. Just bruised."

"Will you let me see? Take off your shirt. Can you manage it without my help?"

He chuckled. "Georgie, are you asking me to strip for you again? I know how much you delight in seeing my body."

She meant to frown, but was too worried about him to be riled by his teasing. "Truly, my lord? You're hurt. Let me help you."

He shook his head again, this time quite serious. "No, you mustn't touch me just yet."

"Oh." She clasped her hands in front of her. "Then you are bleeding. I don't see where."

He ignored her and turned away, his gaze now falling on the headboard and the arrow protruding from it. He turned back and noticed the shattered window. "Where are my dogs? What happened here?"

"Someone tried to kill me again. Charon and Styx pulled me down in time, and the arrow merely sailed over my head." But she knew there was nothing harmless about the incident, and by his darkening expression, he didn't consider it harmless either. "They ran off in search of the assailant. I think they found him. They're not back yet. Perhaps still chasing others."

He leaned out the window and gave a whistle.

In the distance, two dogs barked.

He nodded and then turned back to her. "They are safe. But you're not." He waved his hand toward the window and the shattered panes of glass were suddenly repaired.

"What did you just do?" Her eyes widened in confusion. "Can you repair your tower bedchamber as easily?"

"Yes."

She fixed her gaze on his hands, wondering whether lightning bolts would next shoot from his fingers. "Then why did you not simply do it? Why make your subjects toil on repairing the stonework?"

"Because this is a dark magic to be used sparingly. I should not have used it just now, but I was still enraged and could not stop myself. I have no wish to become what Brihann is, but I know it is my cursed fate. These tasks I assign to my subjects help to remind them and me of the men we once were. Brihann has lost the memory of his heritage. Look at what he has become. I will not go willingly down that path."

He stepped closer and ran his thumb along her cheek. "Perhaps you are the one meant to keep me from this dismal fate. Will you lead me down a new path? Or will you be the one to send me tumbling to my soulless destiny?"

"I would never hurt you." She meant it with all her heart. He was her protector, but he was so much dearer to her than that. That his every touch set her body tingling was only a small part of what she felt for him. He called to her heart, and perhaps had already conquered it, but she dared not answer to his call yet. "Come, my lord. Sit on the bed while I see to your injuries."

To her surprise, he did as she asked with no more than a deep, throaty grumble. She helped him off with his shirt and immediately noticed the reddened welts along his ribs. These would soon form bruises.

She was about to step back while he tended to himself, but he took her hands in his and set her hands, with palms down, upon the welts. "What are you doing?" she asked, immediately responding to the warmth of his skin and the sensual tautness of his body.

"Finding out if you have the power to heal me."

The notion was ridiculous, but he did not appear to be in jest. She nodded. "I suppose there's no harm in trying."

He arched an eyebrow and frowned. "Let's hope not."

He drew a long, obviously painful breath and closed his eyes.

Georgiana did not know what she was supposed to do. Just touch him? That was easy enough. However, she knew there was nothing special about herself. She had no wizard's magical powers. Surely, she would have noticed it by now if she had.

At first, the tingling in her hands was the same sensation she always experienced whenever she touched him. Then the warm tingles began to spread through her body in gentle waves. Still, she thought nothing of it.

He had a splendid body.

Any woman would respond to him this way.

He grinned. "I see you're enjoying yourself. Immensely."

She gasped. "I am not. How dare you–"

She had no chance to finish the thought before her entire body was suddenly sent atilt by a powerful, fiery surge that would have dropped her to her knees had Lord Bloodaxe not caught her in time.

He drew her up against him to steady her. "By the Stone of Draloch! Georgie, you're pale and trembling."

She tried to pull away from him before he was drawn into this maelstrom of sensations, for the room was spinning all around her and sparks were shooting back and forth between his body and hers. Her heart was pounding, its beat intense and frightening. Her limbs were tingling and her throat constricted so that she could hardly speak. "Am I hurting you?" she asked, her voice so hoarse she wondered if he understood what she'd said.

"Hold onto me, Georgie. Don't let go." He held her tightly against his chest as the room continued to spin and gusts of warm air swirled all around them with the force of a typhoon. Her hair whipped wildly about both their shoulders, the loose strands blowing into his eyes. She closed hers and hoped he'd done the same with his. She didn't want to hurt him.

"My lord, what's happening to us?" She held onto him desperately, as though her life depended on it. No doubt, it did. She felt tossed upon a stormy sea, and he was her saving anchor.

He responded by burying his fingers in her hair and tipping her head upward so that her lips met his. His mouth pressed down on hers with blazing urgency, sending the room into a faster spin. Or was she the only one spinning? He dipped his tongue between her lips and then began to swirl it within the warm cavity of her mouth. The movement of his tongue matched the crests and ebbs of her own body with such fervent yearning, that moans of desire suddenly exploded within her and she could no longer keep silent.

She moaned against his mouth, crushed her lips and body to his and would not let go.

"Georgie, I have you. Be still, my beauty. You're safe."

Mother in heaven. Her heart would never be safe from him. She wanted to draw him inside of her and share the intimacy that should only be reserved for a husband and wife. But he didn't want her as his wife.

Nor should she want to be a dragon's mate.

She circled her arms around his neck. If she was going to lose him, then she wanted this moment together. He wanted it as well, she could tell by the gentle desperation in his touch and kiss.

In the next moment, he broke that kiss and stared at her. His eyes were wild and smoldering so that she knew this *thing* that had passed between them had affected him as deeply as it had her.

He eased her arms away, giving each a light caress as he set them off his body. "Forgive me," she said. Heat shot through her cheeks now that her mind was clearing and she realized how wanton her behavior had been. "I didn't mean to be so, um... frenzied."

He grinned.

She melted a little inside. "Are you healed?"

To her dismay, he wasn't. The red welts still ran along his ribs and were beginning to form purple bruises. Her shoulders slumped, and she responded to his grin with a look of dismay. "It didn't work."

"It did, Georgie." He tweaked her chin and kissed her lightly on the nose.

"You're only saying that to make me feel better. It's obvious that I failed miserably. Not a single red welt has disappeared." She traced her finger along the outline of one bruised rib. "See."

His hand still rested on her chin, but he now moved it up to cup her cheek. "Georgie, you healed the part of me that needed healing most. The injury to my ribs is nothing and will quickly repair on its own."

Her eyes widened. "Then what part of you did I heal?"

He lifted her off his lap. How had she gotten there? No matter, she watched him move away to walk to the window. "There's a secret passage out of this fortress. We'll leave upon the darkening of the two moons. We'll travel by foot. No magic will be used for Brihann to track us. Charon and Styx will remain here for now. Brihann knows I never travel without them. Their presence here will distract his spies long enough so that we can escape unnoticed."

"I healed your dragon heart, didn't I?" she said in a reverent whisper. "That is the part of you that needed healing most."

He turned back to her, his handsome face expressionless. "We will travel by night and hide by day so that we are seen by no one, not even my own loyal subjects. Brihann cannot torture information out of them they do not know."

He must have noticed the anguish in her eyes, for his expression softened a little. "My soldiers have already been stationed along the borders of my realm and throughout the hamlets that populate it. Brihann's soldiers will not slip in without notice. They'll be stopped before they can hurt anyone. My captains can be trusted to crush them if they dare trespass onto my land."

He paused a moment, and then a grin spread across his finely shaped mouth. "As for Brihann, I heard the crunch of bone as I slammed into him. He may have bruised my ribs, but I'll wager I broke his."

"You almost had him by the throat. Would you have killed him had the green and yellow dragons not arrived in time?"

Bloodaxe nodded and his expression turned serious once more. "Yes. I'll kill anyone who tries to harm you. I'll smash the Stone of Draloch to bits if that is the fate it intends for you."

Georgiana moved to stand by his side but did not touch him. She did not dare after the intense exchange that occurred when she'd placed her palms on his skin. "That's an awfully passionate declaration from the lips of a soulless creature. Are you certain that I'm not your dragon mate?"

She sensed his anger, although he did not show it. "Do you wish to be my mate?" He gave the low, throaty growl she was coming to recognize as a mark of his frustration. "Mine for eternity?"

"No," she said with a shake of her head. "Not unless you love me."

He peered out the window as though studying a distant point. "Get some sleep, Georgiana. We will be up all night and traveling fast. I need you to be alert should we encounter a problem."

"Then you don't love me."

He took her by the shoulders and gave them a light shake. "By the Stone of Draloch, have you been sent here to plague me? I'm a demon, not some mewling beau paying court to you. Forget your fancy balls and elegant tea parties. Love has no place down here. I do not love you. I *will* not love you. Have I made my meaning clear?"

She turned away. "Not in the least."

CHAPTER SEVEN

"Time to go, Georgie," Bloodaxe said in a whisper, gently shaking Georgiana awake. The red moons were now dark and not a sound could be heard in the fortress, at least none that could be detected by his finely tuned dragon senses.

She was curled in a little ball upon the large bed, like a kitten and purring as well. "So soon? It can't be morning yet."

He'd fashioned a pallet for himself by the unlit fireplace and spent the hours wide awake, hoping she would come to his side again and curl against him, but knowing it was the worst thing she could possibly do.

Fortunately, she hadn't.

"It's the middle of the night. Remember? Wake up, Georgie." He scooped her off the bed and into his arms, always a dangerous thing to do since he never wanted to let her go. "Here, put on your gown." She'd taken it off earlier and slept only in her camisole.

Sweet temptation! The sheer, white fabric hid nothing of her delectable body. Part of her camisole had ridden up to her thighs so that her long, slender legs were on display. The bodice was twisted so that her breasts would spill out if she turned the wrong way. She'd left her hair unbraided and flowing loosely so that it now fell over his arm in a silken wave of gold.

He loved the softness of her body, the warmth of her skin, and her wildflower scent.

He set her down. "Stand still. I'll put it on you."

Her eyes had yet to open. "Put what on?"

"Your gown, my beauty." Indeed, she was that and so much more to him. He eased it over her head, smoothed it down her body, and then tied the lacings. "Sit down." He nudged her onto a nearby stool and knelt beside her to help her on with her boots.

She finally opened her eyes, and he was momentarily stunned by the smile with which she graced him. "Good morning," she said with a soft laugh. "Or should I wish you good night? I'll only need a moment to braid my hair."

She combed her fingers through her wavy tresses and began to work the strands into three parts. Once finished, she tied off the result with a thin, gold ribbon. "Lead the way, my lord."

He hoisted a crossbow, quiver full of arrows, and a small pouch packed with provisions over one shoulder. He'd already secured his battle axe and dagger to the belt around his hips, and was about to open the door and walk out when to his surprise, Georgiana took hold of his hand.

"You know your way through these darkened passages, but I don't."

He nodded. "Stay close. Hold onto me. Keep up."

They moved silently down the stairs and kept to the dark shadows along the great hall before turning down another hallway. He paused at the third door on the left and released her hand to quietly open the door. He'd ordered Thomas to oil the hinges earlier, and breathed a sigh of relief that his reliable steward had attended to it at once. "This way, Georgie."

He felt her nod against his shoulder.

"My library," he murmured, taking her hand once more to guide her to the bookshelf that hid the secret passageway.

"Do you have many books in here? I wish I could see it."

But she couldn't, and he was not about to light a torch to show off his collection. The room was black as pitch, for he'd also ordered Thomas to draw the heavy, dark green velvet curtains.

"Another time, perhaps," she said.

He said nothing.

The last thing he wanted was Georgiana back in the Underworld and prey to Brihann's madness.

The bookshelf groaned as it opened, causing him to curse softly. Had anyone heard? It was unlikely. He'd closed the library door behind him and all the windows were sealed. The noise would be mistaken for any of the common creaking floorboards and groaning rafters that could be heard throughout the fortress.

Fortunately, the bookshelf was much quieter as it slipped back into place once they'd passed through it. "Still with me, Georgie?"

"Right beside you."

Her casual assurance sliced through him like a knife. All at once, the memory of the little girl with rosebud lips he'd kissed to seal their betrothal rushed to the fore. The kiss was a gesture that she was too young to understand at the time, and he was of an age that kissing a girl was an unpleasant chore rather than something in which to take delight.

In that long-ago time and place, had he not chosen to follow his little brother into the bowels of hell, everything would have been different. He would have become the Duke of Draloch, and Georgiana would have stood beside him as his wife.

But he'd made that fateful choice, and now Georgiana was betrothed to another. He would have her beside him for another two days, perhaps three at most. These few days would have to be enough to get him through his entire dragon lifespan.

"Is something wrong, my lord?"

He took her hand and gave it a light squeeze. "No, Georgie. Everything is perfect."

They spoke no more as he led her through the forest surrounding his fortress. Hidden deep within the woods was a waterfall, and beside it, a sheltered glade where they could camp during the day, undisturbed.

They'd sleep by day and travel by night. Only by night, for they couldn't risk being seen even by his own subjects.

Georgiana uttered not a word of protest even though they'd now been walking for almost four hours over uneven terrain. He was used to the warm, clammy air, but she was not, and he knew she had to be tired. But the two moons were rising over the horizon to signal the break of day and their hike would have to end shortly. They weren't far from the glade. However, they would have to step up the pace to reach it before the townspeople living nearby began to stir. "Only a little longer, Georgie," he said, wrapping an arm around her waist when she stumbled. "Are you all right?"

She nodded. "Just a little worn down. I'll keep up. Lead on, my lord." But she held him back a moment and took a deep breath. "It smells like a pine forest, the same as we have back home."

Bloodaxe smiled. "It is a pine forest. There's much in my realm that will remind you of England."

"Will I have the chance to see more? You mentioned that not all souls passing through here are sinful or doomed. I'm curious to learn about them."

He pursed his lips in thought, for the temptation to introduce her into his life was compelling. But it would serve no purpose. She needed to return to her home. The sooner she climbed the Razor Cliffs, the better.

Moonlight began to fill the glade as they stepped into the clearing. The *whoosh* that could be heard nearby was the sound of water streaming down a precipitous, rocky slope, and the *plunks* that followed soon after, were that same water hitting the bottom of the slope to gather in a circular pool. They could wash and slake their thirst from the cascading stream. "Are you hungry, Georgie?"

"A little. But I'm hot and sticky and would love to wash first."

He tucked his crossbow and quiver down on the grass behind a fallen tree and placed the pouch of food on a flat stone out of sight beside his weapons. "Then I'll take you to the waterfall first. I think you'll enjoy it. Do you swim?"

She shook her head. "No. My father didn't believe it was necessary to teach me."

"Then keep to the edges to rinse away the dust of a night's travel. I've packed a cake of soap for you. Best to use it now, for we won't camp in such pleasant surroundings tomorrow. This will be your only chance to bathe." He reached into the pouch and withdrew a lavender soap. "Here, Georgie. I'll walk you to the pool and show you the spots to avoid. But you go first. Don't take too long. I'll return in ten minutes."

Georgiana beamed when she saw the waterfall glistening in the dawning light. "It's beautiful." She walked around the pool's edge and knelt from time-to-time to study the flowers along the bank. "These are lilies. And is that honeysuckle? What are these?"

"Starfire daisies. Touch your finger to the petals."

She eyed him warily. "Will they turn into sharp-toothed creatures and try to bite me?"

He knelt beside her. "Look, I'll touch them." As he did so, they took on a fiery gleam. "They glow like candles in the night. I come here to swim sometimes. These starfires provide a beautiful light, gold like the English sun that used to shine on my face when I was young."

"Do you often think of England, my lord?"

He nodded. "More now that Brihann is intent on decimating it. He won't be satisfied until he controls the world of man."

"But you'll stop him."

"I don't know, Georgie. The prophecy speaks of two black dragon who will unite our worlds. I cannot deny that the urge to return to the place of my birth compels me. But the sun burns me now. I am not the human I once was. I can endure no more than an hour or two under its glare. Whether I will ever be capable of surviving in that light has yet to be determined. I doubt it, though. It is more likely that I will unite with Brihann and return to the place of my birth as a conqueror."

"Like William the Conqueror when he sailed from Normandy into England and changed the land forever. Why would you do such a thing?"

He studied the soft green of her eyes. "I do not wish it, but every day I become more like Brihann. He knows it and is determined to push me harder toward that end. He needs me to join him, for he knows I am the only one who can fulfill this destiny."

"The only black dragon. I thought you mentioned there was a third."

His expression turned as grim as his memories. "That third dragon is my brother and he's sworn to kill me on sight. For that reason, I doubt he and I shall be the two dragons who unite to fulfill the prophecy."

He turned away and shook his head. "Take your bath, Georgie."

Her gaze remained on him as she began to unlace her gown. "Tell me more about your brother."

"Not now. Perhaps I'll speak of him when we settle down to eat."

She smiled. "I must admit, I'm hungry." She peered into the water. "Are there fish in there?"

"No fish. No dangerous creatures of any sort. You'll be safe enough. Just don't wander into the deep end."

"I won't. I can wash up just fine right here." She pointed to a shallow spot immediately beside the waterfall. Still smiling, she waved him off. "I'll be careful. I promise."

Reluctantly, he turned away. Ten minutes was all he dared give her. He knew this place was safe, but what if Georgiana accidentally slipped into deep waters? What if someone wandered into the glade or saw her by the waterfall? What if that someone was one of Brihann's demons?

"Bah," he said and walked away. He would have picked up the scent of Brihann's demons if any were about.

He laid out their cloaks to serve as blankets on an area of flat ground that was devoid of rocks. It also provided a good hiding place, for it was sheltered behind shrubbery and the trunks of several fallen trees.

The day was already warm enough so that no fire needed to be set. Good thing, for the smoke would carry for miles and be a beacon to anyone tracking them. They were safest dining on cold fare, on the bread, fruit, and cheese he'd brought along for their journey.

He shrugged out of his shirt and removed his boots. He heard her humming as she bathed, so he waited the ten minutes and a few more, then made his way to the waterfall. About to call out to Georgiana, he stopped when he saw her step out of the water, naked with droplets of water casting her skin in a silver glow under the brightening moonlight. Her newly washed hair was clinging to her shoulders and swirling over the rose-tipped peaks of her breasts. "By the Stone of Draloch," he muttered, his voice a choked rasp.

Had that monolith purposely gifted him with this unexpected moment? Indeed, it was a gift and at the same time, a moment of agony.

He turned away to catch his breath, for he'd responded as any man would. Indeed, he needed several deep breaths to bring his body under control. But he was no ordinary man. His loins were hard and throbbing, his body longing to mate with hers. Dragon scales began to form along his skin. Dragon lust surged through his body like a ball of fire. "Georgie, dry yourself off and get dressed."

His voice sounded harsh to his own ears, but he was desperate for her to hurry. His control would only last so long. He needed to dive into that cold water to cool his dangerous ardor.

"I'm out," she called from behind a row of shrubs.

"Stay there. Don't move." His voice was still harsh as he stripped out of the last of his clothes and dove into the water.

He swam along the floor of the pool, the sparkling blue water so clear, the moon's rays shone straight through to the bottom. After a moment, he realized that Georgiana might worry if he did not come up for air. Dragons had a great capacity for holding their breath and could do so for ten or twenty minutes with little difficulty.

He broke the surface, swam toward the bank, and then stood in the shallow water, careful to keep the lower part of his body hidden below the water. He combed his fingers through his hair while searching the shrubs where Georgiana had been dressing, and then chuckled when he saw her peeking back at him. Her big, green eyes were as wide as saucers.

While he had accidentally come upon her undressed, she had just been caught purposely spying on him and there was no way she could deny it. "Like what you see, Georgie?"

She blushed furiously. "Must you always ask me that? Are you so uncertain of your good looks?"

"No, my beauty. I know my body is desirable to women. I like that you admire it."

She edged closer, taking a seat on one of the flat rocks beside the waterfall. "You don't need me to tell you that you're handsome. Your nymphs, no doubt, tell you every night."

"They do. But it is your opinion that matters to me."

"It does?" She tucked her legs under her and leaned forward. "I did not realize that the tail of the dragon painted on your back extends below your hip and wraps around your thigh."

"You saw that much?" Mercy, she must have been watching him closely.

She changed the subject. "Here's the soap." She tossed it to him.

He caught it in one hand and began to lather his hair with it, then worked the soap over his chest and shoulders before quickly lathering the rest of his body. He tossed the soap back onto her lap and then dove deep to rinse off. He swam to the other side of the pool and climbed out to grab the clothes he'd left on one of the overhanging rocks.

Georgiana gasped. "You might have warned me!"

He bothered only to don his pants before returning to her side. "Come along, Georgie. Time for a light repast, then sleep."

She took the hand he held out to her. "You really ought to have warned me."

He arched an eyebrow and grinned. "You could have looked away."

Her soft laughter filled the glade. "But where would be the fun in that? I'll need some sensational stories to tell my friends when I return to… If I ever make it out of here."

"You will." He gave her hand a gentle squeeze. "I'll miss you. It isn't often we have an innocent in our midst. You're quite a special girl."

"My lord, please tell me how we know each other. I know we've met before, it must be so. My heart feels at ease when I'm with you. My heart knows yours. Please don't deny it, for I know it is so."

"Very well, I'll tell you when we're on the move tonight. I won't tell you now. You won't sleep if I do. I need you well rested to reach our next stopping point. We walked a mere four hours today. This next leg requires us to walk for eight hours, perhaps more."

They returned to the fallen trees where he'd hidden the pouch and weapons. He broke off a chunk of bread and wedge of cheese, then handed both to her. He motioned to the small sack of water he'd also brought along. "Care for some?"

"Yes, thank you."

"Have as much as you wish. I'll refill it at the waterfall before we leave."

They ate in silence, and when they were done, Bloodaxe stowed away their supplies and then stretched out on his cloak. He'd placed the cloak he'd brought along for Georgiana beside his own. To his relief, she settled on it without protest.

To his surprise, she drew her cloak close and nestled her body against his. "Sweet dreams, my lord."

He knew they would be, for he'd dream of her. "To you as well, my beauty."

CHAPTER EIGHT

GEORGIANA FELL ASLEEP wrapped in Lord Bloodaxe's arms. She awoke hours later to find herself alone, for his pallet was empty. All that remained were shadows caused by the fading moonlight and an indentation on the grass where he'd slept. Her heart shot into her throat. Where had he gone? "Don't panic, Georgiana," she said, hoping to convince herself that there was a logical explanation for his disappearance.

She had the presence of mind not to jump up and start shouting his name, though inwardly she was crying out for him like a lost lamb for its mother.

Don't leave me.

But she was no child and had to keep her wits about her in this dangerous land. She rolled to her knees and carefully peered over the fallen tree trunks that had served as a barrier to hide them from anyone walking through the glade.

She saw nothing but an empty glade.

She turned around to search for their provisions. Were his weapons and food pouch still here? A glance revealed the pouch had been left by her side but his weapons were gone. He'd also left a dagger tucked under her cloak. Did this mean he was going to return?

Or had he abandoned her to fend for herself without so much as a farewell?

No, he was her protector. He wouldn't simply sneak off.

Besides, he had agreed to tell her more about himself and his realm as they walked to their next destination. "Please come back. Please come back," she repeated in a whisper as she tucked the dagger into the belt at her hip and then shook the dust and grass off her cloak.

"Georgie, you're awake."

She gasped, dropped her cloak, and whirled to face Lord Bloodaxe who had come up behind her so silently that she hadn't heard so much as a twig snap. "You didn't leave me." She threw her arms around him and hugged him fiercely.

"What's this?" At first, he appeared confused by her behavior which was no doubt cowardly and ridiculous. But she was no warrior, nor was she quick witted or experienced enough to live off the land. She was the daughter of a duke, and had never fended for herself.

He gave a short laugh and shook his head as realization struck. Prying her hands off him, he took a step back to study her face. He cupped her cheek and his expression turned sober. "I'd never walk away from you without warning. I merely went for a swim and did not wish to wake you. In truth, I expected to have difficulty waking you upon my return, for you were so soundly asleep, you didn't so much as flinch when I sneezed."

"Demons sneeze?"

His expression lightened once more. "Yes, at least this demon does. Although it is not at all pleasant when it happens in my dragon form. It tosses my dragon body off balance and causes me to lose the lift of air beneath my wings. I begin to plummet to the ground, and as if that isn't bad enough, the sneeze also causes fire to snort through my nostrils instead of my mouth. Have you ever munched on a chip of ice and felt the sudden freeze shoot straight upward into your brain? That's how fire shooting through my nostrils feels."

She winced, but at the same time managed a hearty chuckle. "Oh, dear. Not pleasant at all."

"Fortunately, I don't feel the urge to sneeze very often." He glanced around the empty glade. "Do you wish to eat before we begin our trek? I'd like to get away from here as soon as possible."

"Then let's go. I'm not hungry. But I do need to... take care of myself. It will only take a moment." She searched around for a suitable place to relieve herself.

He'd had a swim, but she'd washed thoroughly earlier by waterfall and would manage with just a quick washing of her hands and face before they started on their journey.

"Here, take the soap." He handed it to her and watched her as she walked away. She felt the heat of his gaze upon her all the while, only broken when she walked around the bend to seek her privacy.

After taking care of her needs, she quickly washed up and scampered back to the spot they'd bedded down for the day. The moons were setting and soon there would be no light at all to guide them.

However, Lord Bloodaxe seemed to know every path, hill, and waterway in his realm as though he'd walked it blind.

Georgiana was not afraid of the inky darkness so long as he kept hold of her hand.

"Georgie, do you think you can wait a little longer to eat?" he asked when he heard her stomach growl.

"Yes. My stomach may be howling, but I can hold off for as long as you need."

"Good, because we're almost at the river, and I think we'll make better progress if we travel by boat. We'll eat once we're aboard."

She frowned lightly. "Is this a change in plans?"

"Yes. I caught the scent of Brihann's demons on my land about half an hour ago. They seem to be following us, although it could be mere coincidence. Brihann must have sent several scouting parties to hunt us down. My captains have stopped most of them, but our shared borders are long and it's almost impossible to prevent every incursion. Who knows? This scouting party might have slipped through a month ago, long before our hostilities intensified. They may not even know about you, but I dare not take the chance."

"You think we will be better off on the river?" She'd noticed that he had quickened their pace, but thought nothing of it until now.

"Most assuredly. Brihann's demons don't like water. They won't go in it or anywhere near it. We were fortunate, the little bit of breeze we have tonight happens to be coming from the west. If the wind shifts, the demons will pick up our scent while we're on land."

"But the water will lend us cover?" She was taking two steps for each of his own in order to keep up with his long strides.

"That's right." His arm was now around her waist as he helped her over a small rise. She was out of breath from struggling to match his step, while he did not appear to be struggling at all. "It will lend us good cover, for these demons detest the odor of water."

"Which means they don't like to bathe," she added, grinning, although she doubted he could see beyond his nose in this darkness. "No wonder they smell so bad. Good thing there's a river nearby." However, she sensed he wasn't all that pleased with this forced change in plans. "You don't seem happy about it."

"I'm not. The river will take us east when we must be heading west. Every hour lost gives Brihann the advantage. We'll lose at least half a day."

She understood. The longer it took to reach the Razor Cliffs, the more time Brihann would have to secure that important portal and stop them. "But it would mean I'd have another day with you."

"Georgie, had I been able to get you out yesterday, I would have. You're in danger every moment you spend in the Underworld. Your innocence offers you some protection, but I do not know how much or how long that protection will last."

"Ah, my innocence." It wasn't nearly as precious to her as it appeared to be to him. Indeed, had he bothered to make any advances toward her, she would have surrendered without resistance. She was eager to do it.

However, her casual wantonness extended only to him. She would never allow another man to touch her.

"Do not underestimate its importance. There's an aura of power and mystery that emanates from you because of your innocence. You're an unknown to these demons, and now that you've survived dragon fire, they're certain you are a Chosen One, a mortal girl under the protection of the Stone of Draloch."

She frowned as she considered his words. "Or meant to be its virgin sacrifice."

"Well," he said with noticeable humor in his rugged voice, "I'll fix matters if it comes to that."

"Fix? As in…" She inhaled, which he might have mistaken for a gasp of horror. Quite the opposite ran through her mind, a feeling that his *fix* was much desired flooded through her. The notion that he would be the one to take her innocence felt very right. "How much longer till we reach the boat?"

"Just over the next rise. Can you hear the soft rush of water in the distance?" He paused and wrapped his arm around her waist.

It took Georgiana a moment to hear the gentle ebb and flow over the hasty beat of her heart. Then she heard a languidly rhythmic *thuck, thuck, thuck,* which she realized was the sound of the wooden boat gently striking the dock as the river current flowed beneath it. She also heard the groan of a rope that had been pulled taut and was straining to hold the boat to the dock.

Otherwise, all was quiet as a tomb.

She stood beside Lord Bloodaxe, unmoving and not speaking as the hot, night air encircled both of them. At home, she would have heard the sound of crickets or seen fireflies playfully flitting in the meadow.

Only ominous silence and a breathless dark existed here. "There are no stars in your heaven."

"Heaven? A strange thing to call what lies above us. There is no heaven here, only an endless red sky. No stars shining brightly to light our way. No sunshine to warm our hearts."

After a moment, he took her hand again and wordlessly started up the small rise. It seemed so odd, he was a large man and carried a battle axe at his side along with a shield, bow, quiver of arrows, and a travel pouch slung over his shoulder, yet he made not a sound walking over the ground in his thick leather boots.

She had his dagger still strapped to her belt and carried nothing, but it was her booted feet that slipped and slid as they climbed, and her steps that would be heard were anyone lying in wait for them.

"No one knows we're here, Georgie. It's just you and me and that boat we'll soon reach. We outwitted Brihann in making our escape last night."

"How can you be certain? You said his demons were on our trail."

"They were, but I now think it was mere coincidence they were following us. We lost them a short while ago. I don't think we would have shaken them off if they had been ordered to find us."

"How long do you think we can fool Brihann? His spies will know something is amiss since you didn't come down to your hall today."

"Thomas and my captains are doing their best to make everyone think we're still in our bedchamber. Dragon Lords are known to have lusty appetites, especially after a battle. Everyone saw me and Brihann fight. It will not take much to fool them into believing that I've taken you into my bed and am enjoying the pleasures of your body as my spoils of war."

"Spoils?" She shook her head and sighed. "I'm rather meager fare, not nearly as… er, desirable a prize as your nymphs. I dare say, it will not take his spies long to suspect it is a ruse."

"Do not doubt your worth, Georgie." He chuckled lightly and tweaked her nose. "There is no one like you in all of England or in this realm. Even if Brihann suspects we're on the run and headed for the Razor Cliffs, he'll have most of his scouts and armies gathered there, not here."

She nodded. "Good, then we shall have time to eat and talk without interruption."

She slid most of the way down the other side of the rise and would have landed with a splash in the water had not Lord Bloodaxe kept a firm hold of her hand. "Gracefully done," he teased. "Here, let me help you into the boat. Careful, now. Don't fidget or it will tip over and land us both in the water. Sit on the center bench and hold tight to the pouch."

"I'll keep it securely on my lap. I'm famished. If it falls in, I'm jumping in after it."

"Try not to, Georgie." She felt his grin rather than saw it. "I'm also famished and may rescue the food instead of you."

She laughed. "No, my lord. I know you'll save me."

"Aye, always." His voice was suddenly gentle and husky.

She looked up, wishing she could see his face. "It feels nice."

He set down his weapons and moved to untie the boat from its mooring. "What does?"

"What you just said. Will you truly always be there to protect me? Yesterday, you seemed insistent on never seeing me again."

"We have yet to set off and you're already asking questions." But he didn't seem very much put out as he tucked the oars in their oarlocks. He kept them tilted upward so that they sat above the water.

"I can't help being curious," she said. "There's so much to learn and so little time in which to do it."

"We'll talk on the water."

The boat rocked as he stepped in and settled on the bench across from hers. She grasped the sides and gave a soft yelp when it suddenly tipped hard in one direction. "You do remember that I can't swim. I'd be wailing and howling, resisting climbing aboard with all my might if I were here with anyone else."

"I'm honored you trust me." His hands come to rest lightly on hers.

"Of course, I do." The quickening beat of her heart was for reasons other than fright. The longer they remained together, the more she cared about him.

He squeezed her hand and spoke gently. "Let's eat first. Then you can assail me with your questions."

"Very well." She wasn't going to protest, for she was hungry, and he needed to concentrate on getting them underway.

All too soon, he removed his hands from hers. The oars were now loosely perched on his lap so that he could set them in position quickly if the current caused the boat to drift too close to the shore.

As they floated downstream, he sliced some cheese and bread for her and then for himself. They ate quickly, and once sated, he handed her a small sack. She opened it and inhaled the heady scent. "A honey wine? Do you grow grapes here?"

"Yes, in the midlands of my realm. Our grapes grow by the light of our moons so their flavor is more bitter than the grapes grown in Spain or France that have the benefit of your sunlight. We add honey to cut the bitterness. We do the same for most of our ales." He leaned forward, close enough that their breaths mingled. "The midlands is my farming region. Our grains and orchards are cultivated there. The pine forests near my fortress provide wood for our ships and houses. The Razor Cliffs provided the stone for my fortress."

She wished that they could travel by day so that she could see more of his lands. The night here was unsettling, so dark without starlight or even the bright glow of the two moons that shone only by daytime. "The activities here are remarkably similar to those that would go on in England."

"In many ways they are, because it is important for those who cannot move on, those who have no choice but to reside in the Underworld, to feel rooted in the familiar. But there are important differences between your world and mine. The existence of Dragon Lords, of course, and the knowledge we carry of a powerful, dark magic that is unknown elsewhere. I was eager to learn this magic, but use it sparingly now that I have mastered its power."

She sensed an aching sadness in his words, a longing to be something other than he was. But he seemed to quickly shake out of his morose thoughts and continued to talk about his home. "Our animals and birds aren't quite the same down here. You wouldn't recognize most of them."

She listened, fascinated as he opened up to her. "No grouse or quail?"

"No, our birds come in all sizes, but they're all nasty, as you will recall from your first encounter with those creatures. They have sharp teeth and tough skin, not suitable for eating."

She recalled her surprise on that first day and it instantly made her heart beat a little faster in an unpleasant way. "Is there anything that isn't dangerous here?"

"Many things," he assured, the deep rumble of his voice as smooth as the water upon which they drifted.

"Name one."

"Sausage trees," he replied immediately.

She laughed and shook her head. "I've never heard of such a thing. Now I know you're teasing me."

"No, I'm in earnest. They exist in your world as well, in the arid regions of your continent of Africa. These trees sustain most of the demons living down here as well. Their fruit happens to grow in the shape of a sausage, hence its name." His tone became more serious. "Mordain, the red dragon, and I have maintained our lands so that they and our subjects flourish. But Brihann, Necros, and Python have been swallowed up by the evil of their magic. Their thoughts are filled with war and death so that they no longer think of what is needed to sustain their minions. The demons who live within their realms mostly survive on the fruit and flowers of the sausage trees."

"Will you think me heartless if I'm relieved to know those demons are weakened? And glad that their Dragon Lords are destroying the very evil which gives them power? It cannot be a bad thing."

He sighed. "I suppose it isn't. But the Underworld does not harbor only wicked souls. Many who are here are not unredeemable."

Their conversation seemed to flow as swiftly as the current that propelled them silently down the vast river. She was glad it would take hours to reach their destination, for there was so much to learn about him and this Underworld in which she was presently trapped. "Then why are they here?"

He sighed. "I don't know. Perhaps their anger needs to fade before their souls can return to your world or rise to heaven. Perhaps it is sorrow or pain that compels them here, or a mistake that could not be healed while they lived. Many of them were tormented in life, but few who pass through here are pure evil."

"You seem to understand their suffering."

He grunted. "I'm not that insightful. However, I don't judge the souls who come to me. Here, they are given a second chance. They start afresh once the ferrymen bring them across the river and they set foot on my lands. Many understand the hope of redemption that is offered and do eventually move on to a better place."

"They're fortunate to come to you." She suddenly wondered whether she'd been brought here for the same reason, only he was hiding the truth from her.

He somehow sensed her thoughts. "No, Georgie. You're here for altogether different reasons that will be revealed by the Stone of Draloch in its own good time. Had you not been brought to me, I might have decided to join Brihann in his mad quest. Perhaps you are here to remind me that goodness still exists and ought to be left to flourish."

He took the sack of wine and drank heartily. "Perhaps you've been brought here merely to torment me. The Stone of Draloch is not above cruelty either. It could have–"

He stopped abruptly, and Georgiana ground her teeth in frustration. "What could it have done?"

"Nothing."

She sighed, feeling his sudden tension and knowing he was hiding something.

"Obviously, it is important. Did you ever consider that I was brought here to mend whatever it is that you won't tell me?" In truth, until this moment, she hadn't considered herself important or powerful and that had been a mistake on her part. She'd been chosen by this mysterious Stone of Draloch and put in close quarters with Lord Bloodaxe. Why wouldn't he tell her the reason?

The connection that she'd felt so immediately and profoundly at their first meeting had to be significant. She glanced around in the hope of seeing something of their location as they continued to drift, but saw nothing but an endless blackness. They'd been in the boat for some time now and she didn't want to miss the chance to ask more questions. "I think you must tell me how we are connected."

He was already tense, but the warm, moisture-laden air had suddenly charged. She didn't care if he was angry. He wasn't going to hurt her. He was her valiant protector. "Did you save my life when I was in England? I don't recall it ever being in peril. But I think it must have been and you were the one to save me. Why else would I feel such a strong bond with you? When I opened my eyes and saw you beside me, I wasn't afraid."

He grunted. "You were frightened out of your wits."

"No, I wasn't. Perhaps in that first moment. But I calmed quickly. I knew you were someone important to me."

She paused and was disappointed when he refused to answer. "Very well, if you can be stubborn and irritating, then so can I. I'm not climbing those Razor Cliffs until you tell me what I need to know. So, what do you say now?"

There was another long pause before he finally relented. "Will you promise to climb to the light and never look back if I tell you about us?"

"There was an *us*?" Her heart beat a little faster in anticipation. "Of course, there had to be. Yes, I promise."

He leaned close then and gave her the softest kiss on her lips. As his mouth pressed to hers, she tasted the honey wine he'd taken his fill of earlier. "I kissed you once like this in England."

She held her breath and then released it in a rush of questions. "When? Why don't I remember it? And yet, my heart remembered you. I knew we were connected somehow."

"You were but an infant then. I was just a boy. Our families had grand plans for us at one time. Marriage plans."

"What?" She gripped the edge of the bench so tightly, the splintered wood dug into her fingers.

"We were betrothed, you and I?"

Her head began to spin with wild thoughts.

His words rang true, but her mind could not yet comprehend it. "No, how can it be? I was never betrothed until Oliver." But even as she spoke the words, she knew he was telling the truth. There had been rumors. Whisperings. "Who were you in England? What happened to us, Lord Bloodaxe? Why did my father never tell me this?"

"In that time, I was known as Arik Blakefield, eldest son of the

Duke of Draloch."

"Arik? It's a nice name. May I call you that?"

"No," he said with unexpected harshness, "that part of me is gone. I am no longer Arik but Lord Bloodaxe. Named so for all the killing I've done with my battle axe. Many have been slain by my hand, many who may not have deserved to die. But I took their lives anyway."

She shook her head in denial. "I cannot believe you purposely did harm to anyone. Were you… did you do this in England?"

"Not in England. I was like any other boy then." There was a wistfulness in his voice that could not be overlooked, but he quickly shook it off with his next words. "Well, I was a young and wealthy marquess, so perhaps I was insufferably arrogant."

"You are still arrogant, but I think deservedly so. You're a natural leader and you care for those under your charge."

He grunted. "I learned to kill in the Underworld."

"To protect yourself," she insisted.

"I convinced myself it was so. I no longer know if that is true. I've killed so many, I do not think twice about it now. Nor do I ever suffer from regret for my actions."

"But you take no pleasure from your actions. You don't kill for the sport of it."

"Not yet."

She didn't think he ever would, for he appeared to be too honorable ever to take a life unless his lands and people were under threat. He had yet to harm her, and despite his obvious strength, had never made her feel intimidated or scared.

Were he cruel, he would have used her in the way Brihann had intended when gifting her to him. Instead, he'd gone out of his way to protect her innocence. She could not bring herself to think less of him. His horrific deeds were done to survive in brutal surroundings where the rules of humanity did not exist and survival depended on brute force. "You mentioned Draloch. Your title bears the same name as the stone."

He took her hands in both of his and wrapped them in his warmth.

"Rumors of evil have always swirled around the Dukes of Draloch. Demon blood runs in our family. Somewhere down the bloodline, one of my ancestors must have sold his soul for the promise of vast wealth. Ever since, the Dralochs have been sacrificing their sons in return for continued riches."

"But you were the eldest and meant to inherit." She frowned in confusion. "Our fathers agreed to the betrothal, did they not? Then why would your father suddenly give you over to this evil?"

There was another long pause and Georgiana knew this proud Dragon Lord was struggling to find the words to tell her of a moment that must still cause him great anguish. "I was never meant to be the one sacrificed. My younger brother was taken. I refused to accept it, so I went against my father's wishes and followed Saron into the Underworld."

His voice grew ragged and husky. "They were more threats than wishes, in truth. But I didn't care. I had to save my little brother. I went after him and spent the next few years planning his escape. He suffered greatly in the meanwhile. I could only watch in silence as he endured the pain like a true Draloch."

"Which meant he fought against them every day," she said, knowing that if Saron Blakefield was half as proud as his brother was, he'd never allow his spirit to be conquered.

"He did exactly that and they beat him for it every day. They'd lock him away each night and even now I can hear his sobs and sniffles in my mind as he cried himself to sleep. He was only six years old when he was taken. But every morning, he stood firm and endured the same hardships as valiantly as any soldier who ever fought for a just cause. In the beginning, I fought along with him and endured the same punishment. Then I realized that I had to form a plan or else we'd both suffer the same fate until the beatings finally killed us."

Georgiana felt each of his words like a rip to her heart. She felt an intense sorrow for both sons of Draloch. What father would ever allow his boys to be condemned so cruelly? And for what? The promise of coin?

"Georgie, are you crying?"

"Of course, I am. How can I not be moved by the torments you both endured? What happened to Saron?"

Lord Bloodaxe's laughter was mirthless. "He escaped. He thinks he did it on his own, but he wouldn't have made it beyond Brihann's great hall if it weren't for my help. That's the first time I killed, and I did so without a shred of remorse. I killed every demon who got close enough to dig their talons into my brother. I couldn't fight them all, though. Some managed to grab him, but he was strong enough by then to shake them off."

He shifted in his seat, took one of the oars that sat across his lap, and began to row them toward the center of the river. They hadn't drifted close to shore, but he must have felt the need to do something as he spoke of his bitter memories. "Our dark powers had grown while we were trapped here," he continued, his voice brittle. "Brihann thought he had tamed me and so began to teach me his dark magic. In turn, I taught what I could of it to Saron while he was down here. However, much of his knowledge came from the rage that naturally sprang from within himself."

"Do you know what has become of him?"

"Yes, he is now the Duke of Draloch. Anabelle, the woman I mentioned to you earlier, is his wife. His dragon mate. Hopefully, she is the one who will free him from the darkness."

"Then I must go to them as soon as I escape. The prophecy you spoke of, the one concerning the two black dragons. Why would it not be you and Saron?"

He gave a tug on the oar and propelled them faster down river. "Because he will kill me on sight."

"You've mentioned this before." Georgiana shook her head in disbelief. "Why would he do such a thing when you saved his life?"

"He doesn't realize that I saved him. I don't know what my parents told him about me, surely lies to poison his mind. Then Brihann made certain that he and I would never reconcile."

"What did he do?" Georgiana braced herself for the terrible explanation she knew was to come.

"He killed Saron's son and made it appear as though I'd committed the murder. Saron now believes I killed his boy, Gideon."

Georgiana wasn't certain how much more sorrow she could bear. This proud and powerful family ought to have had an easy existence, residing in a great manor and able to provide their sons with all the luxuries she had been given as the daughter of a duke. Instead, they'd been treated worse than any caged animal. "I'm so sorry."

They were speeding down river now, his oar thrusts ripping through the water as though Brihann's demons were nipping at their heels. Nothing and no one was chasing them at the moment. The demons he was fleeing from were his own nightmarish memories. "Brihann purposely used one of my arrows. I realized his intent but was too late to stop him. When Saron looked up, grief etched on his face as he held Gideon's lifeless body, all he saw was me. He recognized my markings on the arrow and decided I was guilty. He vowed then and there to kill me on sight. He'll do it. Nothing has swayed him from his purpose."

"Yet Anabelle believes in your innocence, and so do I. There must be something we can do to convince Saron."

"There is nothing. Don't you think I've tried? But it's hopeless. Brihann's evil has won the day. Saron and I will never reconcile. The two black dragons that the Stone of Draloch mentions will be Brihann and me, or Brihann and my brother."

"But neither you nor your brother is evil. So how can Brihann succeed in conquering us while you are both able to stop him?"

"Georgie, have you not been listening? My brother and I are dark souls. It will take little to turn us into what Brihann has become. Necros and Python have already succumbed to the madness of evil. Mordain and I cannot be far behind."

"How is it that Mordain has resisted? Who was he in his earlier life?"

He dug the oar once more into the water and gave a powerful thrust so that their boat appeared to be flying like a bird on the wing. "The son of Lucifer," he said tersely. "The fallen angel."

"What?"

"Georgie, there is no happy ending to be found here. Mordain is the devil's own spawn. So, you see, the Dragon Lords are tainted by an evil that cannot be rinsed off by good intentions or by *love*. I don't know why Mordain and I have not turned to rot yet. We are the youngest among the five. We know what we will become in time."

"No, it doesn't have to be that way. You and Mordain must continue to resist," she pressed. "The reason why you haven't succumbed yet is important. I don't believe it is merely a question of your age. What if Mordain has warded off the darkness because he believes in true love? Has he taken a dragon mate? Is he searching for her?"

"Dragon Lords don't attend balls or country weekends looking for love." He snorted in dismissal.

"Then how do you find love? Do you simply fly among the clouds, minding your own business, and it suddenly strikes you between your dragon eyes?"

"Love does not conquer anything, certainly not a Dragon Lord's heart."

"That is nonsensical. It is a momentous thing for a dragon to take a mate. Did you not tell me so yourself? Once they are mated, they must remain true to each other throughout eternity. They *want* to remain true to each other. No one does that simply because they're jolly good friends."

"Are you being sarcastic, Georgie?"

She tipped her head up in indignation. "Well, perhaps a little. Mostly, I'm trying to make you believe in love. What if Saron is saved because he married Anabelle? What if you can be saved because of me?"

"You are not my dragon mate," he said with unnecessary vehemence and almost tipped the boat over with the force of his oar thrust.

She closed her eyes and held on for dear life. "Of course, I am." Her voice was little more than a squeak. "It all makes sense now that you have explained it to me. And if you think that I'm not going to fight for you, fight every day of my life to protect and heal you, then you had better think again."

CHAPTER NINE

G EORGIANA HAD BLOODAXE so riled that his oar was no longer swift and silent as it cut through the water. He was now bearing down on it so hard that even the boat groaned and waves slapped against its hull while he propelled it along the river.

She'd asked to call him Arik.

Arik.

Did she think that his name alone would bring him back to what he once was?

"You are going to wake every creature along the river bank and probably alert Brihann's demons if you don't calm down," she chided. "Not to mention that you'll probably drown me if the boat tips over. You'll never find me in this dark water."

"Then stop riling me, Georgie. No more questions. No more talk of my brother. No more talk of dragon mates. You promised me that you would climb the Razor Cliffs toward the light."

She nodded. "I did and I will keep to that promise. But I haven't promised to sit back on my satin settee and eat chocolates while I conveniently forget you ever existed. I'll never forget you. I'll never compromise my principals again. I'll never marry anyone but you, so what do you think of that, my lord? You had better reconsider your decision or you'll condemn me to a life of spinsterhood."

He groaned, the possessive thought that no one else would touch her, filling him with pride. But she was a beautiful soul, and he didn't wish to see that rare beauty wither and die. It would if she became his dragon mate, condemned to live in this Underworld as he was. "I knew I shouldn't have told you about our betrothal."

"You didn't have to. I sensed it already. My heart knew of the connection between us, but I'm glad you confirmed it. You may as well know that I had already decided never to marry unless it was to you."

"I'm not going to marry you." He stopped himself from slapping the oar into the water again. He needed to remain calm and keep his senses on alert.

Unlike her, he could easily see in the darkness. He noticed every purse of her lips and shake of her head. Now she was shrugging her shoulders. "You're not going to marry me *yet*. There's an important difference."

"Georgie." His voice was almost pleading. "Just go back home and be safe. Let me fight Brihann with a clear head."

"Why should you be the only one to engage in this battle? You saved your brother's life. You tried to save his son."

"But I failed."

"So did he. It isn't your fault or his. But his misconception has gone on too long. It's time he accepted the truth."

"Don't bother. He has the Draloch stubborn pride. He'll never admit he was wrong."

She shook her head and laughed. "He's a married man now. His wife will make him change his stubborn ways. Nor will I ever stop trying to beat sense into your idiotic brother. If Anabelle is as wonderful as she sounds, she will not hesitate to help me. And what of the Stone of Draloch? Must it not account for its actions? It does not deserve to bear your family name."

"Georgie, stop." He growled softly to silence her. "You are not to go near that stone."

She frowned at him. "It bears your name. It should be protecting you. I won't promise to leave it alone. Indeed, I intend to talk your brother into taking me to it right after I tell him what I think of him."

"Bloody hell," he muttered. "And I thought demons were unthinking and deranged."

"Thank you." She cast him a smile.

"I did not mean it as a compliment."

"I know. Your flattering description of me as unthinking and deranged gave you away."

Her intentions were dangerous, especially to her own wellbeing. His brother wouldn't harm her, but there was no telling what the Stone of Draloch would do if she challenged it. A few days ago, it had allowed Brihann's demons to abduct her and bring her to his fortress. She had done nothing to deserve that fate.

But she was now intent on riling that ominous force. This was no mere wasp's nest she was about to poke. What would the Stone of Draloch do if she angered it? Perhaps drop her straight into Brihann's lair in retaliation.

He meant to lecture her, but a soft splash in the distance caught his attention. He placed a finger over her mouth and leaned close to whisper. "Hush, Georgie. We have company on the water. Get down under the bench. I don't want them to see you."

He silently secured the oars within their locks and reached for his crossbow and quiver of arrows. Who was out there? He knew it wasn't one of his ferrymen bringing new souls into his realm. It could not be Brihann's demons either, for they were afraid of water.

"It's only me, Bloodaxe," a male voice filled with amusement quietly called out. "Set down your weapon and allow me to draw close."

"By the Stone of Draloch, curse you." He removed the arrow and put down his crossbow, relieved it was only Mordain. "I almost put a hole through you. How did you find me?"

"Pure chance. You're not using your magic. I had no trail to follow. But since Brihann's armies are amassing between your fortress and the Razor Cliffs, and Necros is patrolling north while Python is flying across your southern border, I thought you might try to approach the Razor Cliffs from the east." He glanced at Bloodaxe's boat. "I heard your oars splashing along the water. Surprisingly careless of you."

Bloodaxe grumbled in response.

"Where's Lady Georgiana? I'm eager to meet the slip of a girl who managed to survive dragon fire *and* get under your skin. Even a deaf-as-a-post dragon soaring among the clouds could have heard you on the water."

Bloodaxe reached down and helped Georgie back to her seat, but she wouldn't stay there. Instead, she skittered to his side so that she now sat beside him and placed her hand on his arm to grip tightly onto him. "Rest easy," he murmured, placing his hand over hers. "This is Lord Mordain. The red dragon I was telling you about."

Mordain nodded in her direction. "A pleasure, Lady Georgiana. I hope he has only good things to say about me."

"He has, my lord."

"Good, because I'm going to travel with you to the Razor Cliffs." He raised a hand to stop both their protests. "You'll need help keeping Brihann's men away from Georgiana while she climbs. You'll likely need help keeping the portal open. Or do you think you can manage it all on your own?"

He'd had his fill of arguments with Georgiana and did not need another from Mordain. "I will have my soldiers in place."

"And now you will have a Dragon Lord at the ready as well. You know Brihann won't be expecting it."

Bloodaxe frowned. "He'll pound your wings to dust once he gets his gnarled talons on you."

"Aye, he'll try." Mordain tied his boat to theirs and settled back down on its bench. "But I'll fight back, for he can't be allowed to succeed."

"Easier said than done," Bloodaxe grumbled, his hand still lightly covering Georgiana's as she listened to their conversation with growing trepidation. He could feel her quiet shudders running up and down her body.

"I know, but Brihann has to be stopped. His madness has gotten unbearable. His best lands are rotting because he doesn't care for them. The soldiers in his armies are disgruntled and growing enraged. Now that Queen Melody has fulfilled the Fae prophecy, they're afraid to invade the realms of the Fae. So, what does that leave them? Either they'll invade the mortal world or we'll have open warfare in the

Underworld, demon fighting against demon. I don't know if Brihann still has the sense to prevent that. But what matters is that he'll unleash his reign of destruction on the mortal world if we don't do something about him soon."

"Mordain, what you speak of is treason."

He shrugged. "I say aloud what you are thinking. We both know that he cannot continue to rule the Underworld."

Georgiana spoke up as he was about to untie Mordain's rope and send his boat on its way. "Lord Mordain, you say that Brihann's demons can't be allowed to invade the mortal world. What cause do you have to protect mankind?"

"The simplest and most eternal of reasons. A young woman," he said with a quiet, but obvious ache. "Brihann cannot be allowed to find her before I do."

"She must be someone of great importance to you." Although Georgiana was now smiling at Mordain, that gloating smile of hers was meant as an "I told you so" to Bloodaxe. "Is this young woman your dragon mate?"

"I've yet to meet her, so I couldn't say for certain, but I expect so. She must be important to me in some way because Brihann is intent on destroying her and we all know his motives are anything but honorable." He turned to face Bloodaxe, his expression grim. "The Stone of Draloch has been talking to Brihann. Beware of it, for I have a bad feeling about its intentions."

"So have I." He glanced at Georgie, wishing she could see his expression and understand how important it was for her to keep away from the monolith that was powerful enough to manipulate Dragon Lords as though they were mere puppets.

She was still clinging to his arm as though it was her anchor. He liked that she instinctively turned to him and did not fear him. However, she did not fear the Stone of Draloch either, and that was a mistake on her part. "Georgie–"

"I know you don't want me anywhere near that stone, but I think you both place too much importance on its powers. Do you have no free will? Is your destiny unchangeable? If so, why are you bothering to take on Brihann?" She turned to Bloodaxe and spoke with aching gentleness. "And if so, why are you determined to protect me? Of what value is your resolve to save me if you have no power over my fate? Perhaps it is not manipulating you so much as it is compelling you to make a choice."

"It cannot be as simple as that," Mordain said, but he was clearly intrigued by Georgiana, which explained why he was here now. Bloodaxe knew that he had come to help her and would be true to his word. Indeed, Bloodaxe was glad for the assistance. However, this was not the reason Mordain had come looking for them. No, Mordain was here because Georgiana had a pure heart. In the Underworld, this was a thing of fascination.

He and Mordain were condemned souls and desperate for salvation.

Georgie was his salvation, he knew it. But that made him all the more determined to protect her. He silently repeated the vow he'd made to himself at first sight of her. He repeated this vow every time he worried for her safety. Too often, for she was constantly in peril. He'd give his life for her. He would never allow her to come to harm to save his soul.

"Lord Mordain," she said, no doubt about to argue with the formidable red dragon about the power of love, but her thoughts were interrupted as their boats suddenly began to rock violently.

Georgie gasped and clung to him with both hands. "What's happening?"

He wrapped his arms around her. "Bloody damned selkies. Hold tight, Georgie. We're about to go into the water."

GEORGIANA WANTED TO SCREAM, but managed to hold on to a shred of composure. She took a deep breath as their boat suddenly surged upward and then flipped over, tossing both of them head first into the black depths. All she felt was panic. It didn't matter that Lord Bloodaxe held her in his vise-like grip. Nor did the knowledge that he would drown along with her rather than ever let her go alleviate her fear.

She did not know how to swim.

And now she was in deep water with no idea how far it was to the bottom.

Not that she expected Lord Bloodaxe to let her drown. He wouldn't. *Thank goodness.* But these creatures were circling around them and she could feel their menace. Lord Bloodaxe couldn't fight them while he held onto her.

What were selkies? She'd heard of them in Irish tales and thought they were seals who changed into human form. They seemed harmless enough in myth. But this was the Underworld and nothing was harmless here.

Did the selkies have sharp teeth? Did they bite?

The water was warm, unlike the cold waters in the lakes near Penrith, but that gave her little comfort. One of the selkies bumped hard against her leg. The urge to scream rose in her throat, but she suppressed it. She was still sinking and couldn't risk her lungs filling with water if she dared to open her mouth.

Air.

She needed air.

Her lungs began to sear with pain, a slow, fiery burn that spread outward into her limbs. She flailed her arms and struggled to kick her feet that were now entangled in weeds. Was she close to the river bottom? She tried to push upward, but to no avail.

Just as her lungs were about to burst, Lord Bloodaxe put his mouth on hers and breathed air into her. She silently cried in relief. However, the breath of life he'd given her would not sustain her for more than a minute.

Her lungs were still on fire.

Another selkie bumped into her with the force of a battering ram.

The pain no longer mattered. Her head was spinning and her body was being sucked into a whirlpool, dragged downward, ever downward so that she had no hope of ever taking another breath.

Was this how her life was to end?

It simply couldn't, for she had yet to save Lord Bloodaxe. He was Arik. *Her* Arik. She had to make it out of the water alive. But how? She was about to lose consciousness.

Lord Bloodaxe pressed his mouth to hers again, and in the next moment, she was shoved upward in a powerful surge. Suddenly, she was no longer underwater.

Air.

She took great, gasping buckets full of it into her starved lungs. She gasped and coughed and her head was spinning, but the warm, clammy air felt delicious against her cheeks. She was alive. Lord Bloodaxe still held her securely while he brushed back the clumps of her wet hair that clung to her brow and cheeks. "Easy, my beauty. You're safe."

She nodded and tried to assure him that she was all right, but all that spilled from her lips was a muffled sob amid her ragged breaths. Selkies still circled them and bumped insistently hard against them. Her legs and hips would be bruised, but it was nothing to her near drowning. "Get me out of the water," she pleaded, clinging tightly to his shoulders and shivering with fright.

Wordlessly, he began to swim her to shore. She calmed as his powerful strokes drew them away from those frenzied selkies. That he remained calm managed to quiet her panic, but her heart was still pounding and her head was in a dizzying whirl. "We've lost everything but your battle axe." She felt that hard weapon in its sheath that was pressing against her leg. "Your crossbow is lost, the arrows as well. We have no food. No boat."

"But you're alive. Do you think I care about anything else?" He lifted her into his arms when they neared the shore and the water was no longer over their heads. He carried her onto the grassy bank and set her down on a soft patch. But he did not settle beside her. "Mordain is dragging the boats to shore. I'm going to retrieve the crossbow and arrows. I know where they went down."

He dove back into those inky depths before she could stop him. Not that she intended to do anything of the sort. The weapons were important to him, and she'd been enough of a burden to him already. Indeed, she'd never felt so helpless or useless. What would she have done if he'd left her to fend for herself in the water?

She didn't want to think of it.

The sky was still black. Darkness surrounded her and an ominous silence filled the air. She understood how someone who was blind and deaf might feel, for she could not see to the tip of her nose or hear a sound, not even Lord Bloodaxe's powerful strokes as he cut through the water. Nor could she hear the selkies that had to be circling around him. She could not even hear Lord Mordain bringing the two boats to shore.

She took more air into her lungs and released it with a loud, rasping cough that could be heard across the wide river.

She closed her eyes to calm herself.

Every moment she was apart from Lord Bloodaxe felt like an eternity. But it could not have been more than a minute or two before she heard the faint sound of someone wading in the water. Then she heard the quiet rumble of male laughter and realized both men were coming out of the water together.

Georgiana rose on wobbly feet. "Are the boats salvaged?"

Lord Bloodaxe responded. "Boats, crossbow, and arrows, all retrieved. Food is gone though."

"So are my bollocks," Lord Mordain grumbled as he dragged the boats up onto the bank. "Damned selkies are in heat. It's mating season for them. They kept coming at me like battering rams aimed straight between my legs. I vow if they try it one more time, I'm going to turn them into toads."

"They caught me a time or two," Lord Bloodaxe said, commiserating.

"Lady Georgiana shielded you from the worst of it. My parts are still rattling." He sighed. "But let's see what is to be done about your boat. Damned selkies put a hole in it. We could fix it with magic."

"No," Bloodaxe responded immediately. "Brihann will be upon us in an instant. But using your magic is not a bad idea. We just need to be clever about it."

"What's your plan?" Mordain asked.

"I must get Georgie close to the Razor Cliffs undetected. You can help by leaving us."

Mordain snorted and then eyed her with renewed interest. "That's your plan? Keeping her all to yourself. Can't blame you."

Lord Bloodaxe ignored the quip. "Once far enough away from us, start leaving traces of your magic about my realm to keep Brihann and his scouts distracted, searching in all the wrong places for us."

"Not a bad plan. I suppose it will amuse me for a few days. How long do you think you'll need to reach the Razor Cliffs?"

"Two days at least. We'll be traveling on foot. Meet us there at the setting of the moons on the third day."

Georgiana remained quiet as the two Dragon Lords discussed their plans. The sky was beginning to lighten and she knew Lord Mordain would soon be on his way. But as it lightened, she was able to see his face quite clearly and was surprised by the handsomeness of his features. Dark hair, firm jaw, and nice bone structure, but his eyes were a reddish gray, like burning embers.

Fires of hell.

Lord Bloodaxe had told her that this Dragon Lord was a spawn of the devil. He had not been in jest.

The two of them slapped each other on the back with thumping pounds. "Very well. I'll see you in three days' time. Keep your Chosen One safe. She may be small and female, but I think she has the *bollocks* to take on the Stone of Draloch."

He returned to his undamaged boat, pushed it back into the water that was no longer black but the dusky gray of morning, and stretched his large frame across the bench. Lord Bloodaxe watched him drift downstream and then turned to her as the small craft disappeared around the bend of the shoreline.

He ran a hand raggedly across the nape of his neck and cast her a wincing smile. "Our boat is in ruins, we've lost our food, we're nowhere near our destination, and our clothes are soaking wet."

She smiled in response. "True, but we're still alive."

He stepped close and cupped her cheek in his large palm. "Life will be quite dull around here without you, my beauty."

He was the one who insisted on her leaving. She knew he was right, but it didn't lessen the deepening sorrow she carried in her heart. They belonged together, a fact that he refused to consider. "I need to remove my gown and let it dry," she said, carefully wringing the excess water out of the soggy fabric that had now grown so heavy, she felt as though she were dragging anchors. "You need to do the same with your shirt."

He laughed with genuine mirth. "Always trying to get me out of my shirt, aren't you?"

She blushed. "Nothing of the sort. Catch a nasty cold for all I care."

He grinned. "There's a cottage not far from here. I use it on occasion when I travel through my realm. It's for my use alone. More of a hut, really."

He strode to the boat, dragged it onto the grassy bank, and hid it behind a row of shrubs and tall grasses. Once well out of view, he used a tree branch to sweep away all trace that anyone had stopped there. "We can't build a fire. Too dangerous."

She merely nodded, too ashamed to reveal her thoughts. They didn't need a fire. They had sparks enough between them to kindle all the heat they'd need. More than enough to keep each other warm in a raging blizzard.

"How do you feel, Georgie? Can you walk?" He took her hand and squeezed it lightly.

She dismissed her wayward thoughts and nodded again. "I'll keep up."

About twenty minutes had elapsed before they reached the cottage, a small and simple wood structure that blended with their forest surroundings. A casual passerby would have to look closely to notice it, assuming anyone ever strayed this far.

Georgiana was too tired to muster much cheer by the time Lord Bloodaxe opened the door and ushered her inside. "Not much to see, but it has a kitchen, bedchamber, and a sturdy roof."

Her near drowning had taken more out of her than she cared to admit. All she wanted to do was remove her wet gown and camisole, set them out to dry, and then fall into a sound sleep.

The kitchen had a table and chairs with a bedchamber the size of a horse stall behind it. The bedding appeared to be clean and the two blankets they found were in good condition.

However, there was no edible food, only an old tin box that contained biscuits they dared not eat, and a wooden cask that held barely enough ale to fill the one cup they'd found in the cupboard. "Take off your boots and clothes and I'll set them by the window to dry. Wrap one of the blankets around you, Georgie. I'll see if I can hunt down some food for us."

Her eyes rounded in alarm. "You won't go far?"

"No, my beauty. I won't go far." He spoke with gentle assurance. "Get out of that wet gown before you catch a chill."

At her nod, he helped her to untie the lacings that were soaked and knotted. Once she was able to slip out of the gown without his help, he bent his head toward her as though about to kiss her. She closed her eyes and tipped her head upward, but he must have decided against giving her a kiss, for he pulled away and strode out of the bedchamber instead.

Disappointed, she moved slowly, now feeling the bruises on her hips and thighs where the selkies had butted their heads into her. She stripped out of her gown and camisole, but kept her boots on, for the floor was not clean and the thought of walking upon it in her bare feet was not to be considered. After inspecting her body and noting the purplish bruising starting to form on her pale skin, she wrapped herself in one of the blankets and walked into the kitchen to spread her clothes over the chairs beside the window.

It took only a moment to accomplish the task. She yawned and returned to the tiny bedchamber, eager to sink onto the small bed.

She kicked off her boots and set them to one side.

She meant to stay awake while awaiting Lord Bloodaxe's return, but her eyelids were as heavy as anvils. She fell asleep the moment her head touched the pillow. She wasn't certain how long she'd slept, but the creak of a chair pierced her dreams and brought her sharply awake.

She sat up and looked around, her heart in her throat as she began to panic.

"It's only me, Georgie. I didn't mean to wake you." Lord Bloodaxe was seated in a chair beside her, preparing to remove his soaked boots. He studied her as she first fussed with her blanket to secure it around her body and then hastily rubbed her eyes to wipe the sleep from them.

She released the breath she had been holding, her gaze now fixed on him. He'd taken off his wet shirt, revealing that magnificent warrior's body that she never tired of gawking at. But he'd kept his trousers on, as though that alone would lend propriety to their situation.

She shook her head. "In truth, I slept lightly. My hair's wet and I'm awkwardly tucked in a blanket. I'm hungry and still feel like a drowned water rat."

His seductive smile suggested he found her much more appealing than she'd described. But she knew he wasn't going to do anything about it. He kept his boots on and stood. "I found us some food. Care to eat?"

She nodded.

"Stay in bed. I'll bring it to you." His voice was warm and indulgent.

Food and him beside her? Suddenly, this cottage felt like heaven. She dismissed the wayward thought, for he'd never think this place was anything more than a convenient shelter. "What did you find?" she asked as he turned to leave and she saw the magnificent black dragon with its blue underbelly drawn on his back.

He laughed lightly. "Sausage fruit. I came upon an open field and found one tree growing in the center of it. This fruit won't taste like the sausages you're used to eating, of course. But it will sustain us for the day."

"A feast fit for a king. You won't hear me complain." She fussed with her blanket once more, trying to keep it tucked around her body, but it seemed to be an impossible task. She was not quite certain how to manage eating while holding up the blanket to protect her modesty. If anything was to be sacrificed, it would be her modesty, she decided. "Have you eaten?"

He nodded. "You were sleeping so peacefully, I decided not to wake you. So, I ate first and then came in here. I was going to take the other blanket and stretch out on the floor."

She frowned. "After all you've done for me, do you think I'd deny you this bed? It's big enough for the two of us to share."

He snorted. "Georgie, look at me. I'm twice the size of you. I'd squash you."

"No, you wouldn't. I could rest quite comfortably if you wrapped me in your arms."

"Forget it. I'm not taking you into my arms while you're naked beneath that thin blanket. That *very* thin blanket." He muttered something unintelligible under his breath. "Forget it. Not going to happen."

He stormed out of the room and she heard the clatter of plates and the *thwack* of his axe as he must have practically cleaved the table in half while cutting more sausage fruit. He gave the fruit another mighty *thwack* that cracked wood.

She was unsettling him. Good, it was about time he admitted that this connection between them was more powerful than any force determined to keep them apart. If that dark force succeeded, she wanted to have more of him than a few restrained kisses.

All of a sudden, her senses perked.

She strained to hear him moving about the kitchen, but heard not a sound.

Drat, had he walked out? Even when overset, he had the uncanny ability to remain silent. She closed her eyes and held her breath, continuing to listen in the hope of catching the squeak of a booted footstep. Nothing.

"Georgie."

Her eyes flew open. The husky croon of his voice had startled her, for he was now standing right in front of her with his hands empty and an unmistakable ache in his voice as he spoke her name.

Obviously, he yearned for her as badly as she yearned for him.

He placed his hands gently on her shoulders and nudged her up against his chest. "Stop me," he said in whisper, "for this is madness."

She circled her arms around his neck. Madness was in refusing this offered moment, this gift that held a wealth of promise. "I won't. You're my betrothed. I never released you from your marriage oath."

"But your father must have. I'm sure he tore up the contract after my brother and I disappeared." But he bent his head and crushed his lips to hers in a kiss that was exquisitely desperate and hungry.

She returned it with equal desperation, loving the heat and muscled tension of his body against hers, loving his unleashed passion. She had to make this moment one neither of them would ever forget. She wasn't certain how to do it, for this would be her first attempt at seduction. "I don't care what your father and mine decided afterward, my lord. I never tore up the contract. I never let you go. How can I ever let you go after knowing you now? My heart will break into a thousand pieces."

Her words angered him, but that anger was mostly directed at himself for wanting her in the same way that she wanted him. "You must forget me, Georgie. I can only offer you danger and misery."

"You could also offer me love."

"No," he said sharply, but he groaned and gave a little tug on the blanket to slip it off her body.

She let it fall to the ground and made no move to retrieve it.

His eyes darkened with passion as his gaze raked over her curves, for all of her was unashamedly open to his view. He sucked in a breath. "Sweet mercy, you're so beautiful." He drew her up against his hard body once again and pressed his mouth to hers with a possessive need.

His hands roamed over her bare shoulders and then slid down her back and hips. He groaned and then wrapped one of his hands around her waist while he cupped her breast with the other so that the weight of it rested in the palm of his hand.

He groaned once more, still holding her possessively as he rubbed his thumb across her breast and teased its straining bud. She gasped when he bent his head to close his mouth over it. His tongue swirled over her flesh. *Mother in heaven.*

Heat exploded within her most intimate depths and radiated throughout her body.

She ran her hands along the corded muscles of his neck. He was trying to hold back. She wanted to demolish his resistance.

He nudged her onto the bed and settled over her, the weight of his big body absorbed by his propped elbows. His mouth closed once again over the bud of her breast and he began to suckle and tease it with his tongue, his onslaught relentless and magical.

She cried out in pleasure.

She needed him, wanted him with a desperation that bubbled beneath her hot skin and turned her thickening blood to molten lava. "I want this," she whispered, fearing he would hold himself back and draw away. "You're the only one for me."

But even as his hand slid between her legs, his fingers rubbing against her core, she knew he would not consummate their bond by taking his own pleasure with her.

She accepted all that he was willing to offer, her body turning to liquid heat at his knowing touch. "Georgie, my beauty," he whispered in wonder.

She closed her eyes and took in each sensation, loving the warmth of his skin against hers and the honey scent of his own rising passion. With each touch and exquisite kiss, each dip of his head to taste and rouse her, she fell in love with him a little more. *I love you.* The words ached to slip from her lips, but she refused to let them pass. As it was, he hated his weakness in wanting her. He'd stop the magic and pull away from her if she spoke those very words he did not wish to hear.

He kissed her with a dragon's passion, his mouth once more on hers as he heightened the pressure of his fingers against that intimate spot between her legs. She moaned, for the sensation was unbearably exquisite. Then he began to trail kisses down her body, first to the sensitive spot at the base of her throat, then down and across each breast, then lower until his lips covered the spot where his hands had been. Fireworks of sensation went off within her.

She knew his own dragon senses were taking in all of her, that need of his to remember the silky warmth of her skin and the heady scent of her. His need was driving him to conquer her despite the dangers to both of them. She wanted to taste him as well, to run her tongue along the muscles of his powerful body and take in the honeyed, salty taste of him.

She meant to respond, to be bold and put her mouth to his body, but she was now lightheaded and boneless and too lost in her own building pleasure to think of anything but the fiery swell of desire now consuming her.

And then the fire did consume her.

His flames. His lips. His taut, rough skin on hers. His gentle arms cradling her as she soared. "Thank you, Arik. *My Arik.*"

Wordlessly, he shifted their positions so that she now lay atop him. "Sleep, my beauty," he whispered, covering them with his blanket. "We have a long walk ahead of us tonight."

CHAPTER TEN

BLOODAXE STARED DOWN at the tempting morsel who was now sleeping soundly in his arms. Georgiana. How was he to keep her safe when she addled his senses? How was he to let her go when his dragon heart cried out to keep her by his side for all eternity?

He watched in fascination, unable to take his eyes off her beautifully expressive face. He'd watched her earlier as he'd roused the passion dormant within her all these years. Her eyes had taken on a gem-like sparkle, those deep green orbs shining as brilliantly as any star that ever shone in the English night sky. Even now, the upward tilt of her pink lips taunted him with their lush softness and tempted him to kiss her again.

And again.

Her breaths were calm and steady now, but he took pride in recalling her breathy moans and the urgent movements of her inexperienced body as he suckled the rosy buds of her breasts and tasted the heat of her essence.

He'd needed to savor her, to brand her into his memory.

No, that wasn't quite right. He needed no reminder of Georgie. She'd been branded into his heart from their first meeting. What he'd felt was the dragon urge to mate with her and claim her for his own. "Get up, Georgie," he said in a whisper. "Night is falling. Time for us to move on."

She purred and stretched her lithe body that was curled around his hard torso. "So soon? But I just fell asleep."

"You've been snoring for hours," he teased. "Honking like a foghorn."

"Oh, dear. I have? Did I keep you awake?" She drew the blanket primly about her as she hurriedly sat up.

"Don't cover yourself, my beauty. Let me see you." He drew her hands off the blanket so that it fell away from her body. Her skin was warm and pink. Her golden hair was a cascading mess, sticking up in spots and flat where she'd burrowed her head against his chest. Her eyes were heavily lidded and her lips were pouty.

She looked rumpled and deliciously sleepy.

His gaze moved lower and his dragon lust ignited.

Georgie had the ability to send him into a mating frenzy simply by being her innocent self.

By the Stone of Draloch! Did a more beautiful female ever exist?

A rustling sound directly outside had him rolling to his feet and grabbing Georgie along with him. Damn. Her clothes were in the kitchen. She had nothing but her soggy boots and the blanket she was once again hastily wrapping around her body with awkward and trembling hands. "Who's out there?"

He shook his head to silence her and then motioned for her to put on her boots. She did so immediately, but didn't have time to securely lace them before a foul scent began to permeate through the wood-planked walls. Brihann's scouting party. They'd somehow picked up his and Georgie's scent and it had led them straight here.

How many were there?

Perhaps eight demons in all, assuming this was the same scouting party they'd avoided earlier.

He donned his boots and grabbed his battle axe, noticing Georgie's eyes widen at the sight of the massive axe he so casually held in his grip. He put a finger to his lips to warn her to keep silent and then placed one of his daggers in her hands before drawing her behind him. It was his smallest weapon and wasn't enough to keep her safe. But she hadn't the strength to wield a bigger one.

Yet, he had to give her something with which to defend herself, for drawing her behind him wouldn't be enough to assure her safety. He didn't know where else to put her. There was nowhere to hide in this simple cottage.

He heard more rustling as the demon scouts surrounded them. They'd burst through the door and windows to come at them from all directions.

He was ready for battle when they did just that, shattering glass and splintering wood as they lunged for him and Georgie, their howls and screeches filling the air, along with their foul odor.

"Georgie, do your best to keep behind me," he ordered, knowing it was no easy task, for he was whirling and smashing his axe into soft, demon heads and frog-like bodies, leaving a splattered mess. Three downed with his first swings. He swung again and killed two more.

Only three left.

They sprang at him all at once, their talons and sharp teeth bared. He stunned them with one hefty swing that struck all three of them, and then dispatched them with precise, killing blows.

In less than a minute, all eight demons lay dead at his feet.

He could have killed them faster had he transformed into a dragon and released his fire, but he had no need to use his magic. He'd done it easily with mere brute force. He was not even breathing heavily as he turned to Georgiana to make certain she was unharmed.

She gaped back at him, her eyes wide and filled with fear. He reached out to touch her, but she surprised him by drawing back. "I didn't have to raise my dagger." She emitted a ragged breath. "They never got near me."

Was she complimenting him for his prowess? In truth, it wasn't much of a battle. His daily training took more effort. But no, she regarded him with horror, as though seeing the beast within him for the very first time. "This is what I am, Georgie."

"I know."

"No time to clean up this mess now. I'll send Thomas here afterward." He lifted her into his arms and carried her to the kitchen where her clothes and his shirt were still draped over the chairs untouched. "Get dressed. Grab a little of that sausage fruit to break your fast. Eat it quickly. We need to get as far away from here as possible."

She obeyed his command, but was slower than he would have

liked. It wasn't her fault that her hands were shaking and she was obviously distraught. He didn't understand why this attack should leave her pale and feeling worse than the others before it. He wanted to ask her why, but not yet. They needed to run and would only be slowed down if she were tearfully chattering and stumbling along.

Most of all, he didn't want to dwell on her revulsion of him and what he'd just done. She was in the wrong. He'd saved her life. Those demons would have ripped her sweet, innocent body apart. That she now looked upon him as no better than their attackers wounded his heart. Curse the fates that had left him a tattered shred of that feeling organ. Well, his heart was truly beyond mending now.

He turned her none too gently to face away from him and quickly laced up her gown. Then he turned her back toward him and bent to securely lace her boots. Her hair was still a glorious tumble, but there was no time to secure it now. He tucked his dagger into the belt of her gown. She'd need that weapon later. "Let's go."

While she had struggled to don her clothes and grab a bite to eat, he'd quickly slipped his shirt on, cleaned off his battle axe, and belted it to his hip. He now grabbed his crossbow and quiver of arrows and slung them over his shoulder.

Losing patience in the face of her continued silence, he scowled and lifted her into his arms once more, carrying her over the kitchen floor that was strewn with shattered glass and splintered wood, to the threshold.

He set her down once they were outdoors and then took her hand. The red sky was darkening and would be ink-black within moments. He'd brought her this far along and did not intend to lose her on this leg of their journey. That she might flee from him hadn't crossed his mind until now, and it curdled his insides to know this thought was surely rattling around in her brain.

So much for her talk of love.

Love was not all powerful and eternal.

Love wouldn't change a damn thing.

They walked in silence for hours until she finally broke it with a sigh. "You're still angry with me."

No, he was angry with himself for believing there could be a happy outcome to his fate. He was even angrier with himself for stubbornly wanting her with an ache that filled the empty cavities of his heart. "I'm not angry."

"Then you're disappointed in me." Her voice was soft and ragged with remorse.

He grunted and paused in their hike. "It doesn't matter how either of us feels now, does it? The damage has been done, Georgie. We had our moment and are both eager to move ahead to our separate destinies."

"Separate?" She inhaled lightly. "You don't want me?"

"By the Stone of Draloch, why are we discussing this? You're the one who showed utter disgust with me. You're the one who now cringes at my touch."

She tugged on his hand. "Are you mad? How can you possibly think that?"

He shook his head and grunted again in disbelief, knowing they should stop talking and move on. The sooner they reached the Razor Cliffs, the sooner she'd be rid of him. "You gave it away by recoiling as I approached you. The look of horror mingled with disgust that you graced me with after I'd slain those demons was another clue."

"I was horrified by my own ineptitude and disgusted with myself for allowing fear to numb my limbs and render me useless to you. What if you had needed my help? I couldn't lift that small dagger much less thrust it at any attacker. I wasn't prepared. Fortunately, you protected me once again. I was, as I said, useless to you. I'm so sorry, my lord."

His heart shot into his throat. "Don't apologize to me, Georgie. You have nothing for which to be sorry."

She tugged lightly on his hand again. "But I failed you."

He held back the urge to roar with laughter. He was a fool. So much for reading her thoughts. He'd read her completely wrong. "Your strength is not in your physical might. You're little and have no muscles to speak of. But don't ever doubt that there is a remarkable power in you."

She pursed her lips and *tsked* to dismiss his words. "I have no idea what power you are talking about. I certainly haven't shown any. Are we friends again?"

He arched an eyebrow. "We were never friends. I doubt a word exists to describe what we are to each other."

"No, I suppose not. But I don't know what else to call us."

He resumed walking, making certain to keep her hand securely in his as he once more hurried their pace. "It doesn't matter."

"It does to me. We are more than friends but less than dragon mates. I'm not even a dragon. And I don't know that I would count as an innocent now that... what we did earlier. You know. I liked *that* part very much."

It was dark, but he could see her cheeks glow like crimson torch-lights in the night. The last of his bile and anger fled from him, quickly replaced by his stirring dragon lust. She'd been so exquisitely respon-sive to his touch. "Ah, *that* part. So did I, my beauty. So did I."

⫸⫷

GEORGIE WAS EXHAUSTED by the time the two moons began their ascent into the red sky. They must have been walking for close to ten hours, much of it over hills that felt more like mountains during the upward climb, and climbing was difficult to do in her gown. Not to mention having to struggle all the while in the dark.

She didn't know where they would hide today, but was tired enough to drop down anywhere and promptly fall asleep. Fatigue even overcame her hunger. "Where will we stop?"

Lord Bloodaxe scanned the horizon, his gaze keen and assessing like that of a hawk. Or a dragon on the prowl. "There," he said, pointing to a crude, stone outcropping that made the hunting cottage they'd left hours ago seem like a great manor house in comparison. "This is all the shelter I dare risk. There's another of my hunting lodges not too far from here. I had Thomas quietly clean it out and stock it with food. But I think it's too dangerous to sleep there now. I'll settle you beside the outcropping first and then go to the lodge to retrieve our food."

Despite her fear of being left alone even for a short time, she nodded. "Any chance he hid a lavender soap and a clean change of clothes for us there?"

Lord Bloodaxe managed an upward twitch of his lips. "Perhaps a change of clothes, but there shall be no scented soaps for you, my beauty. Brihann's demons are prowling all over my lands and will easily pick up the scent of lavender on your body. You smell far too delicious as it is."

She shook her head and laughed. "I must reek as badly as those demons. And kindly do not refer to me as delicious. I have no wish to be their next meal."

He kissed her lightly on the lips. "Hmm, tasty."

"I'm little and bony and will starve if I don't eat soon." She would have to content herself with another cold meal to fill her belly, but didn't mind. They were being hunted and needed to remain hidden. Perhaps he might return with a pouch of water. She could use a little of it to rinse away the demon stench that pervaded the air around them.

"Georgie," he said, wrapping his arm around her waist and drawing her closer. "The Razor Cliffs are just over that distant rise. We'll reach it by tomorrow, unless we're caught."

"We won't be." She had faith in him, although it seemed he was less confident at the moment.

How many demons had he noticed lurking about? They had altered their course several times over the past hours, and at times he'd put his finger over her lips to warn her to be silent. If not for his naturally keen senses, they would have walked into one of Brihann's raiding parties long ago.

"These past few days have been easy in comparison to what lies ahead for you. You and I will part ways soon. You'll have to make the climb alone while Mordain and I distract Brihann's forces. There is no other way to get you to safely back into your world."

She nodded. "I can do it."

A fabrication, of course. But he needed her to be strong and she did not wish to disappoint him. However, the thought of returning to her familiar surroundings, to the Lake District she adored, left her feeling empty. She did not wish to be anywhere but by Lord Bloodaxe's side.

He wanted her gone.

She would comply for now. She still had matters to attend to once she'd made her escape. First, to call upon his brother, Saron. Next, find her way to the Stone of Draloch.

These visits weren't quite the same as calling upon a friend or attending a tea party. She did not know what would happen when she confronted Saron.

She was *afraid* of what would happen when she confronted the Stone of Draloch.

She shook out of the troublesome thought.

Mother in heaven, she would not back out of her plans. Whatever the danger, she would face it. After all, dangers existed even in Polite Society. No one knew what might happen to them in the next hour or the next day. Indeed, anything could happen at any time to anyone. Brihann could even die of old age.

He wouldn't though.

The wicked never seemed to die early deaths. Their rage and bile seemed to keep them going for years.

She glanced at the dagger she carried in her belt.

"Use it on yourself if Brihann captures you," Lord Bloodaxe said, following her gaze and understanding the bouncing trail of her wayward thoughts. "Don't hesitate. He will not go easy on you."

She swallowed hard. "Hopefully, it will not come to that."

They had just walked into the outcropping when they heard the distant sound of barking. Georgiana regarded him curiously. "Your dogs?"

He nodded. "They're chasing demons. I've had them doing so ever since we left my fortress. That they're so close is not a good sign. I warned you that Brihann's armies are closing in on us."

"And where are your armies?"

He cast her a mirthless grin. "Not far either. They're positioned in and around the Razor Cliffs but will not attack Brihann's forces until I give the word. For now, they will only fight if they are attacked first. However, I hope that war between us will be avoided."

"Why? Don't you want to defeat Brihann?"

"Yes, if I can." He nodded. "However, if one succeeds in deposing a king, one has no choice but to kill him. It is not an easy thing to do while Python and Necros remain loyal to him. As for Mordain, he may be willing to join forces with me, but the Stone of Draloch may stop him from interceding. If the prophecy is true, the outcome must be determined by me and Brihann alone. We're the two black dragons."

"Or your brother."

He frowned. "I've told you. He will never fight by my side, no matter how mad and dangerous Brihann might be. He believes I am just as mad and dangerous. If forced to make a choice, he will choose Brihann over me."

She shook her head and sighed. "Men can be such stubborn fools."

"Women can be just as foolishly stubborn. Don't think of returning here once you're safely back home." As the sun began to peek above the treetops, he led her into a cave hidden in the outcropping. They'd had to crawl through the almost unnoticeable entrance, but once inside, even Lord Bloodaxe was able to stand to his full height.

"Is it safe to light a torch in here?" Georgiana had spent the last few days walking in total darkness. One would think her eyes would be accustomed to it by now. Alas, no. She still had to cling to Lord Bloodaxe as he led her deeper into the cave, guiding her with care over the bumps of packed dirt, jutting rocks, and loose pebbles that abounded on the floor.

"No torchlight, Georgie. It's too dangerous. The faintest glimmer will be noticed."

She'd expected his answer, but still felt disappointed. "I feel like a mole wandering blindly in its hole."

"Sit here," he said, helping to ease her onto a long, flat rock. "It isn't a goose-down mattress, but it will serve as a bed for now. Close your eyes and rest. I'll be back in a little while."

"Arik, I–"

He growled, the feral sound arising from low in his throat. "Don't call me that."

She sighed. "Lord Bloodaxe."

"What is it?" He spoke quite gently to her now, no doubt realizing he'd been unnecessarily cross with her.

"I lied to you before. I'm not very confident that I'll make it up the Razor Cliffs. I'm scared, but I'll do my best. If I fail–"

He knelt beside her. "You won't."

She shook her head. "We both know it is likely I will. I'm just sorry that I've put you to so much trouble."

He rested his palm against her cheek. "Aye, you've been nothing but trouble from the moment you appeared in my tower bedchamber. It now lies in ruins. So does my south bedchamber. And my hunting lodge, although it was already fairly run down." He caressed her cheek. "It is a good thing Dragon Lords like trouble. We thrive on it."

"Do you love it?" Of course, she was asking if he loved her.

By his low growl of annoyance, she sensed he understood precisely what she was asking. "When the time comes, just start running up that cliff face. I'll be watching out for you, ready to shove that dainty arse of yours upward if you falter. Understood?"

He turned and strode out of the cave before she could answer.

She sighed and stretched her exhausted frame upon the hard rock. He would never admit he loved her. Should she confess she loved him? It felt right to do so.

She yawned and closed her eyes. It was nonsense to think about these possibilities. They could talk about it until the end of time and he would resist her all the while.

They would mate if it was meant to be.

CHAPTER ELEVEN

"GEORGIE, WAKE UP."

Georgiana felt Lord Bloodaxe's hand on her shoulder shaking her urgently. "I'm up. For pity's sake, I'm up." She tried to roll to her feet but he wouldn't stop shaking her. Then she realized it wasn't him but the ground rumbling beneath their feet. "What's happening?"

He dragged her into his arms and wrapped her firmly in his embrace, all the while muttering a string of blasphemies that would make the basest knave blush. "It's the cursed Stone of Draloch."

"What is it doing?" She threw her arms around his neck. If that force meant to tear her out of Lord Bloodaxe's arms, she refused to give up without a struggle.

"Expressing its displeasure."

"At us?" She looked up at him in disbelief, but could make out nothing of his features. The cave was too dark and the ground was still dangerously shaking beneath their feet. "We've done nothing wrong."

"It isn't about right or wrong. It's about the destiny that awaits us," he said loudly against her ear, for the roar of the moving earth was drowning out their voices.

She tried to shout above the din. "Only we can chart the course of our destinies. That slab of marble can't do it for us."

He drew her up against him as though wishing to take her inside of him and mold them into one. She wished it, too. "It's bluestone, not marble. You cannot understand the force it wields. More powerful than that of the five Dragon Lords together."

She suddenly screamed. "Arik, the ground's opening up."

"I know, my beauty. Hold tight to me. We're in for an unpleasant ride."

She closed her eyes and pressed her body to his muscular frame with as much of her strength as she could muster. He hadn't growled at her for calling him Arik.

She supposed it didn't matter now.

Were they going to die?

Although her eyes were still firmly shut, she could tell that they were hurtling through a vast expanse. The air was cooler than that of the Underworld, and there were brilliant flashes of light behind her closed eyes. She was curious about those lights, but didn't dare open her eyes while she was tossed and dragged through a sweep of air that felt like nothing she'd ever experienced before.

She was afraid to let go of Lord Bloodaxe for fear of drifting apart from him forever.

After several minutes of hurtling through this void of brilliant lights and strong winds, they suddenly stopped and began to drift languidly, as though sailing downstream on the boat they'd taken the other night. But this was no gentle current of water. She peeked open one eye and was amazed by the sight she beheld. Thousands of stars twinkled like diamonds. Swirls of pink, orange, green, and violet vapor that drifted before them in all shapes and sizes. "What are those?" she asked, pointing to several dark orbs overhead.

Lord Bloodaxe followed her gaze. "You wouldn't believe me if I told you."

"What are they?"

"Planets. Mars. Venus. We're drifting in celestial space."

She shook her head. "It cannot be."

"Georgie, there are worlds that exist beyond your mortal world and my Underworld. We see only the space before our noses, but there are countless others. Pathways, I would call them. The Stone of Draloch gathers its strength from all of these forces. Even my formidable powers are puny compared to that of our guiding stone."

Her heart, already pounding through her ears, began to beat even more violently. "And now I've angered it."

"Perhaps. We'll know for certain in a moment. We're almost there."

"Where is it sending us?"

"The Fae king's palace. The Stone of Draloch sits in his great hall." He gave a mirthless laugh. "All my planning to get you safely out of the Underworld seems to have been unnecessary. You were never meant to cut your soft hands climbing the Razor Cliffs. Brihann was never meant to stop you. All along, the Stone of Draloch intended to snatch you away."

"And you as well."

He kissed her on the forehead. "I don't think I was meant to join you for the ride. It cannot be pleased that I have done so. Don't be surprised if we are soon parted."

His words ought to have worried her, but she felt elated instead. "Are you suggesting that we've changed the course of destiny?"

He frowned at her. "What?"

"If you weren't meant to accompany me, but now you have, then what does that signify? Something important, I think. Do you wish to know what I think?" She hurried on without awaiting his response. "We're meant to be together and no force is powerful enough to conquer our love, not even that of your guiding stone."

He groaned. "I don't know whether to kiss you again or throttle you."

"Do I have a say in the matter? Because you know which I would choose. The kiss, of– ack!" They landed with a rattling thump in the center of a great hall. Fortunately, it was dimly lit, for after all the days of darkness she would have been blinded by ordinary light.

Despite the dim light, she could make out the magnificence of the hall.

Lord Bloodaxe eased her out of his arms, but kept hold of her hand. He circled his other hand loosely about her waist to quietly assure her of his presence. Georgiana was relieved to have him standing beside her. He'd obviously taken this journey before and was familiar with the giant monolith that towered over them and glowed eerily as they slowly approached it.

Logic would suggest that they not approach it at all, but Lord Bloodaxe still had his hand about her waist and was gently propelling her forward, even closer to the gleaming stone. "Can you stand on your own, Georgie? I know this sort of travel can be difficult for those not used to it. Are your legs still wobbling?"

She nodded. Even if her legs did not feel like crumbling piles of sand, she would have said they did just to keep him by her side. Having him close gave her the courage to speak out, even though she felt quite small and insignificant within this elegant, marble-floored chamber. Indeed, it was vast and splendid, but devoid of any furnishings that might have added any warmth.

The Stone of Draloch began to hum softly.

"Oh, dear. Is it supposed to do that?" She burrowed against Lord Bloodaxe even though she was already standing practically atop him and gripping his hand so tightly, her knuckles were turning white.

"It can do whatever it wishes."

She frowned. "Does the hum have significance? Is it talking to us?"

He nodded. "Aye, my beauty. It is talking to me."

She gasped and looked up to study his handsome features. His jaw was clenched, his day-old beard accentuating his masculine appeal. His eyes were a darkening crystal blue and his aquiline nose was flared. The muscles of his iron-hard arms were taut and flexing.

He reminded her of a dragon about to engage in battle.

"What is it saying to you?"

He gazed at her. "The Stone of Draloch is saying that I need to let you go."

"No!" Her legs still felt as though they were going to crumble. Now her hands were shaking and chills were shooting up and down her spine. "No," she said more quietly. "We're meant to be together. Why bring me to you if only to force us apart?"

"Brihann brought you to me."

She frowned at him. "His weak mind was manipulated by the Stone of Draloch. You thought so yourself. I won't allow it to manipulate me."

The hum grew louder and sharper so that it hurt her ears.

She released his hand to cover her ears and immediately realized her mistake. In the instant of time that passed before she could rectify her error and grab his hand once more, he was gone. The deed had been done so fast, her mind could not accept that it had really happened.

She looked around the empty hall, frantically searching for him. He was big and muscled and would be easy to spot even if this hall were filled with people. But she was alone. "What have you done to Lord Bloodaxe?"

Angry and worried, she rushed forward and began to pound on the cold bluestone with her fists. She'd never felt so puny or insignificant, not even when faced with a dragon blowing fire at her. "Don't hurt him! Bring him back to me. *Please.*"

She wanted to say that she'd do anything to save him, but this was the very manipulation that she'd scoffed at moments ago. She'd promised herself that she would never succumb, and yet she was willing to fall to her knees and give up her life for this Dragon Lord. She was not afraid to do it. "What devil's bargain will you have me make to save him? Give me your terms."

She tipped her chin up and kept her hands curled into fists as though ready for a fight. It was laughable to think she held any power whatsoever over this cold stone and its obvious force that she had badly underestimated. "I love him."

Why hadn't she been brave enough to tell Lord Bloodaxe what was in her heart? And yet, she hadn't hesitated to reveal it now. She was talking to a rock.

She felt the ground shudder beneath her feet.

Her heart shot into her throat. Was she about to be carried off to somewhere else? Or dropped into an endless void where she'd be left to drift alone until she died?

You dare to call me a rock.

What? The stone was talking to her. Rather, it was conveying its angry thoughts to her. She spoke in response. "Yes, I do. A rock has no feelings and you've shown none in taking Arik away from me."

He is no longer Arik. That boy was lost years ago and no longer exists.

Georgiana felt a rip to her heart at the stone's cruel words. "He still lives within Lord Bloodaxe's noble heart. How else could he protect me? Why else would he save me from the perils of the Underworld?"

He is only Lord Bloodaxe now.

"It does not matter what you call him. He is the one I love. What have you done to him?" She might have asked, "What have you done to him lately?" For there was no doubt in her mind that Arik's brutal journey and his years of suffering were the fault of this evil stone that bore his family name.

I am not evil.

"How dare you deny it after all you've put him through. He is a Draloch, one of your own. What cause did you have to make him endure so much pain?"

To make him strong.

"If you're as powerful as everyone believes, then why not simply cast your magic and make him strong? Fast, painless. Done with a snap of your fingers, or whatever you have. You understand what I mean."

I do not have the power to alter souls. Nor do I have the power to save worlds. Only you have the power to save your mortal world.

"Me? Are you saying that we have the power to save ourselves from Brihann's attack?"

"No," a female voice said from behind her. "The power lies within you alone, Lady Georgiana."

Georgiana whirled on her heels to face the person who had spoken to her. She was surprised to find a young woman who might have been mistaken for an ordinary Englishwoman, although she was prettier than most. She had rich chestnut hair and sparkling green eyes. The green of this woman's eyes was an emerald green, much darker and more vibrant than her own moss green. "Who are you?"

The moment the words sprang from her lips she realized who she was. The Fae queen, Melody. Groaning, Georgiana bowed to her. It was a meager way of showing respect to this simple vicar's daughter of legend. Melody's journey must have been similar to her own, but there was an important difference. Melody had saved the Fae. Georgiana had yet to save anyone. "Forgive me, Your Majesty."

"There is nothing to forgive, Lady Georgiana." She spoke kindly as she took Georgiana's hand and gave it a friendly squeeze. "Tell me all that has happened to you. We were quite worried when we heard you'd been taken into the Underworld. I'm glad to see that you are unharmed." She frowned lightly. "I hope it is so."

Georgiana nodded. "It is. Lord Bloodaxe kept me safe."

"Ah, so this is about you and Lord Bloodaxe." Her frown eased. "Does he look as bedraggled as you?"

"No." She shook her head and laughed. "He looks magnificent. He always does." But her moment of mirth lasted no more than a few seconds and her smile quickly faded. "He brought me here, but the Stone of Draloch sent him away. I don't know what's happened to him or where he's been sent. Or if he wished to go."

"I don't think he has come to harm."

"But how can you be certain?" There was a kindness about Melody, in the gentle tilt of her mouth and the understanding that seemed to glow in her eyes. Georgiana could not help but warm to her. She began to pour out her heart to this woman she'd known less than five minutes, unable to stop herself from relating all that had happened after being abducted from her Penrith home. "He was determined to lead me safely back to my mortal world," she said, finally reaching the end of her tale. "He didn't want me in the Underworld with him. Not that I blame him. I was useless there. More of a burden than a help."

Melody put her arm around Georgiana's shoulders and gave her an encouraging smile. "Ah, I see how it is. I had a similar problem with my husband. It took him far too long to admit that he cared for me. Good thing he came around to it in time to save me from Brihann's fire. I was meant to roast like a stuffed pig in order to fulfill the Fae prophecy."

"But you changed the course of destiny."

"The Fae destiny." She nodded. "Perhaps. Who knows whether I did? The destined outcome may have always been for the Fae to win. But I think the lesson to be learned is the importance of finding the strength within yourself to fight for what you believe in and protect those you love."

Georgiana sighed. "I'm willing to fight, but Lord Bloodaxe doesn't want me anywhere near him when war breaks out between mankind and demon. In truth, he hopes to prevent it from ever happening. But that means he must fight Brihann." She paused and began to wring her hands.

Melody glanced at her hands. "What are you thinking, Lady Georgiana?"

"Please, call me Georgiana or simply Georgie."

"Very well, and you must call me Melody when we are conversing in private. Of course, I must be Queen Melody when we are among others. But I was born a vicar's daughter and must admit that I'm still not used to being a queen."

Georgiana silently expressed her gratitude in meeting Melody, for she could be a strong ally. "A moment ago, you asked what I was thinking. In truth, I don't know what to think. Now that Brihann believes he can never win against the Fae, he has become obsessed with conquering the world of man." She turned to frown at the Stone of Draloch. "And this stone is encouraging his madness. *Two black dragons shall reign supreme. Two black dragons shall unite the worlds of demon and man.*"

Melody was quick to defend the Stone of Draloch. "The prophecy has been inscribed in the stone for thousands of years. It did not merely appear overnight. But the Fae and Brihann – for he was once a Fae prince – thought only of the words that concerned them. Only after he was defeated did Brihann turn to thoughts of conquest elsewhere."

"I see." But Georgiana was still confused by all that was happening. She didn't understand why the Stone of Draloch existed and whether it served to protect the Draloch family. It did not seem to be so, for

Saron and Arik had suffered greatly. Yet, Saron was now the Duke of Draloch and Arik was Dragon Lord Bloodaxe who ruled in his own realm in the Underworld.

Perhaps strength was forged out of adversity, but what these two sons of Draloch had endured was more than anyone should be forced to bear. She did not know Saron, although she was determined to meet him.

However, she'd learned a little about Arik and his transformation into Bloodaxe and had no doubt that he'd always had a noble and brave heart. That nobility did not need to be beaten into him. It was a part of who he was and ingrained in him since birth.

"Come, Georgiana. I think you need a hot bath, good food, and some rest after your travails. Let me show you to your guest chamber. I think a change of clothes is in order as well. We're about the same size. You ought to fit into one of my gowns, I'm certain."

She was grateful for the welcome, but did not wish to waste a moment of precious time on sleep. She needed to know that Arik was safe. Afterward, she would visit his brother and kick sense into him.

Melody held her back a moment, expression troubled. "He is no longer Arik. You only hurt him by thinking of him as he once was, of someone he can never be again. He is Lord Bloodaxe now and this is always how you must think of him."

She had received the same admonition from the Stone of Draloch as well as from Lord Bloodaxe himself. All those times she'd called him Arik and his response to her each time had been the same. *Don't call me that. I am no longer Arik.* She had been unwittingly cruel in stirring up memories of a past that had forever changed him. "I owe him an apology. He'll have it from me as soon as I see him again."

But would he allow it? How could he bear to be in her company?

She had not only been useless to him, but hurtful. "I must see his brother and Anabelle. Will they accept my visit? Can it be arranged as soon as possible?"

"Yes. My husband and I will arrange it." They walked at a brisk pace through the palace, Georgiana paying only slight attention to the elegant rooms and the dragon designs that were on display in each chamber they passed.

"Dragons seem to be everywhere in your decorations."

Melody nodded. "Cadeyrn explained it to me when we first met. Fae are demons, just like those who exist in the Underworld. As Fae king, he is of an upper class of demons who have the ability to shift into dragons. I use the term 'upper class' loosely, for Brihann, Python, and Necros also have the knowledge to shift into dragons, and we know they are foul creatures."

"You did not mention Bloodaxe or Mordain."

"On purpose. I think of them as knights of the Underworld. They keep order where none might otherwise exist. They protect the souls who are only meant to pass through their realms and then move on to their final destinations."

Georgiana nodded. "That is a good description of Lord Bloodaxe. A chivalrous knight. My knight."

"You have stars in your eyes, Georgiana. He may have been gentle with you, but he is a demon. You mustn't think of him as a man, although that is an important part of what he is. But remember, he also carries a darkness in his heart."

Melody led her down a long hallway as she continued to speak. "At one time, we thought my husband, Cadeyrn, might have been the other black dragon referred to in this prophecy. But it cannot be. When he shifts into a dragon now, which is rarely, his color is sapphire blue."

"Now? Was it something else before?"

Melody nodded. "His dragon color was black before he met me. At first, we did not understand why the Stone of Draloch settled on this new dragon color for him. But now we do. Being a dragon is not what defines my husband. He is first and foremost king of the Fae. In truth, he avoids shifting into his dragon form as much as possible now. It is a dark power that steals a little of your soul with each transformation. Only love can replenish what is lost. Even so, that love would have to be powerful indeed to heal the damage done. Not even Ygraine, most powerful of our Fae, was able to save Brihann, the husband she loved."

"Lord Bloodaxe mentioned her to me."

"We all loved her. She was mother to all Fae and their best healer. She is the reason I am here today. She saved me. She saved Cadeyrn. She saved all Fae, although I am given the credit for it. Perhaps it was our combined powers that saved the day."

"What chance is there for me? I have no powers. Even my mortal talents are dismal. I can't embroider a straight stitch. My singing is abysmal. So are my skills on the pianoforte."

"I'm sure I was worse." Melody's trill of laughter filled the hall, but she soon turned serious. "Doubt is a poison that must not be allowed to work its way into your blood. I know because I was filled with doubt and nearly did not overcome it. If not for my love for Cadeyrn, I might not have succeeded. If you love Lord Bloodaxe, then believe in that love and remain true to it. Let it give you the strength to do whatever you must."

Melody's words once more lent comfort to her and helped her to firm her resolve. "Loving him is the easy part. I knew we had a connection from the moment I awoke in his chamber and our gazes locked. So did he, I think."

Melody rolled her eyes as she opened the door to the guest chamber. "But he refuses to admit it. Isn't that the nature of men? They go forth and conquer. They don't surrender. But to admit to having feelings for you—even worse, to admit to loving you—is the same to them as surrendering. It is a momentous thing for them to overcome."

Georgiana was ushered into a chamber that was exquisite even by her elevated standards. "This is a guest room?"

Melody regarded her with a glint of mirth in her eyes. "You're in a palace. My husband is king of all Fae. It certainly is better than sleeping in a cave."

"Indeed." She'd be happy anywhere if Lord Bloodaxe were beside her, but these offered comforts were much appreciated and too splendid to pass up. "Your guests must never want to leave."

"Most don't," she said, her merriment infectious. "But I think you're already eager to be on your way. Nevertheless, take a few hours to restore your strength. You have a lot of work to do to save mankind."

Georgiana nodded. "I'll do all I can, but the task is daunting. I have no special abilities. Are there any you can teach me?"

"I'll try." She motioned for Georgiana to follow her as she stepped into the room and sat casually on the large, rose silk canopied bed that dominated the chamber. Georgiana sank onto the wooden chair beside the bed. She was too dirty and would stain the counterpane if her soiled gown touched the delicate fabric. "However, I doubt I can teach you enough in a few hours to make a difference. It is more important for you to keep your thoughts on Lord Bloodaxe. Only by saving him will you save all of us. Brihann must be destroyed, and your Lord Bloodaxe is the only black dragon who can do it."

"But Saron is a black dragon as well."

"He does not know the Underworld as his brother does. He does not respect it as his brother does. No, Lord Bloodaxe is the key."

Georgiana nodded. "And what am I? His key chain? Isn't that how husbands sometimes refer to their wives? The old ball and chain? Perhaps I'm that annoying loose key that dangles beside him on the chain and no one can remember its purpose."

Melody shook her head and laughed. "If you must know, and forgive my crudeness, I'm certain you are the lock he must stick his key inside of to open the door to his destiny."

Georgiana blushed furiously. "He hasn't stuck his *key* or any other part of himself inside of me. Since we are speaking bluntly, I'm ashamed to say that it wasn't a lack of willingness from me. I would not have denied him entrance."

Melody's response was cut short by the sound of a man clearing his throat.

"Goodness," Melody cried, obviously as startled as she was. "My love, we didn't see you standing there. How long…" Her voice trailed off, for he must have heard too much.

Heat shot into Georgiana's cheeks as she studied the handsome king standing at the threshold with his arms folded across his broad chest. He was tall and had dark hair and vivid blue eyes, much like Lord Bloodaxe. But his features were elegant, while Lord Bloodaxe's were ruggedly masculine.

By his crown and the doting glance he cast Melody, she would have quickly guessed that she was in the presence of the Fae king. That she'd addressed him as 'my love' completely gave his identity away. "Welcome to our palace, Lady Georgiana. I've obviously arrived at a bad time. I merely wished to greet you."

She jumped to her feet. "It is a pleasure to meet you, Your Majesty."

Melody returned his doting glance. "Stay, my love. Our conversation is important. There's little time to lose in getting down to the business at hand."

"Quite so." His dark eyebrows shot up to denote the understatement. "Brihann has been setting the Underworld ablaze looking for you, Lady Georgiana. How ironic that you're the one who survived dragon fire. Glad to see you're still alive. Unfortunately, Lord Bloodaxe isn't doing as well as you are just now."

Georgiana forgot about sleeping or eating or bathing in the steaming, scented bath that had been offered to her. "What's happened to him?"

"Brihann and his minions have attacked his lands. We don't know where Mordain has disappeared–"

She gasped and curled her hands into fists. "Is this more mischief from the Stone of Draloch? Mordain was willing to support Lord Bloodaxe. Who else would stop him from doing so? And what of you, Your Majesty? Can you not help him?"

"No, but it isn't from lack of wanting to." His expression turned serious. "The portals are all sealed. I can unseal as many as we need from our side, but someone must unseal the other side. Brihann won't do it now, for he knows our forces will come to the aid of Bloodaxe. If anything, he will have his demons guarding every point of access. He's probably destroyed most of the portals already. He will stop at nothing to prevent Bloodaxe from opening one of them and letting us come through to help him."

Georgiana shook her head. "There must be another way. The Stone of Draloch brought us here. Obviously, it has the power to move us at will. Can it not unseal the Underworld portals for us?"

His expression now turned grim. "To do so would interfere with our destinies."

"Interfere?" Georgiana gasped in outrage. "It has done nothing but interfere. Why stop now? We are nothing more than chess pieces on a celestial board. It moves us from square to square at will."

Melody placed a hand on her shoulder to calm her agitation. "At times it may seem so, but its purpose is not to choose a side and make it win. I'm not certain how to describe its existence. It is powerful, that is without question. I would describe the Stone of Draloch as a symbol of faith."

"A religious symbol?" She hadn't considered it to be one.

"No," Cadeyrn said. "It does not ask you to seek faith in a higher being, but in yourself. For this reason, anyone can seek its guidance. The journey it will show you is your own. What you make of that journey is up to you."

Melody moved to stand by her husband's side. "The point is, the Stone of Draloch responds to the power within ourselves. It is guided by our strength. Our love. Our fortitude. Those who look to it for easy rewards will be sorely disappointed."

Georgiana did not know whether their words were true, but Melody had believed them to be so and she'd led the Fae to victory. It would be foolish on her part to ignore the wisdom she'd just received. "I must speak to Lord Bloodaxe's brother as soon as possible. May I impose on you to take me to him?"

"We will do so gladly, but give yourself a chance to rest. You'll be of no help to Lord Bloodaxe if you fall ill." Cadeyrn glanced at her hands that were now clasped together in front of her. "Even your hands are shaking with fatigue."

"But Bloodaxe–"

"Has fought with Brihann before," Melody said.

"Open warfare such as this?"

Cadeyrn frowned. "These are mere skirmishes yet. Brihann will not risk declaring war, for he or Bloodaxe could be killed. He still hopes to lure him into conquering mankind. To that end, he needs to draw out the darkness within Bloodaxe. Fighting is an easy way to do it. They both enjoy battle. Indeed, they thrive on it."

Thrive on it.

Bloodaxe had used those same words.

Now that she was apart from him, would the darker side of him take over? Would he forget her?

Her thoughts were brought to the present as servants arrived wheeling a tub. Others carried pails filled with steaming water and gleaming silver platters laden with food.

Melody motioned them in and then turned to Georgiana. "I'll have a fresh gown and slippers brought to you shortly. Gwyneth will remain behind to attend to you. I'll return in a few hours to fetch you and we'll formulate our plans then."

She nodded, hoping it would not be too late by then.

Mother in heaven. She was no savior. How could she be when she couldn't even manage to untie the knotted laces of her own gown? She gave it a try, though. And failed. "Gwyneth, will you please help me?"

CHAPTER TWELVE

GEORGIANA ALMOST DIDN'T recognize herself as she gazed in the mirror to inspect her appearance before leaving her chamber to meet with King Cadeyrn and Queen Melody. The few hours of rest had turned into six precious hours lost in helping Lord Bloodaxe. She suspected that she'd been given a sleeping draught and was reluctant to admit she'd needed this time to restore her weary body.

Still, she was disappointed in herself. She was a failure as a dragon mate. A few days on the run and she'd been completely worn down.

In other circumstances, she might have been pleased by her reflection in the mirror. Her hair was clean and simply fashioned in a braided chignon at the nape of her neck. Her bath had been scented with lavender oil that smoothed her rough skin and left its subtly lingering scent on her body. Her gown and matching slippers were a deep amber velvet, a fabric too heavy to be worn in the Underworld, but suited to the English winter.

The Fae royals meant to return her to England, hopefully to meet Saron Blakefield, the Duke of Draloch and his wife, Anabelle. She needed to see her father as well, for he had no doubt suffered greatly over her abduction. She supposed she would have to see Oliver, too. Hopefully that would be an easy meeting, a quiet chat with him accepting to quietly call off their marriage. Her father would pay him off if Oliver demanded a settlement.

Indeed, it would likely be necessary. Oliver hadn't proposed marriage because he loved her. He'd wanted her fortune and the connections her father's title would bring.

She turned away from the mirror and followed Gwyneth downstairs to the great hall. After opening the door for her, Gwyneth took her leave. Georgiana walked into the large chamber, her heart pounding faster as she approached the Stone of Draloch and the dozen or so Fae that had gathered beside it.

Breaking with decorum, Cadeyrn and Melody came forward to greet her and quickly introduced her to Cadeyrn's Fae council. She met Fiergrin and Lothair, their eldest counselors, and Beogrin, a handsome, young Fae who appeared to be more of a warrior than a statesman.

Among the last to be introduced was a young faerie called Edain, easily one of the most beautiful women ever to exist. She had delicate, spun gold hair and eyes that were a vivid mix of azure and teal, the colors of a tropical ocean. Georgiana had never seen such an ocean other than depicted in paintings on display in the British Museum. "I am *well* acquainted with Lord Bloodaxe," Edain said, startling Georgiana with the obvious emphasis in her words.

How well did this beautiful faerie know him?

Georgiana struggled to control the heat creeping into her cheeks, a sign of her own petty jealousy. It did not matter what had happened in the past. Assuming anything at all had happened.

Melody regarded her sympathetically. *Pay no attention to Edain. She speaks of truce meetings between Lord Bloodaxe and our council, that is all.*

Still, Edain appeared the sort one would choose as a dragon mate. Beautiful and wise, for why else would she be a member of Cadeyrn's council? Whereas she hadn't sat on any boards or councils, not even the Penrith annual harvest fair committee. The closest she'd come to any decision-making duties was judging their annual mince pie contest.

Melody frowned lightly. *Do not doubt yourself.*

She wasn't. She was merely questioning herself. It wasn't really the same thing, was it?

She had no time to dwell on her failings, for the doors of the great hall opened once more and Mordain appeared. He walked toward them with the confident stride of a Dragon Lord, his black cloak billowing around his large frame.

To Georgiana's surprised, he grinned when he saw her standing beside the royal council. "You're safe. I wasn't certain what had happened to you. I only meant to test the portal, but it suddenly opened up and sucked the both of you into the void."

"You did that?"

He winced as he nodded.

She was relieved to know it had been an innocent mistake, and nothing more sinister. But what of Lord Bloodaxe's sudden disappearance once they'd reached the Stone of Draloch? Had he caused that as well? "Have you seen Lord Bloodaxe? Is he safe?" Georgiana's heart raced, for she was worried about the perils he faced upon his return.

"I've only heard that he's back in his realm. Haven't had the chance to pay a call on him yet. But you needn't be alarmed, he knows how to protect himself from Brihann's rages." He turned to address the royal pair and their council. "Saron must be warned. Brihann has decided to break his pact."

"What pact?" Georgiana asked.

Mordain appeared surprised. "Did Lord Bloodaxe not tell you?"

She curled her hands into fists at her sides. "Obviously not."

He glanced at Cadeyrn. "Tell her, Lord Mordain. It is important that Lady Georgiana understands."

He nodded. "Lord Bloodaxe was the eldest son of the Duke of Draloch and meant to inherit the dukedom. Saron, his younger brother was meant to be taken into the Underworld. He was taken, but Bloodaxe followed after him."

Georgiana nodded. "He told me a little about that."

"He battled his father and Lord Brihann for years, stubbornly refusing to leave the Underworld without Saron. As his father grew ill and lay close to death, Lord Brihann and he finally reached an understanding. Bloodaxe would remain forever in the Underworld and rule as a Dragon Lord over his realm while Saron would be allowed to return to England and assume the English dukedom."

"Allowed?" She shook her head in confusion. "Lord Bloodaxe had to help him escape."

"They made it appear so. Brihann couldn't let any of the lost souls brought into the Underworld believe he was capable of showing mercy. In truth, there was no mercy in what he did. Bloodaxe gave up his soul to save his brother. In exchange, Brihann agreed never to harm Saron."

Georgiana felt a wrenching tug at her heart. "Then Brihann broke that pact and killed Saron's son."

"Aye," Mordain said, "and ever since, he and Bloodaxe have been battling. But the damage was done. Bloodaxe no longer had the ability to survive in the mortal world, and even if he could survive, he had a brother who would kill him on sight."

Cadeyrn stepped toward her. "Brihann had almost succeeded in turning Bloodaxe into that black dragon of prophecy, for Bloodaxe lost a piece of his former self every time he waged battle and every time he shifted into a dragon. Losing the love of his brother was a stunning blow. Brihann believed he had finally won and grew too confident. He abducted you, for you were the last innocent vestige of Bloodaxe's early life. He thought Bloodaxe would steal your innocence and then discard you to be used by his soldiers."

Georgiana shuddered. "It could have happened."

"No," Mordain said, "not even Brihann has the power to break a bond so pure. The darkness that had consumed Bloodaxe over the years was wiped away the moment he saw you."

Melody nodded and then turned to smile at Georgiana. "That's when Brihann realized his mistake and came after you. But he's failed, Lady Georgiana. You are the one who survived Necros' fire. You did that on your own."

"I did," she admitted, but it was only a matter of luck that she had done so. They believed she had managed to survive because of a supposed strength of will. She hadn't done anything brave. But she had done something wonderful in restoring Bloodaxe's damaged soul, if the story she just heard was true. "Saron must hear this news as well. He must be made to understand what his brother has done for him."

She turned to Mordain. "Will you return to the Underworld

soon?"

"As soon as I can. I have other matters to attend to first." He did not bother to explain what those matters were, and she knew by his expression that he would not confide them to her if pressed. "Bloodaxe can hold off the three Dragon Lords until my return. They won't dare kill him yet."

Yet? But they would kill him soon if she did not do something to prevent it. She cast an imploring gaze at Melody and Cadeyrn. "May we go now? Any plans we make will depend on Saron's response. He must be included in this discussion."

To her relief, they agreed. "Perhaps he'll believe this story if he hears it from all three of us," Cadeyrn said, glancing at his wife.

At Melody's nod, Georgiana was suddenly taken into Cadeyrn's arms. She held on for dear life as the floor beneath them began to give way. This journey was faster than her first and her landing more jarring.

When she opened her eyes, she found herself in the well-appointed study of an elegant London townhouse. Cadeyrn and Melody were beside her, looking upon her with concern. "Travel through these portals is not easy in the beginning," Melody said kindly. "Eventually, you will become used to it."

Georgiana's stomach was still lodged in her throat. Her legs were wobbling and her head wouldn't stop spinning. "I just need a moment." Perhaps more than a moment, she realized after trying to take a step and stumbling into a small table and knocking over the decorative lamp that stood on it. The vase beside the lamp fell over as well and shattered on the polished wood floor.

The noise it made when smashing into pieces brought a gentleman running into the room. "What the...?"

Georgiana put a hand to her mouth and inhaled sharply. "You're Saron."

Her words spilled out in a muffled mumble, but everyone understood them.

Saron resembled his brother and might have been mistaken for him at first glance. They were both broad shouldered and ruggedly muscled. Saron's hair was as dark as his brother's. His eyes were the same vibrant blue. She kept her gaze on him as he approached, and she noticed that his eyes held the same shadow of darkness in them.

He glanced at the Fae king and queen before concentrating on her. "And who are you?"

Her initial surprise having passed, she lowered the hand she'd clamped over her mouth and gave a quick curtsy. "Lady Georgiana Wethersby. I'm so sorry I broke your vase."

His manner was gruff and suspicious, but he took a moment to close the door behind him and then stepped closer to study her once more. Finally, he shook his head and turned to Cadeyrn. "Your Majesty, why have you brought Lady Georgiana here?"

"Do you not know who I am?" Although he'd been but a boy when her betrothal to his brother had been announced, she thought he might have remembered. Obviously, he hadn't. "I'm the daughter of the Duke of Penrith."

His eyes widened in surprise. "The missing girl?"

She nodded, hoping he might now make a connection to that long-ago arrangement between their families. But she noted not a flicker of recognition. "I asked to be brought to you."

He folded his arms across his chest and frowned. "The question remains, why?"

"Is your wife here? She ought to hear my reasons as well." She met his look of impatience with a steady resolve of her own. If he thought to intimidate her, he'd soon learn it would not work. His brother's aspect was far more fearsome, and she hadn't been afraid of him. Of course, Bloodaxe had gone out of his way to be kind and protect her. "I was betrothed to your brother when he was Arik."

"When he... Arik...?" The blood seemed to drain from his face. After a moment, he turned to Cadeyrn in anger. "What trick is this?"

"None, Your Grace." Cadeyrn took a step forward to stand directly beside her. "It is vitally important that you listen to what Lady Georgiana has to say. Summon your wife. Duchess Anabelle must hear the news as well."

Saron's arms remained folded across his chest, a sign of his stubborn resistance. "It isn't possible. She is indisposed."

"Is she ill?" Melody asked with concern, coming to stand on the other side of her to create a united line of support for her cause.

The door to the study squeaked open just then and a young woman with lush red hair and an engaging smile stepped inside. She frowned at Saron, but was quite gracious to the three of them. "I am not in the least indisposed." She glanced at her stomach and Georgiana noticed the obvious bump. "Seven months along," she said, her eyes aglow with love for the child she carried and its still scowling father. "What have I missed?"

Saron sighed and finally unfolded his arms. He rubbed the back of his neck as though disconcerted. "Sit down, my love. Watch out for the broken vase."

She arched an eyebrow and addressed Georgiana. "Your first time through a portal?"

Georgiana blushed. "My second."

"You're still a beginner." She took a seat in a cushioned, oversized chair. "You did me a favor. It's a hideous vase."

Saron cleared his throat. "Penelope gave us that vase."

Anabelle nodded. "I adore her, but that vase was hideous."

He finally cracked a smile. "Yes, I suppose it was." But that was the extent of his pleasantry. He was scowling once more when he turned to Georgiana. "Arik is dead and your betrothal died along with him. Why are you here?"

"He isn't dead and you know it. He may go by Lord Bloodaxe now, but he is still your brother and needs your help." She turned to Anabelle whose gaze was far more sympathetic than her husband's. "He tried to tell you. I think you believed him. It was Brihann who killed Gideon."

Saron surprised her by grabbing her by the shoulders and turning her toward the door. "Out. Get out. Don't mention my son ever again."

Anabelle shot to her feet. "Stay," she insisted, hurrying to block the door and openly defying her husband. She refused to move away when he asked her. "I will not. How many times must you hear the truth before you will believe it?"

She turned to Georgiana. "Lord Bloodaxe tried to tell me what happened. But it was not an easy thing to communicate with him and all I could understand was that Brihann had done the terrible deed. He'd tried to stop him, but was too late." She paused a moment and then crossed to her husband's desk and withdrew a parchment from one of the drawers.

"A painting? What does it represent?" Georgiana asked, glancing at the paper depicting a black dragon amid a scene she couldn't quite make out.

"Saron's cousin, the Earl of Eastbourne, has a nephew with a connection to the Fae as well as a talent for painting. It is said that he can foretell the future, but I don't believe it is quite true. Eastbourne's wife, Julia, brought me this drawing yesterday. It is of you and a black dragon. There is no doubt that you are this girl, for he's painted the exact gold shade of your hair and the green of your eyes. It shows the dragon protecting you."

Saron's grip gentled on Georgiana's shoulders. "What is your version of what happened to Gideon?" he asked.

"It is the same as your wife says. Lord Bloodaxe would never hurt your son. Everything he did was to protect you, the brother he loved. He gave up everything, even his very soul for you. And still, you refuse to see the good in him."

His hands slipped off her shoulders. "Because there is no good in him."

Georgiana balled her hands. "Don't ever say that again or I'll plant you a facer." She held up her fists which were puny compared to his own. "How do you think you escaped the Underworld? A mere boy managing to climb the Razor Cliffs on his own, all the while chased by Brihann's demons. Who do you think shielded you?"

He regarded her in astonishment. "Shielded me? Shall I show you my back? The demon talons flayed my skin raw. Is this how my brother protected me?"

"He wasn't much older than you. He'd been there less time than you and endured the same beatings. He did the best he could. It may not have been easily done, but you made it through the portal. Why do you think Brihann never came after you?"

Saron began to pace. "He sent Bloodaxe to bring me back. My— Bloodaxe, that is, searched high and low. He would have delivered me back into Brihann's hands if he'd found me."

"You know in your heart it isn't true. Your brother would have easily found you had he wanted to. He knew you'd taken refuge with your Aunt Penelope." She shook her head and sighed. "Please give her my apologies for shattering her gift. I'll replace it, of course. The point is, you were free and he meant to keep you that way."

Her voice began to falter, for the risks Bloodaxe had taken for the love of his brother suddenly overwhelmed her. "He gave up his soul for you. This is the pact he made with Brihann. His soul for your freedom. How do you not see it? How can you allow Brihann to win?"

She could see that her words were beginning to penetrate. Saron would not look at her, but he concentrated his gaze on Anabelle who had been nodding in agreement with her all the while. She continued, relieved for the opportunity to speak of all that had remained unsaid between the brothers for too many years. "Brihann abducted me on my wedding day, a mere hour before the ceremony was to take place. He gave me to your brother."

Anabelle's eyes rounded in alarm. "Gave you to him?"

She repeated the entire story, hoping she'd left no detail untold… other than the night of pleasure he'd given her. "Lord Bloodaxe's behavior was at all times chivalrous. Even now, he refuses to have me as his dragon mate, thinking to spare me from the life to which your Draloch ancestors have condemned him. But I know he loves me, just as he has always loved you. You are his little brother. He will never stop loving you."

She was doing her best not to cry, but Anabelle's sudden burst of tears weakened her resolve. Soon, she was crying too. Blast! She had to be strong. Saron would not take her seriously if she continued to cry.

He still refused to look at her. He now had his arms around Anabelle and was comforting her. "What if Bloodaxe has tricked us all? What if this is a monstrous ruse to destroy us all?" But his voice was strained and she knew his composure was about to shatter into a thousand pieces like the vase she'd knocked over a few minutes ago.

"I know in my heart it isn't," Georgiana said, her voice shaking as she struggled to maintain her control. "It can't be. Bloodaxe is the Dragon Lord who shepherds lost souls through the Underworld. He protects them until they find their rightful place. Do you think a monster is capable of that? It is no surprise that he and Mordain have been entrusted with this task."

She thought on it a moment longer before proceeding, knowing the fragile hold Saron must have on his feelings. After so many years of hating his brother, it was no easy thing to suddenly shed all that enmity and accept his love again. "I do not know if the Stone of Draloch gave him and Mordain this assignment or if they were chosen by a higher authority. I'm no religious scholar. But I think I know the heart of your brother. Unlike Brihann, Necros, and Python, he is not lost to evil. But he will be if we fail him."

"I must think on this," Saron said with a quiet soberness.

"It's all I ask." Georgiana held back her elation, for Saron was still far from convinced. But he'd agreed to think about it and this was more than anyone had ever gotten from him. "In any event, I'll need a day or two to see my father and straighten out the matter of my wedding to the Marquis of Linwood."

Anabelle's eyes rounded in surprise. "Do you intend to go through with the wedding?"

"No, of course not. How can I, now that I'm in love with Lord Bloodaxe? He's the only one I'll have." She cast Anabelle a wincing smile. "Even if he won't have me."

"We'll fix that," Anabelle replied. "The Draloch men are stubborn, but so are we. Your father and the marquis have returned to London.

My husband and I will escort you to your father's residence. I'm sure the two of you will have much to discuss, but don't hesitate to call upon us if you need our assistance, especially in dealing with the thorny problem of disengaging from Linwood."

"Thank you." She hesitated a moment. "I've lost all sense of time. How long have I been away? What day is this?"

"The fifteenth of February," Saron said, his manner far gentler now. "You've been missing for almost two months."

She swallowed hard and nodded. "I must see my father right away."

GEORGIANA SAT IN the imposing Draloch carriage with her hands tensely clasped on her lap. The ducal crest emblazoned on the gleaming black carriage had stunned her for a moment. It was the same crest drawn into Bloodaxe's back and the sight of it had brought a jolt of yearning that had yet to subside. Her heart was still racing and her composure was dangling by a slender thread that would snap at any moment.

"We're here," Saron said, his brow furrowed in concern. "Perhaps I ought to go in first and ease your father into the news of your return."

Georgiana thought it was an excellent suggestion. In truth, she'd been worried that the sight of her would shock him into apoplexy. He was not in the best of health, one of the reasons she'd decided to give in and marry the Marquis of Linwood, a man she didn't love. At the time, she'd felt it was important for her father to know that she would be settled and cared for, and perhaps he would even see a few grandchildren before he passed on.

Indeed, his health was delicate. Anything in him might rupture. He didn't have a strong heart and she wasn't certain how much of a surprise he was able to endure. She was relieved that Saron had taken on the responsibility of easing her father into her return. He was the right person for the task. He'd been stolen as a child and understood the upheaval and strain of loss and recovery better than anyone else. "Yes, it is a good idea."

She sat in the carriage with Anabelle, glad to have made her acquaintance and knowing they would become good friends in time. She'd wed a dragon shifter and yet managed to hold her own in the marriage. More than that, she'd kept her good nature and that was no easy thing to do against the dark power of a dragon.

They didn't have long to wait before her father ran out of their townhouse, wrenched open the door to the carriage, and swept her into his arms. "Georgiana, thank goodness!" He was openly weeping.

Soon, so was she.

Her father invited Saron and Anabelle to stay for supper, giving them no opportunity to beg off before ushering them all in. In truth, Georgiana felt it was for the best that the duke and duchess remain. There was much to explain, and at the same time, so much that she could not explain. Indeed, she hoped Saron would take the lead in relating details of her abduction and return. Her father would never believe stories of the Dragon Lords or the Fae. It was best to keep the details simple.

"Your daughter was the unwitting victim of an intrigue gone bad," Saron related when they sat down to supper and the soup course was served. "I cannot say more, for it is a matter of the highest sensitivity. I do not have royal permission to reveal more."

"Ah," her father said, "a top-secret matter. Involving Napoleon, no doubt?"

"It was a clandestine matter." Saron spared her a glance. "One of my operatives rescued your daughter."

"His brother," Georgiana said, not wishing all to be completely swept under the rug. She stared into her bowl as she spoke. She'd eaten little of the leek soup that had been hastily cobbled together by their able cook. "He was very brave and he saved me. It is thanks to him that I am unharmed."

Saron shot her a glower.

Her father's eyes widened in surprise. Perhaps he appeared to be horrified. "Draloch, I did not know that you had a younger brother. I only know of… the elder, Arik. A very good lad. One of the best. You were but a child when he died."

Georgiana closed her eyes and groaned. So stupid of her. *Stupid, stupid.* Of course, he'd remember Arik. He'd negotiated their betrothal, after all. "Brother-in-arms is what I meant. Of course, the duke does not have an actual younger brother."

"No, only an elder," Anabelle said, setting down her spoon. She hadn't eaten much either. Georgiana supposed it was because the topic was not an appetizing one.

Her father patted her hand affectionately to gain her attention. "Georgiana, my dear. I never told you about Arik Blakefield. You may have heard whispers about him as you grew up and made your way in Society, but I did my best to hide his existence from you."

He stared at all of them as though about to relate shocking news. "Draloch, did you know that your brother, Arik, and my Georgiana were betrothed when she was but an infant? Then both of you disappeared and all sorts of disquieting rumors began to emerge. Wild gossip of devilry and pagan worship."

Saron nodded. "I heard those wild rumors as well."

"But as you can see, His Grace and I are happily married," Anabelle chimed in.

"And very much in love," her father said with a nod of approval. "The story we finally heard is that you were both ill and that you survived but your brother did not. By that time, my wife and I were most concerned that more had transpired than a mere illness. We did not trust your parents to tell us the truth and thought it best to keep Georgiana and ourselves away from your family."

"You did well, Penrith. My childhood was not a happy one and my parents were… they were not the loving sort as you and your late wife obviously were. It is plain to see that Lady Georgiana loves you very much."

Her father beamed and patted Georgiana's hand once more, for he'd kept it clasped in hers as though needing the tactile assurance that she was real and had returned. "I'll ask no more questions. I can see that my daughter is well." He frowned and his face became flushed as though he were embarrassed. "Ah, em… Georgiana, if you feel the need for us to summon a physician to…"

"There is no need, Father. I was unharmed… in every way." Dear heaven, she hated that he was worried about this delicate topic. "However, I cannot marry Oliver."

"Cannot?" Her father grew concerned once more.

"Will not," she amended. "My absence has made me realize the mistake our marriage would be. I don't love him, Father."

"No, I never got the sense that you did. You accepted him because you thought it would make me happy."

"You've always had my best interests at heart. I thought it was the right thing to do at the time. Nor does Oliver love me. I think it is my dowry that he loves most."

Her father shook his head and gave a mirthless laugh. "Then he is a fool, Georgiana. You are the treasure, not your trust fund or my title. Are you certain about this?"

She nodded. "I am."

"Then I shall summon him here tomorrow and deal with disposing of your betrothal. I fear he will not take it well."

Saron allowed the butler to remove his soup bowl and then turned to Georgiana's father. "If you wish, I shall accompany you. The dark rumors about the Draloch family can be put to good use. Linwood will not give you a problem if he sees the Dragon of Draloch standing by your side."

Georgiana nodded enthusiastically. "It is a good suggestion, Father. Oliver is known to be a prankster. Who knows what vindictive jest he might play on either of us? He isn't a bad fellow, but he can be petty at times. And who knows if he will behave as a gentleman and even allow us to end the betrothal? The duke's presence will assure it."

"Very well, you've convinced me. Yes, Draloch. I would appreciate your coming with me." He shook his head and sighed. "Odd how life has come full circle. Georgiana, I wish you had known Arik. He was a good lad. I think you would have loved him."

Georgiana maintained her smile even though her heart was about to burst with grief. "I know I would have, Father. You chose well for me."

CHAPTER THIRTEEN

G EORGIANA PACED IN FRONT of the parlor window of the Weth-ersby townhouse impatient for Saron's carriage to roll up the street. She was leaping out of her skin and eager to learn the outcome of the conversation he and her father had held with the Marquis of Linwood. "Georgiana," Anabelle said, setting down her cup of tea and easing her awkward frame gently onto the settee, "your fidgeting won't make them return any faster."

"I know, but neither will sitting quietly and sipping tea calm my nerves." She drew her woolen shawl tightly about her shoulders, for the rose silk drapes were drawn aside and a chilly wind howled through the thick panes of glass even though the window was closed. The day was unusually cold even for February, and she felt the draft of a stiff breeze prickle against her cheeks. "I appreciate your waiting with me, Anabelle. But how can you remain so calm? Saron picked up my father hours ago."

The men had arranged to meet the marquis at noon at his home, and now it was almost four o'clock and still there was no sign of them.

Anabelle chuckled. "Saron and I fought for months before we'd ever met each other. And we fought for months afterward. A few hours is nothing. These matters are delicate and will take time. Who knows? All might have progressed splendidly and now they've gone off to your father's solicitors to draw up the contract ending the betroth-al."

"Or to the bank to secure the funds to pay off Oliver," she mut-tered, doubting Oliver would be gracious or honorable about losing the chance to marry a wealthy duke's daughter. He'd been lured by her funds and would likely demand a hefty price to be bought off.

Perhaps she was judging him too harshly. His family had wealth of their own and he was no pauper. At least, he spent as though he had blunt to burn. His father must have provided him a generous allowance.

She peeked out the window again and saw nothing but a gray sky overhead and a street coated in white, the remnant of this morning's snow still on the ground. Hoofbeats and the clatter of a carriage suddenly caught her attention. In the next moment, the duke's carriage drew up in front of her home. "They're here."

She wasted no time in scurrying to the front door ahead of their butler and throwing it open. "What did he say?"

Her father and Saron, showing more discretion than she had shown, ushered her back into the parlor and closed the door behind them. Georgiana settled beside Anabelle and took hold of her hand, finding she needed a bit of Anabelle's confidence.

"It went surprisingly well," her father said, striding to one of a pair of decorative cabinets lining the wall and opening it. He kept his decanters of port and bottles of whiskey in there. "Care for a drink, Draloch?"

Saron nodded. "Port will do for me."

Her father grabbed two crystal wine glasses and poured the dark ruby liquid into each of them. "I feel like downing the entire bottle," he muttered, handing one of the glasses to the duke. "He agreed to end the betrothal. There will be no marriage."

"Thank goodness," Georgiana said in a whisper. "But at what price, Father?"

"It cost me nothing. That's the part that makes me uneasy. His father holds a tight rein on the family wealth. Linwood isn't wealthy in his own right and I know he has debts. I offered to pay them off, but he declined."

Georgiana felt bad about that, but was heartened that Oliver had proven himself to be more honorable than she had expected. Indeed, far worthier than she'd given him credit for. "Oh, dear. Perhaps your presence," she said, nodding toward Saron, "had more of an effect on him than we realized. You do have a fearsome reputation. He must have been quaking in his boots."

Her father nodded. "I shall wait a brief period and quietly offer again to pay his debts."

"And I shall write him a letter," Georgiana said with a nod. "I owe him at least that much. Now I feel terrible that I misjudged him. It doesn't change my mind, of course. But he always played these silly pranks on his friends that I considered childish and annoying. I'm glad there's more to him than I believed."

Saron regarded her thoughtfully. "I think your first impression of him was correct. What struck me as odd about our meeting is that he never once asked after you."

Her father shook his head. "But we started our conversation by assuring him that Georgiana was returned unharmed."

"Still, he asked no questions." Saron turned to her. "Yours may not have been a betrothal forged in love, but you were to be his wife. You disappeared mere hours before your wedding. Even the wedding guests will be asking more questions than he did once they learn of your return. More important is the question of his honor. Had I been the intended bridegroom, I would have asked to see you if only to make certain for myself that you were not injured."

Anabelle took his hand. "My love, who is to say how one might respond to such news? He might pay a call on Georgiana once he has had a chance to think matters through. Perhaps he believes she wants nothing more to do with him."

Georgiana groaned. "Oh, dear. I ought to write to him at once. I was so caught up in my own circumstances that I didn't consider how the *ton* might view our broken betrothal. I don't wish to make him a laughingstock."

Her father swallowed the last of his drink. "I'll put in a good word for him."

"So will Saron and I," Anabelle said, arching an eyebrow at her husband as an obvious warning not to countermand her wishes. "There will be unpleasant gossip about you as well. Unfortunately, quite nasty rumors will abound. You were gone for two months. Society is not as forgiving to ladies as it is to gentlemen. Indeed, not forgiving at all."

"It doesn't matter to me. I won't–" Georgiana stopped herself before she'd said too much. She meant to return to Lord Bloodaxe, but how could she explain it to her father? Negotiating an end to her and Oliver's betrothal had sapped his strength. She could see that he'd lost his vigor and his hands were shaking.

How would he respond when she told him that she'd fallen in love with a demon, no matter that he'd once been Arik and was now a Dragon Lord? The news would kill him.

She'd only intended to spend a day or two before asking King Cadeyrn to return her to the Underworld, assuming he had the power to send her there. But she'd have to put those plans aside for now. Her father needed her and she couldn't simply disappear mere days after showing up. "There's time before the Season hits full stride to worry about the gossip and address it. Most families won't return until late March or early April. Some even later. I'd rather return to Penrith, anyway. I have no desire to partake in the social whirl this Season."

Her father reluctantly agreed. "I'll engage additional footmen to guard you. You may have been abducted by mistake, but I won't take the chance that it may happen again."

Georgiana nodded.

How was she to tell her father?

Hiding the truth from him was despicable. But was telling him the truth any better? By the end of the day, she retired to her bedchamber and continued to mull her course of action. She decided to sleep on the matter, hoping that she would awaken with a plan in mind about how much to disclose to her father.

Georgiana was still contemplating her course of action the following morning, another bleary day, when the Wethersby butler interrupted her musings by knocking at the parlor door. "Lady Georgiana, a messenger just delivered this note. He is awaiting a reply."

She took the offered envelope and saw that it was from Oliver. "Thank you, Hawkins. I'll respond at once."

She was pleased that Oliver had written to her.

Her father had retired to his study after breakfast, and she'd come into the parlor intending to write to Oliver as well. Instead, having trouble deciding what to say, she'd whiled away the hour simply staring out the window and watching the icy rain fall, hoping inspiration would soon strike.

It hadn't.

"It's quite ugly outside, Hawkins. Escort the messenger into the kitchen and ask Cook to offer him tea and a bite to eat. I'll be done shortly." Once alone, she went to her writing desk and withdrew her notepaper, quill, and inkpot before opening Oliver's missive.

But once she'd read it, she knew her answer was simple. His mother had invited them to tea tomorrow afternoon and in his note, he pleaded with her to join them. He felt it was important that they break the news to his family together. He hoped it would soften the blow, for his parents thought quite highly of her and had looked forward to welcoming her into the family. If she were willing, he'd come around in his new phaeton and drive her to the Cranfield residence. It would give them a few minutes to talk in private beforehand.

His phaeton was not appropriate for cold weather, but Georgiana knew she'd be warm enough in her cloak, hat, and muff. Also, she'd be seated on the driver's bench beside him for everyone to see, so there was no question of lack of propriety. The Cranfield residence was not far from here. It would be a short ride.

She wrote back her acceptance.

BLOODAXE SAT WITH his captains on the dais of his dining hall merely picking at the roasted venison on his plate. Only a few days had passed since he'd last held Georgiana in his arms and already his ache for her was growing unbearable. But to show weakness in front of his soldiers was impossible.

"Lord Bloodaxe, is anything wrong?" his capable steward asked, offering to refill his goblet with the honey ale he'd probably imbibed too much of already.

"No, Thomas. Just thinking ahead to the next battle." He hoped the explanation would appease anyone listening. His men had to remain disciplined and strong to fend off the constant raids and ambushes planned by Brihann. They had to know his mind was on those raids and not on the golden-haired girl he could not get out of his dreams.

"Very well, my lord." Thomas refilled his cup and those of his captains as well. "But while you're thinking, may I instruct the nymphs to begin their entertainment? Your men are growing restless."

Bloodaxe shook his head and chuckled. "Aye, you are right as always. Now that their stomachs are full, I can see that they're eager to satisfy their other appetites." The castle nymphs were just as eager to oblige them. Better they attend to his men than seek his attention.

Although he hadn't taken Georgiana as his dragon mate, he'd quickly found to his dismay that it made no difference. He could not rouse his desire for another. The beautiful nymphs who had nightly pleasured him no longer held any appeal.

The dragon in him would have none other than Georgiana to ever warm his bed.

One of the nymphs began to dance around him, rubbing her breasts against his shoulder. Charon growled at her and she hastily shifted her attention to his more appreciative young captain, Dalgwynn.

He patted Charon's head.

His dogs were under the dining table, seated beside his feet.

"I know you miss her, too." He tried to put Georgiana out of his mind while he returned his attention to the latest raiding party they'd just encountered. Brihann was tossing demons at him without much purpose other than to irk him. He was using them as little more than cannon fodder. Necros and Python, always his toadies, had their demon soldiers doing the same.

Dalgwynn and Artemis had each wiped out a raiding party earlier this evening and suffered no injuries among their men. Indeed, each had returned victorious from yet another foray. He'd congratulated his men and made certain they were met with a hearty meal and entertainments to keep their spirits high.

But he did not like this increase in tensions among the Dragon Lords. It did not bode well for maintaining the fragile order in the Underworld. Most who resided within the five realms were damaged souls and easily led astray. Brihann was intent on waging war on mankind, but by his actions was more likely to unleash a war here in the world of demons that would destroy them all.

"My lord, will you not have one of these nymphs?" Artemis asked, enjoying the companion who was rubbing herself across his lap.

He grunted and then turned away, having no interest in listening to those beautiful creatures sing or watching them dance to the delight of all in the dining hall. "Charon. Styx. Come."

His dogs scrambled to their feet at his command. Before Georgiana, he would have taken no less than two nymphs upstairs with him. With his dogs growling at every one of them who dared approach, they all backed away and left him to himself. He smiled inwardly, amazed that his dogs seemed to have chosen Georgiana as well. "She has gotten to all of us," he remarked, not surprised when both nodded.

It did not seem to matter that he'd returned her to the safety of the Fae king's palace as innocent as she had come to him. *Almost as innocent.* He did not regret the intimacy they'd shared.

"My lord," Thomas called out to him in a breathless rush just as he'd reached the stairs leading to his tower bedchamber and was about to climb them. One of his young scouts followed close on Thomas' heels.

He acknowledged the scout. "Is something amiss?"

"I'm not certain, my lord. King Brihann's soldiers are now amassing on our border, a force larger than a mere raiding party. We spotted some of their scouts near the river. They were watching the ferrymen bring across the new arrivals."

"Blast it. Follow me." He returned to the dining hall and summoned his captains. "Brihann means to attack those who have not yet the power to fight back."

He noted the surprise of all three of his captains. These were fighting men and were as disgusted as he was by the targets Brihann was now choosing. "Where is the honor in that cowardly act?" Andronicus said, running a hand through his dark hair.

Artemis scoffed at him. "When has the High King ever shown honor? Brihann's intent is to goad us and he will use any means necessary. He's attacked us three times already this evening."

Dalgwynn glanced longingly at the nymph who'd been most attentive to him in the dining hall. "I suppose she'll have to wait."

"Artemis and I will take this battle," Bloodaxe said, feeling a surge of power flow through his body. He was eager for the clash of swords and already exhilarated by the thought of smashing his fists into the soft, frog-like bodies of Brihann's demons.

"We'll join you." Andronicus frowned. "I lost my chance at redemption, and I'll be damned if I allow Brihann to harm these new souls before they make their choice."

Andronicus would remain damned whether or not he saved those helpless souls, but Bloodaxe did not point it out to him. Andronicus knew it anyway. "No, Artemis and I will protect them. You're to take your men and position them along our border directly across from Brihann's forces. Don't engage unless they are about to strike. Then do whatever you must."

"Dalgwynn, station your men near the Razor Cliffs. Do not allow Brihann's demons to open the portal into Friar's Crag. Same for Necros and Python. Those mindless toadies are always doing Brihann's dirty work."

His captains nodded, the gleam in their eyes evidencing their readiness for battle. But Bloodaxe doubted there would be significant fighting tonight. Amassing soldiers along the border and sending raiders to attack the newly arrived souls on his shore were merely feints by Brihann to lure them away from his true target.

Bloodaxe didn't know what that true target was yet.

Perhaps there wasn't one.

After dismissing his two captains, he gave instructions to Artemis who responded with a gravelly "Aye, my lord" and strode off to gather his soldiers and ride to the river.

Bloodaxe climbed to his parapet and emitted a roar that could be heard across his realm as he began to shift into a dragon. If Brihann wanted a fight, he was ready to give him one. He roared again as a lightning surge of power flowed through him and began to harden his flesh. Within moments, his limbs and torso were covered in scales as black as obsidian. His blood began to heat and he felt himself filling with a dragon rage. He snapped his whip-like tail and spread his mighty dragon wings to soar toward the red sky.

First, he circled his fortress to make certain no enemy approached, then he gave a mighty flap of his wings and began the hunt for Brihann's demons. They would be easy to spot from his vantage point.

His blood was hot and thrumming.

The hunt.

He enjoyed the hunt.

He enjoyed the kill even better, for that's what he was. A beast. A predator.

Don't harm the defenseless souls.

He had to remind himself.

He had to think of Georgiana.

For now, the mere thought of her was enough to calm the dragon rage within him.

But the constant raids and his own counter raids would eventually wear him down. He and Brihann were playing a game of cat and mouse. By constantly attacking his lands, Brihann meant to bring out the darkest part of him, the savage part that hunted and killed.

So far, these were petty raids. Some fiercer perhaps than usual, but they were easily countered. He and his armies were always prepared.

Indeed, he could play these simple war games for centuries and never succumb to the darkness. Continuing these games for even half a century was all he needed to allow Georgiana to live out her life in peace.

The same for Saron.

They were all he cared about.

How long before Brihann realized his tactics were not working and came up with new ones?

He heard Brihann's dragon roar in the distance.

Brihann himself? What did the mad Fae want now?

Truce, Lord Bloodaxe.

He much preferred this useless game of raiding each other's lands. Allowing Brihann to draw near under the guise of peace was far more dangerous. He roared in response and flew toward him, carefully circling him. *Why call a truce now?*

I am ill and dying, Lord Bloodaxe. It is time for us to reconcile.

He'd heard it before. Reconcile and then pledge fealty to the High King. The moment he did so, Brihann would declare war on mankind. They'd be the two black dragons of prophecy, and together they'd conquer and extend their dominance over two worlds.

It was a mad quest that would lead to the destruction of the Underworld. Their demon armies might flood through the portals under cover of night and spill the blood of an unprepared population, but what would happen when the sun rose and burned these same demon armies to ashes? Not even the Dragon Lords were immune to the power of the sun.

Not even he, once an English duke's son, was immune to its bright, burning light.

He'd tried to regain the ability to stand in sunshine.

He'd secretly tried for years, but it was lost for good. He could no longer move about in that glorious sunlight, that golden brightness as beautiful as Georgiana's shining hair. He was a lord of darkness, now and forever.

What are your terms, Your Majesty?

Were Necros and Python so mindless that they could not see the obvious flaw in the plan?

They continued to circle each other, two black dragons silhouetted against the red sky. Python and Necros soon joined them, but did not approach too closely. They merely made their presence known and circled in the distance.

There was no sign of Mordain. Where was he?

Lord Bloodaxe, meet me by the Razor Cliffs. You and me alone. I'll withdraw my armies, but you must withdraw yours as well.

He still didn't trust Brihann.

He'd sent men to guard the portal at the Razor Cliffs, for it was the largest portal in the Underworld and opened within the red mountain known as Friar's Crag. The Fae king had defended this spot within England's Lake District for thousands of years. He would be on the alert and ready to battle any demons who came through its volcanic depths.

So why had Brihann chosen this location?

Any portal would have served his purpose with far less risk. Perhaps Brihann chose it knowing he would not agree to meet anywhere else.

Very well. I shall meet you here in a week's time, Your Majesty.

Brihann roared his displeasure at the delay. *Why not now?*

Bloodaxe had no specific reason other than the fact that Brihann seemed too eager for them to meet now. It had to be a trick. If so, he needed to prepare his realm for the battles to come.

One week's time, Lord Bloodaxe. I shall hold you to your word.

Bloodaxe did not bother to respond. Promises in the Underworld were meaningless. It took honor to uphold them and Brihann had never known the meaning of the word. The old bastard had broken their pact when he'd killed Gideon. Bloodaxe had never forgiven him for that foul deed and never would.

He circled Brihann once and then flew toward Necros and Python, slamming his body into them for no reason other than he was angry and they were mindless toadies. Python snapped his teeth at him and tried to bite him. He easily avoided the green dragon's pitiful attempt.

Necros fell off balance and began to plummet to the ground. He regained his wings but not before bruising his big, yellow body on the prickly branches jutting from the treetops. *We'll have our revenge, Bloodaxe. Just you wait and see. You'll be sorry.*

Python ordered him to shut up.

Bloodaxe slammed into each of them again and then flew back to his fortress. They weren't going to come after him. Not now, not ever. No, they were going to go after those he loved.

Georgiana and Saron.

Saron could defend himself, which meant they'd go after Georgiana first.

He had to stop them.

CHAPTER FOURTEEN

GEORGIANA DONNED ONE of her favorite gowns, a vibrant Venetian blue wool trimmed in ivory white silk. She then allowed her maid to fashion her hair into a loose chignon at the nape of her neck with loose curls draped lightly at the sides of her forehead.

"You look lovely, m'lady," the young girl said, casting her a smile and nodding her approval.

"Thank you, Mary. You have a talent for styling hair." She grinned. "I couldn't have done nearly as well."

Mary blushed. "Oh, I'm sure ye would have done far better." She handed Georgiana her hat, scarf, and gloves, and then fluffed out her fur muff. "It'll be cold atop that phaeton," she said with a *tsk*. "Make sure you're bundled up."

Georgiana laughed as she held up her accessories. "I shall be so bundled, I'll hardly be able to move."

She hurried downstairs when she heard voices at the front entry and recognized Oliver's bark of laughter. But she paused on the last step, hesitant to come forward to greet him. This first meeting would be awkward.

He was standing beside the door that their butler had shut to keep out the cold wind and was talking to her father. "I shall take good care of her, Your Grace. You mustn't worry. I will not tear through the streets of London with your precious cargo."

Her father released the breath he'd been holding. "Good lad. Georgiana is all I have. I couldn't bear to lose her again." He patted Oliver's shoulder. "You're a good man, Linwood. I'm truly sorry it did not work out between you and my daughter. I hope you find the happiness you deserve."

"I will, Your Grace. Rest assured." There was a hint of bitterness behind his words, but Georgiana certainly understood the reason for it.

She may have been abducted, but she hadn't been the only one to suffer. Oliver and her father had suffered worse, in truth. While she had found love during that time, they'd experienced nothing but fear and frustration.

They had no idea where she'd been taken or how she was being treated. They could do nothing to bring her back and must have felt quite helpless. The blow to Oliver was doubly hurtful, for she'd lost her heart to another during that time.

"Oliver," she said with genuine affection, striding toward him. "I'm truly sorry for all that's happened. I hope you are well."

He nodded. "As well as can be expected."

He showed no expression other than bland acceptance, but a chill shot up her spine nonetheless, for she sensed a bubbling anger. "How are your parents? I look forward to seeing them. These were a hard few months for all of us."

"They are eager to see you." He helped her on with her cloak and then took her arm and led her outside to his shining, dark blue phaeton that was waiting for them at the curb. His family crest was emblazoned on the door, a wild boar above which hung two crossed and bloodied daggers.

It was an ugly crest, she decided.

He helped her to climb up and waited for her to settle on the bench before he strode to the driver's side and climbed on as well. He caught the reins in his hands and gave them a sharp snap. "Why won't you marry me?" he wasted no time in asking.

Heat rose in her cheeks. "I had plenty of time to think about the course of my life while I was gone."

It wasn't a lie. But she wasn't going to mention Lord Bloodaxe. Her heart beat faster at the mere thought of him. She wanted to be in his arms again.

"Obviously, you decided I wasn't a suitable mate for you."

She was surprised by his mention of the word 'mate' but she supposed it was mere coincidence. He could have said 'husband' or 'bridegroom' as well as any other descriptive words. "In your heart, you know that we aren't suited for each other. We are friends and nothing more."

"Friends?" He snorted.

She studied him as he wound the carriage through the fashionable Mayfair streets. "Oliver, you know that you don't love me."

He clenched his jaw and ground his teeth, then turned to her. "I never pretended I did. Nor did you. So, what has happened to change your opinion?"

"As I said, I had time to think of what was important to me. Both of us were marrying for reasons other than love. But I realized it was a mistake for me to do so." She sighed, emitting a vapor trail that dangled in the cold air. "I need to marry for love."

"Love." He snorted in disdain once more, his lips curling in a sneer. "What will you do if you never find it?"

She shrugged. "Then I will never marry."

He stared at her in frowning disbelief. "You say that now, but you shall change your tune when your father dies and you're rattling about all alone in your elegant townhouse. Your father's title is one of those rare grants that allows everything to pass through the female line if he has no male heirs. Will you waste that boon and allow your cousin to inherit it all?"

"And why not? Jacob Wethersby is a worthy heir. Besides, he'll merely inherit the entailed properties–"

"A fortune by itself."

She nodded. "And the title along with it. But I'll inherit plenty on my own. I will not ever lack for anything."

"Other than the heat of a man's body against yours. Or the thrust of–"

"Oliver! You forget yourself!" She clutched the side of the phaeton as he took a sharp turn and headed away from his parents' home. "What are you doing? You're going in the wrong direction."

"No, I'm taking you where you deserve to be. Do you think you can make a fool of me?" He snapped the reins again and raced his matched bays at a reckless pace down the busy street.

He was going too fast for her to jump off. She'd break her neck if she tried. "Stop! What's wrong with you? Take me home at once. I'll send apologies to your parents."

His bitterness flowed freely in his laughter. "My parents never invited you. There's no tea party. They're not even aware you've been found and returned to your father."

"What? Are you mad?" She fought to quell her rising anger. "What are you thinking? Dear heaven, what are you planning to do?"

He'd turned onto the mews behind his own townhouse, his bachelor quarters that would have become their home once they were married. "I just told you, sending you where you belong."

He might have frightened her had he spoken to her in this fashion before her abduction, but she'd faced fire-breathing dragons and foul-smelling demons. She'd traveled through portals that defied the laws of space and time. She'd fallen into deep waters and been attacked by odd birds and creatures of myth.

And she now carried a dagger in her muff.

She wasn't afraid of Oliver.

However, she wasn't expecting the two accomplices he'd hired who now came out of the shadows and helped him to lead his horses and carriage into the barn. The barn door shut behind them, plunging them into darkness. She was about to draw out her dagger and stab it into Oliver's hand, but in the next moment, one of the men lit a lantern and she saw that it would take more than that to successfully make her escape.

She might hurt Oliver, but the two men were big and mean. Dockside thieves, no doubt. They were blocking her means of exit. She'd never get out… unless. "What is he paying you? I'll double it."

"You bitch!" Oliver's slap caught her by surprise and she chided herself for being unprepared for it. "We've been promised untold riches. Do you think your puny allowance will ever satisfy us?"

She rubbed her cheek to ease the sting of his slap. "Who would pay a fortune to have me?" But she knew the answer before the last words had slipped from her mouth. *Brihann.*

He had found the greedy mortals who would do his dirty business for him. She had nothing to lose now. She withdrew her dagger and plunged it into Oliver's hand, then quickly drew it out and jumped down from the phaeton while he was distracted and howling in pain.

The barn door had not been latched shut, only slid closed. To escape, she merely had to elude these two big men and then run for her life around the corner and onto the busy street.

The horses were now between her and these men, for they'd rushed toward Oliver when he began to howl.

She slapped the rump of one of the bay geldings and screamed at the top of her lungs. The horses startled and began to rear up on their hind legs, jostling the carriage and flailing their front legs so that the two men had to jump back to avoid being struck in the head by those massive hooves.

Georgiana had at least two or three seconds lead on them. It was enough, for she was a fast runner. Anyway, she was running for her life. That was incentive enough to sprint like a deer out the door.

She grabbed the rough-hewn wooden door and shoved it open.

Instead of freedom, she ran solidly into a wall of demons. Ugh! They smelled foul enough to make her gag. But she had no time to dwell on them or their odor. She swung her hand in an arc and tried to fell as many of them as she could with her dagger. She used her muff as a shield to fend off their sharp talons, but it wasn't much of a shield and was quickly ripped apart.

She only needed to drive a small path between them and run through it.

She kept swinging her dagger, darting forward and then feinting back, but couldn't clear that path before Oliver and his dockside knaves came up behind her. She gave one of them a swift kick between his legs. He cursed her as he dropped to his knees in pain. Oliver put a handkerchief to her nose and pressed it hard against her nostrils.

He'd doused it with a sickly scent.

She tried to draw it off her nose, but that scent was already having an effect. Her legs buckled out from under her. She vaguely recalled managing to stab Oliver again.

Then everything fell dark.

"A PORTAL HAS just opened up," Dalgwynn said in a rush, finding Bloodaxe sparring with broadswords in the courtyard with Artemis. "My lord, King Brihann has unsealed the portal at the Razor Cliffs and allowed Python through. We tried to stop him, but he used his dark magic on us. We stopped most of Python's demons though. Only a handful managed to get by us."

Bloodaxe muttered an oath. "He's been sent after Lady Georgiana. So much for his supposed call for truce. There's no time to lose. Position your men around that portal and don't allow any of his demons through. If Python returns, don't allow him to seal the portal. Keep it open as long as you can to allow the Fae king and his armies in."

He began to run to the parapet, still shouting orders to his captains. "Artemis, stay here and guard the fortress. Andronicus, add your forces to Dalgwynn's, but leave Dalgwynn in charge of them. You're to go to King Cadeyrn and tell him we need his help. Let him know the portal is open. Ask him to give us as many Fae as he can spare."

"What will you do, my lord?" Artemis asked.

"Try to stop Python before he captures Lady Georgiana and hands her over to Brihann." He grabbed his crossbow and quiver of arrows and called to his dogs. "Charon. Styx. Come." It didn't take him long to reach the Razor Cliffs, for the demon portals that were passageways within the Underworld alone still worked and he knew them all.

He'd gone through them often.

His dogs easily kept pace by his side. "Follow Georgiana's scent."

Their noses were far better than his and could pick up her wild-flower scent anywhere in London. He knew she was there, hopefully reunited with her father.

He didn't know what she had decided to do about her betrothed, the Marquis of Linwood. He'd abide by whatever decision she would make. *No. Hell, no.* She was his dragon mate. He'd be a fool to let her go again.

His dogs led him to a barn in one of the fashionable sections of London. Three men were just getting up off the ground, one of them clutching his bleeding hand and yelling at the others. "Fools! He won't pay us now. All is lost because you couldn't subdue one small girl on your own."

His large companions shot daggers at him with their eyes. "Ye didn't tell us she fought like a demon. Look what she did to ye, Lord Linwood. She almost plunged her dagger into m'heart as well."

Bloodaxe pushed the men aside. "Linwood." He grabbed the cur by the throat and held him in a stranglehold. "If Brihann harms a hair on her head, I'll slice you into pieces and then feed you to my dogs for supper."

Charon and Styx growled low in their throats as though to emphasize his point.

Even the dockside rogues shuddered. "That big man took 'er. Large, 'e was. Ugly creature. But 'e ain't got more than a step or two head start."

Bloodaxe dropped Linwood to the ground. "Harm any of her family and I'll kill you all."

He whirled back through the portal, desperate to find Python before he had the chance to call for reinforcements.

His dogs howled as they raced back through the portal alongside him. They must have caught the scent of Georgiana in the lingering wake. "Take me to her," he commanded them.

In the next moment, they'd made it back to the Razor Cliffs. He saw Python just ahead of him. He was carrying Georgiana over his shoulder and screaming for Brihann and Necros to attack.

Georgiana was lying so still, she had to be unconscious. Then he heard her low moan and saw her trying to lift her head. She was coming around. Not in time though. She was still too listless to defend herself. Probably too nauseated from the drug she'd inhaled to do more than drop to her knees and heave the poison out of her system. He'd caught the foul scent of it as they'd passed through the portal.

He turned to face Brihann. "Don't hurt her. This doesn't have to turn to war between us."

But he knew this was exactly what Brihann wanted, to stir him into a blind rage and turn him into the monster these other three Dragon Lords had long ago become. Brihann killing Georgiana would accomplish it.

Out of the corner of his eye, he saw Python still holding Georgiana. Necros was winging his way toward Python. *Blast.* He raised his crossbow and reached for an arrow out of his quiver, but Brihann used his magic to knock the weapon out of his hands. Knowing Brihann would never allow him to get off a decent shot, he left the crossbow on the ground and dropped his quiver of arrows beside it.

He had no choice but to shift into dragon form. It was his only chance to defeat this unholy threesome.

Python still held Georgiana and had no intention of releasing her to join in the dragon battle. He'd have to rely on Charon and Styx to keep that foul elf from disappearing into his castle with Georgiana... or worse, delivering her to Brihann's castle lair.

How long could Charon and Styx delay him? A few seconds at best?

Bloodaxe shifted as fast as he could, but had no time to stretch his wings before Brihann and Necros descended on him. Brihann slammed into him while Necros lunged for his neck. He easily dodged Necros and soared up into the sky.

The pair chased after him.

He turned and slammed into Necros with the full force of his body, momentarily stunning the yellow beast.

Brihann roared in anger.

Bloodaxe dropped low and then pulled up fast, hitting him squarely in his soft, black underbelly. Brihann floundered and began to fall.

All too soon, he recovered. "Fools!" Brihann shrieked. "We are three against one, but he flies at us as though we are weak, old women!"

Incredibly, Python threw Georgiana to the ground and shifted into his dragon form in order to join in the fight. She'd have a nasty bruise on her head, hopefully nothing worse. Charon and Styx had already taken up positions on either side of her to prevent any of Brihann's minions from getting close.

Then Andronicus and his men protectively surrounded her and he completely lost sight of her, not even able to catch a glimpse of her golden hair. Brihann's minions were swarming along the Razor Cliffs toward them, but his own soldiers were already in place to battle them.

He had to trust his men to protect Georgiana, but his soldiers were battling three demon armies. How long could they hold out?

Fae reinforcements would be welcome.

He knew the Fae king would come to his aid, it was just a matter of time. Precious time. The three Dragon Lords were now regrouping and preparing to come after him. He turned to face them, quickly sorting through his options. Necros was the weakest link, best to get him out of the way first.

Then Python.

Brihann would be a formidable opponent, for he was twice as large as any of them and no longer merely playing at fighting. This time, Brihann would kill him if he didn't give in and pledge fealty to the High King in the war against mankind.

The three dragons flew at him together, and Bloodaxe found it easy to parry this first assault by flying into Necros and knocking him into Brihann just as Brihann opened his jaws. Instead of clamping onto Bloodaxe's neck, he snapped them into empty air.

Since that assault had been a failure, they came at him from separate directions next. He twisted out of the way so that Python and

Necros collided, but Brihann landed a powerful blow that sent him reeling. They went on like this, dragons jousting in the red sky, as battle continued to wage on the ground below. Time seemed to slow and the scent of death filled the air even though they were soaring to heights where the air was thin. Dragons rarely flew this high up, for dragon fire required their lungs to fill with air. At this height, they had little air and would only wind up with a burst of pain across the chest.

He'd lost count of how many passes they'd made against each other. Twenty? Perhaps more. He scanned the ground below, searching for Georgiana to make certain she was unharmed amid the chaos, but could not find her. Andronicus and his men were still standing in a circle while battling Brihann's demons. Georgiana had to be in the center of that circle.

Was she safe?

Brihann slammed into him, cracking a bone in his wing.

Damn.

His fault. He'd taken his attention off the dragons. A searing pain shot up his wing as he tried to move it. He'd done the same to Necros and Python, for the most part rendering them useless. But Brihann was unscathed.

This wasn't good.

Brihann came at him again and he narrowly missed being crushed in his jaws. Just darting out of the way caused him dizzying pain.

Brihann slammed into him again, tossing him against Necros and Python. They were exhausted, but he'd fallen into their clutches and it took nothing for them to tilt their heads and snap their jaws. They missed his neck, but managed to bite his wings. He bit back and shook them off, but not before they'd caused more damage.

He wasn't going to win this fight.

Georgiana.

He had to get her safely into Fae hands before he died. Where was the Fae king and his armies? Why hadn't they come through yet? Had the portal somehow closed?

He dove for the Razor Cliffs.

His men were outnumbered, and more demons were still climbing up the cliffs. Then he saw the problem. They'd pushed back his men and sealed the portal. He dove toward it and with the last of his strength, shot his dragon fire to clear the opening to the portal. Brihann's demons scrambled away to avoid the flames.

Bloodaxe shoved open the portal with all his might and then tumbled off the cliff.

The Fae came through.

He searched for Cadeyrn, knowing he was likely to be in the vanguard. *Save Georgiana.*

He needed to distract Brihann while Cadeyrn got her to safety. He ignored the jolts of pain now coursing through his body and flew upward to engage the three dragons once again. They pummeled him, but he didn't care. In this moment, they'd forgotten Georgiana.

Brihann clamped his massive jaws around his neck.

This was it, the killing blow.

I love you, Georgie.

Could she hear him?

His wing was crippled. He had no breath left in his lungs to blow more dragon fire. He felt Brihann's teeth begin to sink into the soft flesh beneath his scales. But the killing bite never came. Brihann suddenly howled in pain and released him.

What had just happened?

Brihann began to dance oddly in the air.

Then he saw the reason.

A crossbow arrow shot through his tail.

His crossbow arrow.

As Necros and Python hurried to pull it out of Brihann with their teeth, Bloodaxe searched the ground for the soldier who had shot it. Amid the circle of his men stood Georgiana, her gold hair tumbling about her shoulders as she struggled to reload the crossbow and shoot another arrow.

Although it pained him, he burst out laughing, the sound emanating from his dragon snout as an odd, high pitched roar.

Georgiana looked up.

Their gazes met.

I love you, my lord. I'm not leaving you.

Blast the stubborn girl.

He frowned at her. *Get out of here.*

She shot another arrow that whizzed past him and would have struck Python had he not seen it in time and dodged it.

She reloaded.

Bloodaxe wanted to pick her up by his teeth and shove her through the Fae portal, but not even he could get near her. Cadeyrn and his finest Fae soldiers had added another circle of protection around her and he knew Cadeyrn would take her to safety if that circle began to collapse.

He heard the shriek of angry dragons behind him.

The three crazed Dragon Lords were coming after him once more.

He meant to fight back, but his wing was too badly broken to allow him to dart and weave as he needed to elude them. They easily surrounded him and began to attack him from all sides. They were like vultures descending on their prey.

They were too close to him for Georgiana to shoot her arrows.

He'd taken too many punishing blows. His wings gave out and he began to hurtle toward the ground.

Suddenly, an angry roar filled the air and he was caught in the wingspan of a black dragon and lifted upward once again. There was only one other such dragon, but it couldn't be. Saron would never fly to his rescue. Would he?

Need some help, my brother?

If dragons could grin, he'd be grinning at Saron right now. He didn't know what to think. His heart was bursting with joy. His little brother was here. How was it possible? Georgiana, of course. *No, I have them on the run.*

Saron snapped his dragon tail. *Right, and pigs fly.*

Bloodaxe regained his wings and attempted to get in front of Saron to shield him from Brihann's rage. Brihann and his toadies would indeed have to kill him before he allowed that Fae maggot to harm his little brother.

Saron turned to him, his dragon eyes bright. *Let me do this, Arik. You've protected me long enough.*

He was no longer Arik, but allowed himself a wrenching moment to fall back to a time when he was that boy and could run beside his younger brother in the sunshine filled Draloch meadows. He was too far gone to weep, but he felt the sweet pang of his heart beating against his chest. Saron was beside him. His little brother. *I'll always protect you, to my dying breath.*

Saron nodded and gave an angry whip of his dragon tail when Necros dared to come too close. *As I should have done for you. I'm sorry. I'm here now.*

It was enough.

He gazed with pride upon Saron, for they were the two black dragons of prophecy. Their blue underbellies glistened in the light of the Underworld moons.

Brihann realized it at that same moment and rent the air with his anguished roar. *This is not over, sons of Draloch! I shall hunt you both and destroy you. I shall–*

Another arrow whizzed past his head just then and flew up Brihann's nostril. Brihann shrieked in obvious pain and retreated to his castle lair. His toadies, Necros and Python, followed him.

Bloodaxe winced. *That had to hurt as badly as a dragon sneeze.*

Saron emitted a dragon roar that sounded suspiciously like a laugh. *Remember the time we stole Father's snuff box?*

I recall. You couldn't stop sneezing for a week. Bloodaxe's tension eased and he laughed along with his brother, not caring that pain shot through his body with every little movement.

But it felt good to laugh.

He'd been burdened and miserable for so long.

Brihann's demons retreated after their furious and raging king. Within an instant, the battle ended and an eerie calm surrounded the Razor Cliffs. Indeed, all was calm except…

Bloodaxe looked down and saw Georgiana still shaking her fist at Brihann's retreating minions. "And don't come back you deranged cowards," she was shouting as his dogs leaped up and down beside her, barking to emphasize her point.

Bloodaxe did not know what would come next, but this prophecy had been fulfilled.

Two black dragons shall reign supreme.
Two black dragons shall unite the worlds of demon and man.

More important, two brothers torn apart by lies and intrigue were now reunited. His soulless, demon heart soared even as his dragon wings gave out and could no longer support his flight. He held them out long enough to glide to the ground and then he shifted back into himself. That his soldiers saw him naked did not trouble him, for they'd seen him shift before. But he'd never been injured as he was now. He did not like that they saw how badly he'd been hurt.

Saron alit beside him but retained his dragon form. *Do you need help?*

No, nothing that a Fae healer cannot cure.

Good, then meet me at the Fae king's court in a week's time. The Prince Regent will want my report and there are a few loose ends to take care of, a few loose demons to toss back into the Underworld. He lifted off the ground and started toward the Fae portal. *Remember, one week. I will bring Georgiana's father, for they'll have much to discuss. I'll also properly introduce you to my Anabelle.*

As Saron disappeared into the portal, Thomas, his ever-efficient steward, appeared out of nowhere with clothes. With his capable help, Bloodaxe donned his trousers and boots. He was about to put on his shirt when Georgiana reached his side. "Do not put it on."

He arched an eyebrow and grinned. "Very well. I know how you enjoy seeing me shirtless."

She tried to appear stern, but he could see the joy and relief in her eyes. "I only mean to inspect your injuries."

He opened his arms to her. "So you say. But I know how you like to see me undressed."

She rushed into his embrace with a sob. "I thought he was going to kill you."

"What's this? No tears, my beauty. Today has been a good day."

"I missed you so much." She wiped a stray tear from the corner of her eye. "I'm sorry I almost shot you."

He began to laugh in earnest. Blast, that hurt. But it also felt so good to have her in his arms once more. "You did well, Georgie. I could not ask for a better dragon mate."

"Right, you—" She gasped. "Are you asking me to marry you?"

"I'd fall on bended knee, but I fear I won't ever get up again if I do. Yes, I'm asking you to marry me."

She cast him a smile as bright as sunshine. "Why, my lord? Why do you wish to marry me?"

"Must I say it? Can you not see how my heart beats only for you?" He bent his head and kissed her with a desperation that could leave no doubt about his feelings for her. "But I will say it because you've won the day and changed the course of destiny. You've united the house of Draloch and changed the balance of power. Brihann is now hiding in his lair, every dragon scale on his thick hide quaking." He kissed her again, feeling at peace as he'd never felt before in all his days. "I love you, my beauty. I've loved you from the moment our lips first touched."

She gave a merry trill of laughter. "I was but a toothless and drooling babe in my cradle."

"But you looked at me with your soft, green eyes and I knew in that moment that ours would be a love match."

She leaned her head against his chest and gave him a careful hug. "One for the ages, my lord."

He nodded. "Throughout the years, through all my changes, I never stopped loving you."

She was pensive a moment. "Nor did I ever stop loving you. My heart was searching for yours all this time. I'm glad you never forgot me."

His arm was broken and he suspected several of his ribs were cracked as well. He wasn't certain what other injuries he'd sustained. Georgiana must have felt him suddenly begin to weaken. "Sit a moment. Let me fetch King Cadeyrn to heal your wounds."

"No, my beauty. I don't need him when I have you beside me."

She looked up at him, her brow furrowed. "I have no magical powers."

He took her hands and placed them palms down on his injuries. "Give it a try."

He closed his eyes and inhaled her wildflower scent. Her hands felt so good against his skin, better than any mage's potion. Better than any Fae magic.

"My fingers are tingling," she said in wonder. He opened his eyes and gazed at her. "Ooh, my entire body is now tingling. Do you feel anything, my lord?"

He nodded and smiled at her. "Aye, but it has nothing to do with mending broken bones. It was worth a try, my beauty. You had better summon King Cadeyrn."

She sighed. "I've failed."

"You healed my heart. You saved my damaged soul. I'd say you've done a fine day's work." After his bones had properly knitted under the power of the Fae healing spell, he took Georgiana back into the circle of his arms. "Do not fret, the skill to mend bones will come to you in time." He arched an eyebrow. "So, I made you tingle?"

"Yes, my lord." He loved the light blush on her cheeks. "You know how I enjoy your body."

"As much as I enjoy yours, I hope."

She laughed once more. "I don't know. Perhaps. The matter needs more thorough exploration."

"Indeed, my beauty." He took Georgiana back to his tower chamber, prepared to do just that.

CHAPTER FIFTEEN

*H*E'D ALLOWED HER *to call him Arik again.*

Georgiana stood before him in his tower bedchamber, her clothes cast aside. Now it was his turn, and she watched in fascination as his muscles rippled and flexed while he casually stripped out of his garments, his seductively graceful movements like that of a beast on the prowl. Even the dragon etched on his back appeared bigger and more powerful, seeming to spread its black wings and soar with his every twist and turn.

He was still a beast, one of the black dragons of prophecy and that would never change. But he was more now. "Georgie, do you realize what's happened?"

"Other than my rescuing you?" she asked with a grin. "Or the fact that you're about to shamelessly seduce me?"

"Yes, other than that." He chuckled. "I'm the dominant male now. I will assume the throne as High King of the Dragon Lords. Brihann is defeated. His madness is such that not even Necros or Python dared follow him into his castle lair. They retreated to their own realms and summoned their demon soldiers home."

"I'm so glad." She called his name softly again, *Arik,* as a gentle rain began to fall outside, its droplets striking the window panes in a rhythmic *plunk, plunk.* But she was warm and cozy in their bedchamber, her gaze fixed on this man she loved with all her heart as he approached, his body eager for their joining.

He did not seem quite comfortable with the sound of his boyhood name on her lips. He'd been Bloodaxe for too long. But it was important for her to call him Arik, for this is how she'd first known him, and this is how she always saw him. Not as a beast. Never as a beast. Always as the man who'd captured her heart.

"Come, my beauty."

He swept her up in his arms and placed her in the center of the bed. He stretched his body over hers, propping himself on his elbows to ease his weight off her, but she wrapped her arms around his neck and drew him closer, for she loved the press of his powerful body against her own slender one.

They spoke no more. Heavens, Georgiana did not think she had the wits to put a sentence together. His hot skin inflamed her senses. She inhaled the honey scent and maleness of him. Her heart took flight as he lowered his mouth to hers and stole her breath in a devouring kiss. This would be their first mating.

She wanted him.

"Don't hold back, my love," she said and returned his kiss with equal ardor. His mouth was warm as velvet. She ran her hands along his back, feeling the corded muscles of his body that was hard as iron. He held her and kissed her, and her joy knew no bounds when he finally entered her.

He had now claimed her as his own.

But in claiming her, he'd been claimed as well. "Georgie, it shall always be you. Only you. It has always been you." He began to move inside of her, carefully at first, but as her body adjusted to his and turned to fire, his thrusts came faster and he embedded himself deeply.

She moved with his body, closing around him as he rocked in and out.

A fiery pressure built within her and so did her abandon. She clutched his shoulders and cried out his name.

He suckled her breasts, his tongue licking and swirling across their taut peaks. She cried out again, this time clutching his head and holding it tight to her heaving chest as he continued his merciless onslaught to drive her to ecstasy.

Her body was an inferno of hot dragon flames that spread like wildfire throughout her limbs and centered its heat at her core.

She cried out once more, aching for relief from the volcanic pressure building within her. He'd touched her and pleasured her in the hunting cottage, but this was different. More intense. More spectacular because he was on fire, too.

He arched his back and continued to thrust into her, his eyes closed and the golden sheen of his body now glistening with heat. "I love you, Georgie."

"I love you, too."

A wave of pleasure swept over her, lifting her in its molten crest and carrying her along with explosive force toward a distant shore. While fire still raged within her, his own molten explosion came. His body grew taut and his muscles strained. He spilled his dragon seed inside of her in pulsing waves.

"My beauty," he whispered, shifting their positions so that he now lay on his back and she was now atop him, resting her flushed cheek against his solid chest. Their legs were entwined and their hearts were beating fast.

Her heartbeat was still rampant while his began to calm. He turned pensive, absently caressing her hair, but she knew his thoughts were focused and not merely drifting. "What is the matter, my love?"

"Nothing, just thinking about today. Did I dream my brother's presence? Will he meet me next week beside the Stone of Draloch? King Cadeyrn has offered to hold our wedding ceremony then. I'm sorry, Georgie. I could not hold back and wait to be properly wed before I claimed you as my mate."

"Nor could I." She smiled and kissed his chest. "But you have a point. Perhaps we ought to refrain from further... *that*... and wait until our wed–"

"No. You are too precious to me, my beauty." He gave a laughing groan, but quickly turned pensive once more. "I was thinking back to the day my father brought me to Wethersby Hall to seal our betrothal. Even then, your hair was as golden as sunlight and your big, round eyes were a soft, moss green. I thought of you in those dark days after Saron was taken to the Underworld and I followed him. I don't know what sustained him, kept him defiant through the years of his captivity. But I thought of you throughout mine. *I will get back. I must get back. I am betrothed to that girl with sunshine hair and moss-green eyes. She is waiting for me.* That's what I told myself with the break of each new day."

"Arik." Her voice was a ragged whisper.

"Then I sold my soul. I lost the ability to survive in sunlight. I lost the ability to shed a tear. But I never lost my ability to love you. *Protect Georgiana.* I knew we were no longer betrothed and you would eventually belong to another, but it didn't matter to me. *Protect Georgiana.* That's what I told myself from every day forward after that. *She is my beloved dragon mate. She is my destiny.*"

THE END

Dear Readers,

I hope you enjoyed the Dark Gardens series Book 4, *Garden of Destiny*. I've also given you a taste of the other three books in this series, *Garden of Shadows*, *Garden of Light*, and *Garden of Dragons*. I hope you'll read all the stories in the Dark Gardens series. I look forward to your comments and reviews. Please be kind! These paranormal romances are a labor of love for me. It took years and years for the publishers to give this genre the attention and respect it deserves, and now I can't wait for you to read the entire Dark Gardens series. So, join me on a journey into the Lake District where bluebell gardens serve as portals into the realm of the Fae. An ancient Fae prophecy is about to unfold, a prophecy etched in the Stone of Draloch. The salvation of the faerie king, Cadeyrn, and his subjects is at risk and lies in the hands of a simple vicar's daughter. But who is she? Will Cadeyrn find her in time? And how is the Duke of Draloch and his lost brother connected to the prophecy? Book 4, *Garden of Destiny*, resolves the fate of the Draloch brothers, two proud men who endured hardships and betrayals that scarred them for life. If you happen to be in the mood for romances with humor and heart, also look for my light-hearted Regency historical romances in the Farthingale series. The first is *My Fair Lily*, but there are five sisters in all, and a swarm of meddlesome, well-intentioned family members that I hope you'll come to love.

Hugs always,
Meara

ABOUT THE AUTHOR

Meara Platt is a USA Today bestselling author and an award winning, Amazon UK All-star. Her favorite place in all the world is England's Lake District, which may not come as a surprise since many of her stories are set in that idyllic landscape, including her paranormal romance Dark Gardens series. *Garden of Dragons*, Book 3 in that series, is a Romance Writers of America Golden Heart award winning story. If you'd like to learn more about the ancient Fae prophecy that is about to unfold in the Dark Gardens series, as well as Meara's lighthearted, international bestselling Regency romances in the Farthingale Series, please visit Meara's website at www.mearaplatt. com.

Made in United States
North Haven, CT
12 October 2025

80730145R00120